GOD BLESS THE BROKEN ROAD

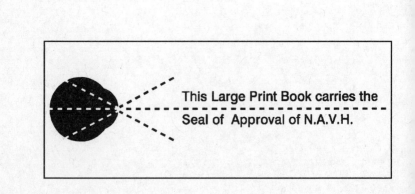

GOD BLESS THE BROKEN ROAD

JENNIFER DORNBUSH

THORNDIKE PRESS
A part of Gale, a Cengage Company

GALE
A Cengage Company

Farmington Hills, Mich • San Francisco • New York • Waterville, Maine
Meriden, Conn • Mason, Ohio • Chicago

Copyright © 2017 by Jennifer Dornbush.
Thorndike Press, a part of Gale, a Cengage Company.

Thorndike Press® Large Print Christian Fiction.
The text of this Large Print edition is unabridged.
Other aspects of the book may vary from the original edition.
Set in 16 pt. Plantin.

**LIBRARY OF CONGRESS CIP DATA ON FILE.
CATALOGUING IN PUBLICATION FOR THIS BOOK
IS AVAILABLE FROM THE LIBRARY OF CONGRESS**

ISBN-13: 978-1-4328-4200-0 (hardcover)
ISBN-10: 1-4328-4200-5 (hardcover)

Published in 2017 by arrangement with Howard Books, an imprint of Simon & Schuster, Inc.

Printed in the United States of America
1 2 3 4 5 6 7 21 20 19 18 17

To all the men and women in the
United States armed forces —
past, present, and future.
And to those who love and support them.

Truly I tell you, if you have faith as small as a mustard seed, you can say to this mountain, "Move from here to there," and it will move. Nothing will be impossible for you.

Matthew 17:20 (NIV)

Chapter One:
Spring Cleaning

Day 429

As soon as the alarm goes off, Amber forces herself to say it.

"This is the day the Lord has made. I will rejoice and be glad in it."

Today, Amber actually believes it. She's so close to the end.

She shakes off the night and her covers. Her bare feet touch the cool, glossy oak floor. The floor she and Darren sanded, stained, and polished together when they bought this old Victorian eight years ago in Clarksville, Darren's hometown.

Amber flies around their king-size bed to the en suite bath with the claw-foot tub she found at a vintage store the summer after they bought the place. She loves this tub. She loves soaking in this tub. She loves looking at this tub. She hates cleaning it. And boy, does it need a scrubbing.

Amber grabs her robe from the hook that

hangs next to Darren's. His robe hasn't moved in 429 days. Neither have his toiletries on the top two shelves of the medicine cabinet. Even his shampoo bottle is still propped up on the rim of the shower stall, just as it was the morning he left for Afghanistan.

Amber enters Bree's darkened room and sits on the edge of her daughter's bed. She lightly touches her eight-year-old's shoulder. Bree's eyes flutter open as she rolls onto her back. Most of her long, brown, wavy hair still covers her face, and Amber brushes it aside to look at her gorgeous brown eyes. A gift from her father. Nothing like Amber's fair skin, blond hair, and blue eyes.

Amber sings, *"This is the day . . ."* She waits for Bree to echo the response.

"No, Mom. I'm tired." Bree pulls the covers over her head.

"*This is the day . . .* Come on," Amber teases.

Bree's head shakes from under the quilt. "It's Saturday."

"That the Lord has made." Amber echoes that part on her own: *"That the Lord has made."*

Amber pulls the covers off Bree's face.

"I wanna sleep in."

"You can't hide. Time to get up." Amber

tickles Bree's sides. Bree squirms under the quilt.

"Keep singing," says a muffled voice.

"This is the day that the Lord has made. Let us rejoice and be glad in it."

Bree peeks out from under the covers and joins in on the last line. *"This is the day that the Lord has made."* Bree stretches her arms above her head, reaching her fingers to touch a photograph she knows is taped to her headboard. Her father in his military uniform.

"Is today the day?"

"No. But not too much longer."

"How long?"

"Ten days."

"That's a lot."

"It's less than two weeks, Bree. We have so much to do before then."

"Like what?"

Amber thinks about the roof that needs repair, and the yard that needs raking, and the fence that could use a coat of white paint, and the house that needs a good spring cleaning. How did she let so much go over the year?

"We're gonna clean the house and rake the yard today," says Amber, who knows she's biting off more than they can chew. "And afterward we'll go downtown and get ice cream."

Bree hugs her pink camouflage butterfly pillow, a gift from her dad from the post exchange on base. "I have an idea. Let's make pancakes and watch cartoons instead."

Amber opens the blinds, sending the sun streaming into Bree's room against the powder-puff-pink walls, filling the room with warmth. Outside she notices the daffodils and tulips have bloomed overnight. She cracks the window open and warm spring air flows in, smelling like moist soil and fresh grass. The yellow ribbon she and Bree placed around their big oak tree that stands in the yard at the end of their house flutters in the breeze. It's looking faded. She should replace it before Darren gets home. Glancing across the lawn, she notices for the first time all winter that it's no longer brown and crumpled. Instead, a light-green hue has cropped up overnight. In a couple of weeks the grass will be long enough to mow.

And Darren will be home.

Amber starts to sing lightly, *"This is the day that the Lord has made."*

"Why do we have to clean the house? It's just gonna get dirty again."

Amber laughs. Bree's spunk and sense of humor make the long days without Darren more tolerable. What would she do without her daughter?

"No more arguments. Up and at 'em, kiddo." Amber goes to Bree's closet and selects two outfits. "Which one?" Amber holds up a hot-pink shirt in her left hand and a yellow-sailor-striped one in her right.

Bree slides out of bed, slipping her feet into her oversize pink elephant slippers. She points to the one on Amber's left.

"You always pick the pink one."

"It's Dad's favorite."

"Can't argue with that. Let's get it on." Amber hangs the sailor shirt back on the bar. Bree treads over to her mother, elephants slapping the wooden floor with each step. Amber lifts her pjs over her head and slides the shirt on in their place. "Brush hair and teeth, and meet me downstairs for breakfast."

She sends Bree to the bathroom and heads back to the master, entering as she hears her phone. She dashes over to find she's missed a call from Darren, hits redial, and prays she can get a connection. Pacing back and forth, Amber wills the call to go through.

"Come on. Come on. Pick up. Let's see, it's nine o'clock here, which means dinnertime there. Come on, Darren. You were just there." After the fourth ring, Darren's line goes to voice mail.

Amber doesn't bother leaving a message. It's happened this way a million times before. By now she should be used to the missed calls and cutoff conversations. But she isn't. It's been more than a week since she's heard his voice.

She shrugs off her momentary letdown. In ten days they'll be able to talk and talk and talk. No interruptions.

CHAPTER TWO:
CHOIR REHEARSAL

The next morning, Amber enters the sanctuary of her church to find her choir members have already arrived and are standing in groups of two and three in the choir loft. Bree darts ahead of her.

"Take a seat next to Mrs. Capers. And don't bug her," Amber instructs Bree, who's already halfway down the aisle. She shuffles up to the piano, where Mrs. Capers slides over and pats the piano bench for Bree to sit.

"Good morning, Miss Bree. Can you help me turn pages?" says Mrs. Capers.

"I was hoping I could play the tambourine this morning," Bree says, with an eye to her mother.

"You can do both. We only need the tambourine for the first song," says Amber. Bree grabs the tambourine from the percussion box next to the piano.

The pastor's wife, Karena Williams, spots

Amber and whisks her way across the loft. Karena's petite stature belies her large personality. With a broad smile, she wraps her arms around Amber. "Good morning, hon. Listen, I don't mean to hit you with this right off the bat, but we're missing the Petersons."

"What happened to them?"

"Their daughter went into labor last night. They're at the hospital."

"That's great news."

"Not for the choir. We're already short on sopranos."

"Then the sopranos will have to take it up a few decibels." Amber checks her watch. "Especially if Bridgette doesn't show. Where is that girl?"

"Haven't heard from her. But she better get here."

"I want details on her date with Isaac last night."

"Hey, that reminds me. We need to plan a girls' night out before Darren gets home. I have a feeling we won't be seeing you for a while once he sets his feet back on American soil."

Amber grins sheepishly. She has definitely indulged in fantasies about their reunion.

"You have me for the next nine days. How 'bout this coming Wednesday?"

"Painting? Shooting? Or binging Netflix?"

"My budget's a little snug right now. Can we do Netflix? My house? You bring your amazing chocolate mousse, and we'll see if Bridgette can make her baked ziti."

"Ladies, ladies, ladies!" a singsongy voice from the back of the church calls out.

Amber turns to see her best friend, Bridgette, coming down the aisle in her nude heels and camel-colored pencil skirt. She's wearing a salmon silk blouse and a delicate gold chain with an infinity charm that Amber's never seen before. She wishes she had even half the energy Bridgette has on a bad day.

"I had the *best date ever* last night!"

Karena nudges Amber with a smile.

"I was expecting at least a text last night," says Amber with a little wink. "You must've gotten in late."

"Isaac took me to that new restaurant that overlooks the lake, and he ordered this amazing seafood platter with oysters, mussels, and escargot."

"You know that's snail, don't you?" Karena says. "Did you tell that boy you don't eat food from the ocean?"

"Turns out, I do." Bridgette glows. "And he got me this." Bridgette runs her fingers over the gold necklace. "Isn't it precious?"

"Precocious, maybe," says Karena.

"This was your second date, right?" Amber is wary.

"He spent over two hundred dollars. I got a glance at the check."

"That's tacky, girl." Karena clicks her tongue.

"What's he got planned for your third date? Skydiving and caviar?" says Amber.

"Hey, I'm just saying that it pays to give people a second chance," Bridgette says.

"Sometimes. And some people," Karena says. "He's trying to buy your affections. You see that, don't you?"

"Can't a girl enjoy a little spoiling?"

Amber smiles. Bridgette is on that dangerous precipice: turning thirty and getting desperate to be married. "Bridge, we wanna do a girls' night on Wednesday."

"This coming Wednesday? Um, can't. Isaac wants me to go with him to some company dinner."

Amber and Karena wag their heads. "Meet his coworkers? Already?" asks Amber.

"Things are moving super fast. You see that, right?" Karena says.

"It's just dinner."

Amber and Karena exchange a look. It's time.

"May I remind you that after Ethan, you

18

begged us to monitor your dating accelerator pedal. Here's your warning. Step off the gas," says Karena.

Bridgette thinks about it for a second. "But he's so cute."

"Bridge," warns Amber.

"Okay, okay. I'll ask Isaac for a rain check. So what's the plan for GNO?"

"My house. Netflix binge."

"Perfect. I'll bring my ziti."

"Don't make it so spicy this time," says Karena.

"The spice makes it mine." Bridgette turns to Amber. "Hey, girl. Ten days. Are you excited?"

"Nine days. And yes."

"You're almost there. Home stretch."

"I know, I know. I want things to be just perfect, but the house is a mess."

"Your house doesn't matter. All he's gonna care about is holding you and Bree in his arms," says Karena.

"I know, you're right." Amber checks the time again. "We'd better get started. I want to make sure we get warmed up and cleared out before the parishioners arrive."

Amber's learned that it's not uncommon for people to show up half an hour before service starts just to make sure they can get a front-row seat to hear Pastor Williams.

19

Karena and Bridgette take their seats as alto and soprano. "Hey, everyone. Good morning. Let's get in place and warm up with 'Jesus Paid It All.' This will be our opening song this morning. Sopranos, you're gonna have to really use your voices today, because Mrs. Peterson's about to become a grandma."

She gets oohs and aahs from the choir. Amber checks for Bree. She's right where she asked her to stay, chatting it up with Mrs. Capers.

"Bree, lemme hear you on that tambourine." Bree gives it a long, hard shimmy. The choir laughs.

"Okay. You got it. Put it down. Watch for my cue." Amber is grateful for such a good kid. She and Darren want to have more. Maybe it'll happen once he gets back home. After years of unsuccessful trying before he left for Afghanistan, Amber stopped wrestling with why and surrendered to trusting God's perfect plan. Besides, Bree is blessing enough.

Amber takes her place as choir director at the podium. She finds her baton and taps out the beat to a modern arrangement of "Jesus Paid It All" that she wrote with Mrs. Capers.

Mrs. Capers comes in with the opening

bars. After the eighth measure, Amber prompts the singers to come in. The sopranos need a little coaxing to up their volume. Bridgette, still giddy from her date, channels that energy to her vocal cords and carries the melody.

Amber then points to Bree, who uses her whole body to shake the tambourine. Amber motions for her to tamp it down, and sends her a wink of approval when she obeys.

As they move into the second verse, Amber gestures for the rest of the choir to lower their voices to a hum as Karena and Bridgette soar into a duet. Their perfectly pitched melody is sure to have the right effect on the crowd.

Amber scans the choir, getting ready to cue them to come in on the chorus. With just three measures to go, Amber returns her gaze to Karena and Bridgette. Karena's expression has taken a turn for the worse, causing Amber concern. When Karena's voice drops off as the choir enters with the chorus, Bridgette glances over to see what's wrong. Her voice thins out, and Amber lowers her hands. The rest of the choir tapers off, looking to Amber for instruction.

"Karena, are you okay?" says Amber. Karena's answer is in her gaze. Bridgette is also transfixed on something at the rear of the church. Amber turns to look.

It registers slowly. Two people are coming down the center aisle. Two men. Tall men. Two soldiers in full dress uniform. Solemn. Marching in perfect step.

Amber feels their expressionless eyes focus on her. She watches as they pace toward the choir loft. In her mind it's slow motion, and she barely notices that Karena and Bridgette have moved to her side, flanking her like bodyguards.

"What is this? What are they doing here?" Amber says, her voice shaky. Bridgette doesn't answer. Karena puts a hand around Amber's arm. It does little to steady Amber's quaking insides.

"Just take a deep breath," Karena whispers. "Don't jump to any conclusions. Let's just see what they want."

Movement at the rear door causes Amber to notice Pastor Williams enter. His eyes are lowered to the ground, but he glances up at his wife. Amber sees the pastor and Karena exchange a disturbing look. Her gut hollows, as if she's been socked hard under the rib cage without warning.

The soldiers move to the front of the church, arriving respectfully to face her. Amber finds it hard to look at them. They wait for her to compose herself. Waiting for eye contact. Everything in the church falls silent.

"Mrs. Amber Hill?" It's all fuzzy in Amber's ears. She struggles to focus on them, her eyes shifting back and forth between their faces.

"I'm Sergeant Miller, and this is Private Kasich. We are here on behalf of the United States Army, and we regret to inform you that your husband, Sergeant Darren Hill . . ." At his name, she retreats, sobbing in heavy gasps. Her chest starts to compress as she stumbles back. Her legs give way, and she collapses.

Amber feels four hands grip her arms and back as she falls to the floor.

"Amber? *Amber?*" The multiple voices calling to her fade away. As she passes out, Amber's brain picks out only one thing: the sound of a tambourine hitting the floor.

CHAPTER THREE:
SUNDAY BRUNCH

Two Years Later

It's now 11:38 a.m., and Patti Hill sits in her silver Cadillac just outside the country club where she and her five girlfriends have a standing reservation for Sunday brunch. The six of them have stuck together since high school, weathering five decades of everything life has dished out. Patti tries to compose herself as she scrolls through the pictures of Darren on her phone.

A lump forms in her throat as she clicks to the phone function to call Kim. She's going to cancel. She hits the voice mail button by mistake, and her eyes go immediately to the last voice mail on the list. It was left exactly two years ago tomorrow. When the call came through it showed up as an unrecognizable number, and because Patti had been at lunch with a friend, she had ignored it and let it go to voice mail. But the annoying caller rang twice more before

Patti stepped outside to answer. It was Karena Williams, the pastor's wife from Amber's church. She was sorry to be the one to tell Patti that her son had been killed and her daughter-in-law was in the hospital.

Patti had rushed to Clarksville Memorial, where Amber was in the emergency room recovering from shock. Bree was there at her side, white as a ghost in the one-size-too-big yellow-striped sailor shirt Patti had bought for her. She spent the day with Amber and Bree until Amber was released that evening. She offered to take Bree overnight, but Amber became hysterical at the idea.

Patti can remember only faint details about the days following. Receiving Darren's body. Funeral arrangements. Memorial services. Paperwork. Interviews. People popping in at all times. Her freezer swelling with ready-made meals from friends and customers. And then silence. Everyone retreated back to their workaday lives. Amber succumbed to a dark place and took Bree with her. Patti found that dark place, too. She shut herself up for a week in her bedroom until Kim dragged her out of the house and back to Sunday brunch. Patti went, but she wore sunglasses to hide her swollen eyes. She donned a black dress and spent the first half hour of brunch in the bathroom. When Kim coaxed her to the table, she saw that her friends had shown up in black, too. And she decided to stay. They were gentle and gracious throughout the whole two-hour meal. Patti didn't remember any of their conversation. Only their kindness.

The next week, Kim picked her up again. And the next week. And the next. By week four, the sunglasses came off. Patti's appetite returned. She started to work again. She owned a successful MyWay cosmetics business that kept her busy during the week.

It was weekends, especially Saturdays, that were too hard to take. To compensate, the brunch ladies started a bowling team so she would have something to look forward to on Saturdays. Her life started to have a familiar flow. Business. Bowling. Brunch. Business. Bowling. Brunch. Weeks turned into months. At Christmas the bowling team disbanded. They didn't regroup after the holidays, but Patti didn't mind. By now she was stronger. Almost herself. And although she would never admit it to the girls, she never really enjoyed bowling that much to begin with.

Patti is surprised how hard the second anniversary is hitting her. The grief reaches deep into her gut and throbs. She needs to lie down. She'll call Kim from home. As she puts the car into drive, Kim rings in.

Patti assures Kim that she's on her way. She pulls the car up to the valet. Kim is waiting for her in the foyer.

After juice and coffee are poured, Bethany, married thirty-six years, three kids, two grandkids, brings it up. "We know this is a hard week for you, Patti. And we just want you to know that we love you and we haven't forgotten Darren."

Patti looks around the table. Her gut has stopped clenching. She is grateful for these strong, beautiful women.

"We know you don't like to dwell on the negative. But we also know you, Patti Hill. We know your heart is still breaking inside," says Kim, longtime divorcée, mother of one, and one of Patti's MyWay associates. Kim is, hands down, Patti's closest confidant. That stubborn lump returns, and Patti is near tears. Kim reaches for her hand. "It's been long and hard, but we're glad to see you living your life. Darren would have wanted that." Patti manages a nod.

"George and I made a sizable donation to Disabled American Veterans in Darren's memory," says Joanne, cancer survivor and mom of four.

"Thank you, Jo. That means the world to me," Patti says.

"We thought it would be a good idea to dedicate this brunch to Darren. Maybe share some memories of him together," says Gayle, widowed attorney, no kids, two dogs. "What do you think?"

"Only if you want to," adds Karen, mid-divorce, three kids, five grandkids.

Patti looks around the table. "I don't know if I'm up for it, but I think it'll probably be good for me."

They fill their plates at the buffet and spend the next hour recalling things about Darren, from his double broken arms when he jumped off the roof to his high school wrestling championship to the day Bree was born.

By the third round of coffee, stomachs are sore from laughing and eyes are dried out from crying. Bethany, Karen, and Joanne announce they have to leave for family duties. Patti sends them off with a round of hugs, assuring them that today's brunch has healed another little piece of her heart.

After they've gone, Gayle asks, "So how are things between you and Amber? Any changes?"

"It's still a lot of excuses. She works a lot. Frankly, I think she's in a bit of financial trouble. That house is going to shambles. I don't know how she can keep up with such a big place."

"You ever get to see Bree?"

"No. It's always Bree's busy. Bree's busy? With what? What kind of social calendar does a child have?"

"She never even calls for you to babysit?" asks Gayle.

"She did once or twice right after it happened. But no. Nothing now."

"Where does Bree go when Amber's working?" says Kim.

"I don't know. Friends' homes, I'm guessing. I really don't know. When I call, I get voice mail. Once in a blue moon Amber will text me a two-word response. *At work. Talk later. Bree's good.*"

"It's time for you to step up the game. You need to arrange a face-to-face," says Gayle.

"That's what I've been telling her," says Kim.

"Yes, but what exactly do you see this arrangement entailing?" says Patti.

"Go to the diner. Ask to be seated in her section. Check in on her."

"I promised myself I wouldn't be that meddling mother-in-law. I want to give her the space and time she needs."

"Patti Hill, I'm calling you out on this one. It's been two years. You have a right to see that grandbaby of yours," says Kim. "And Amber needs to know she still has you to lean on."

Patti finds herself at a bit of a loss when it comes to relating to her daughter-in-law. "Amber never seemed to need me, even when Darren was alive."

"She does. She just doesn't know it yet," says Gayle.

Patti pulls a MyWay lipstick tube from her purse, Copper Penny, a perfect complement to the brassy tones in her hair. "Here's the God's honest truth, ladies. I'm not sure how to handle this. I don't know how to get through to that girl." She presses her lips together, spreading the color across them. "There. I said it."

Gayle and Kim exchange looks, as if the answer is the most obvious thing in the world.

"Patti, just do what you do best," says Gayle.

"I don't understand." Patti returns Copper Penny to her purse.

"You were named last year's top-rated MyWay saleswoman for a reason," says Gayle.

"Yeah, because I poured all my grief into

my work."

"Because you know how to lift people up," says Kim as she takes Patti's hands, squeezing confidence into them.

"Believe in beauty. Believe in you." Patti flippantly quotes the MyWay motto.

"And that's exactly what Amber needs," Kim says.

"You've got to sell her on the idea that her life will be better with you in it," says Gayle.

"Sell?" Patti's lips part in an illuminated smile. "That, I can do."

CHAPTER FOUR:
JUST ANOTHER SUNDAY

Inside the house, the master bedroom remains unkempt, and Amber lies wide-awake, staring out the window. Her face reflects the burden she should never have had to bear.

The alarm goes off on her nightstand. It's after 9:00 a.m. Even ten hours of sleep leaves her groggy. She hits the snooze button for a sixth time, knowing that if she doesn't get going in the next five minutes, she'll be late for her midmorning shift.

Her eyes are drawn to her guitar case, forgotten, dusty, and leaning in the cobwebbed corner. She rolls over, and her look settles on Darren's framed flag and 101st Airborne mug shot. Next to that, their wedding photo. They were too young, according to most. But blissfully happy. So unaware of the road that lay before them. And next to that is another picture, taken just ten months later, when Bree arrived at Clarksville Memorial Hospital. Amber had been worried Darren would be a nervous daddy. Far from it. His eyes glisten with pride and confidence as he cradles his tiny daughter in one arm and wraps the other around his new bride. Instant contentment as a family unit.

With great exertion Amber sits up in bed and shakes off a chill. The alarm sounds again, and this time she reaches over and smacks it. No more snoozing. Her gaze turns to a dusty Bible on the nightstand. Sticking out from the middle is the corner of an unopened envelope addressed to her from Darren and postmarked in the United States. Ten days after she received the news he was gone.

Amber tugs at the corner and slides it out. For a brief second she considers opening it.

But not today. There's no time. And she's still not ready.

She steps over to the window and gazes down at the flower bed along the front stoop. Its fallow soil is still barren from the winter. Spring feels hopelessly far away. A saggy, faded yellow ribbon on a tree in the front yard flutters in tatters in the rainy breeze. She should have replaced it, or torn it down. Another dreary day. Without Darren.

"Mom. It's my turn to bring the Sunday school snack," says Bree, sticking her sleepy head into the doorway.

"What? It is? You sort of failed to mention this."

"No. I told you. You just weren't paying attention."

That seemed to be a common theme in her life lately.

"Can you make something?" Bree asks.

Amber sets the envelope down on the Bible and swings her legs out of bed. Her feet hit the cool wooden floor, and she quickly searches for her slippers.

"We're already running late."

She sees disappointment cross Bree's face.

"I don't know what I have in the house, but I'll see what I can do. Now scoot. You gotta get ready for church."

Bree dashes off. Amber puts it into high gear, grabbing yesterday's soiled waitress smock. She rummages through her dresser drawer for a pair of socks and realizes how desperately she needs to do the laundry. She grabs a mismatched pair and rushes into the bathroom.

Amber opens the medicine cabinet and glosses over Darren's toiletries — unmoved and collecting a thin film of bathroom grime. She reaches around them for her things. Like she has every day since he left.

When Amber arrives in the kitchen, Bree is already at the counter eating cereal straight from the box.

"Don't you want that in a bowl with some milk?"

"I didn't see any in the fridge."

Amber opens the fridge. Sure enough, an empty milk container is shoved all the way toward the back, behind several Styrofoam take-out containers from Rosie's. Amber grabs the empty milk jug and a quarter-full box of orange juice.

"Want some juice?"

"Sure."

She checks the expiration date — "Never mind" — and dumps the contents into the sink. Bree crunches away at her breakfast, engrossed by pictures in her children's Bible.

Amber heads to the cupboard hoping to find a box of brownie mix she can quickly whip up. A quick check of the pantry paints a bleak inventory. A can of black beans. A package of French onion soup. Noodles. A box of crackers with a single cracker stale at the bottom. An old bag of stiff mini marshmallows. A half-eaten box of Froot Loops. And a bottle of gummy vitamins. She tosses one to Bree.

"Here. Eat this."

Bree gobbles it up.

Necessity being the mother of invention, an idea springs into Amber's head. She grabs the marshmallows and Froot Loops.

"Are you done with that?"

"I guess so."

Amber takes the box of puffed-rice cereal from Bree's hands. "Head upstairs and brush your teeth and hair."

"What are you making?" Amber ignores Bree's skeptical look as she slips off her chair and joins Amber at the counter.

"New recipe . . ." She thinks fast. "Um . . . They're called . . . crazy crispies."

Amber empties the contents from both cereal boxes into a large mixing bowl. She heats up the marshmallows in the microwave and pours them over the cornucopia of cereal, stirring until they're all coated. She then presses the concoction into a pan and smooths it out to the sides.

Bree gives the mixture a strange look.

"That looks gross."

"Bree, it's the best I can do right now."

"Lemme taste it."

Amber hands Bree the spoon to lick. Spoon in mouth, Bree nods. It'll do. Amber takes the spoon from Bree's mouth.

"Okay, kiddo. Teeth and hair. Let's go." Bree trudges out of the kitchen.

Amber slaps a layer of foil over the top. Hunger pains prick at the sides of her stomach. She really needs to get a few bites in before heading off to her shift. She checks the to-go containers in the fridge. Limp salad. Moldy scrambled eggs. Shriveled french fries. Trash. Trash. Trash. She finds a soft apple crammed into the corner of the crisper drawer and snatches it.

Bree pops into the kitchen and grabs her Bible from the table. "Okay. I'm ready."

"Okay. Meet you in the car."

Bree rushes out of the house.

Amber tucks the crazy crispies under her arm and finds her purse and keys hanging in the foyer. Through the window of the front door she can see Bree at the end of the sidewalk talking with a strange man dressed in a suit and tie. Stranger danger!

Amber hurries out the door as she hears the man ask Bree, "Your mom home?"

"Hi. Can I help you?" Amber is halfway down the front step. The man looks up.

"Are you Mrs. Amber Hill?"

"Yes, I'm Amber." She reaches out and takes Bree by the shoulder.

"You've been served." Before Amber can

respond, the man shoves an envelope in her hand.

"What? Excuse me?"

The man turns quickly, heading for his vehicle.

"Excuse me. Served for what? Hey. *Who are you?*"

He doesn't turn around as he dives into the driver's side and speeds off.

"Mom, who was that?"

Amber tries to put on a brave face as she looks at the return address. The bank. She knew she was late on her payments, but . . . this can't actually be happening. The shock turns her cold.

"Mom. You okay?"

"Uh . . . yeah."

"What's 'served' mean?"

"Never mind. Doesn't matter. Get in the car."

Bree heads for their rust-bucket minivan and hops in. Amber shoves the envelope into her purse. As she pulls away, Amber surveys their gorgeous Victorian home set against gray skies. She'll get to the bottom of things first thing tomorrow. She's not about to lose anything more.

CHAPTER FIVE: WELCOME TO CLARKSVILLE

Clarksville. 7 miles.

"Less than ten minutes till we begin our sentence in purgatory." Cody addresses an air freshener in the shape of a purple cheetah hanging from his rearview mirror. The scent, Noir Musk, faded two months ago. But the cheetah looks as fearsome as the day it came out of the plastic wrap.

"And the stock-car world is abuzz this morning after Cody Jackson was pulled from the active-driver roster for next week's race in Phoenix. Could this be the end of Cody's career, Bill?" an announcer's voice crackles from the old-school dial radio rigged into the dash of Cody Jackson's car.

The subject of the offending report pounds the steering wheel defensively. "It certainly is *not* the end of my career, Bill. And shame on you for starting rumors."

"Sure looks like it, Gene. His spectacular crash on turn four at last week's Interstate

500 may have been the last straw for team owner Gibbs."

"Spectacular? Got that right. Can't argue with fifty thousand clicks on YouTube. I'll take that as a compliment." Cody tips his head toward the radio in a cocky motion.

"But I guess Gibbs must see something in this kid if he's willing to give him a second chance, Bill."

"More like a tenth or eleventh chance. But then, Gibbs can afford to blow money on a crash risk like Jackson. Just pray he's got another hopeful lined up for the seat. I doubt we'll see Jackson back on the track anytime soon."

"Oh, that one hurt. But watch your back. I'm coming to get you. Soon." Cody snaps the radio dial to the left. "Enough trash talk." He turns the knob to a country music station.

Cody Jackson flies past the city's welcome sign in his '67 Pontiac Firebird, a rusted red (emphasis on rusted), work-on-it-as-I-get-the-dough junker. He revs the engine loud and proud, drawing daggered looks from a couple pushing a sleeping toddler in a stroller.

The town looks pretty much like it did from Google Earth. Except greener. And with more lawn ornaments. He speeds past a gnome entourage marching across a yard.

Cody wonders if he can get a decent burger in this town. He zips past Rosie's Diner, cuts a sharp left — tires burning rubber — and punches it down a tree-lined street of Victorian homes, coasting through stop signs. On the fourth coast, he hears the squeal of sirens behind him.

"You've got to be kidding me!" He slows and sees the squad car's strobe lights in his rearview.

"Pull to the right, please," a megaphoned male voice instructs.

Cody puts the gearshift in neutral and coasts to a stop. "Bless the Broken Road" plays from his speakers. "Appropriate song for the times we find ourselves in. Right, cheetah? Just not so sure this road's a blessing, exactly." The cheetah swings back and forth. Cody reaches into the glove box for his registration card.

"You wanna turn that off, please?"

Cody looks up at the officer who now stands at the driver's-side window.

"The radio. Turn it off, please, sir."

Cody turns down the dial. "Man, you really came outta nowhere."

"You plan on getting the muffler checked?"

Did that couple with the baby call the

cops on him?

"Are you kidding? That muffler cost me cash. Best feature of the car." Cody sees this does not sit well with the officer.

"Those were stop signs back there."

"Yes. I saw them, sir."

"You ran four of them."

"I'm a very conscientious driver. I do the whole left, right, left thing before crossing."

"You need to come to a complete stop when you come up to a stop sign."

"Thought that was more of a suggestion when there's no traffic for miles."

The officer is less than amused. "It's not a suggestion. It's the law. License and registration, please."

Cody hands over the documents and resists the temptation to turn up the radio. He glances at the officer's badge. Brice.

"Officer Brice. You like racing?" Brice starts to write something on his tablet. "You know, like stock-car races?"

Brice lifts his gaze to Cody. "What's your point?"

"I'm a race car driver. Cody Jackson. Maybe you didn't quite recognize me with the scruff." Cody strokes the new beard he's been growing. "And if you and your family are interested, I could score you some tickets to an Interstate event."

"I know who you are, Cody Jackson. I saw your last crash live. And then again on YouTube. And then my buddy also e-mailed me the Asian-spoof version."

"There's a spoof version? Cool."

"You're not trying to bribe me with tickets, are you, Mr. Jackson?" Brice leans over, and Cody gets a good look at the serious expression on his face and the body camera attached to his lapel.

"Oh, no. No, sir. Just a kind offer." Cody smiles coyly for the camera.

"I'll pass. Thank you. In the meantime, since you're new to town and I know that Joe Cartier is expecting —"

"You know Joe?"

"I know everything and everyone. Don't forget it. And don't forget that I'm letting you off with a warning."

"Appreciate it."

"But this is it. You get only one free pass."

"I understand. Thank you." Cody reaches into the backseat and pulls out a rolled-up poster. "Do you have sons?" He starts to unroll the signed poster of himself and his race car.

Brice puts his hand up, shaking his head.

"Daughters?"

"Welcome to Clarksville, Mr. Jackson. Enjoy your — hopefully brief — stay." Officer Brice turns and heads to his car.

Cody sticks his head out the window. "Hey, excuse me? Officer Brice? How do I get to Joe's from here?"

Cody roars into the parking lot of Joe's Auto. The throwback car repair shop with its 1950s signage is the first thing Cody likes about this town.

"This looks like the kinda place we could hang for a while," he tells the cheetah. "Things may be looking up."

He parks the car in front of an open garage bay, swings his door open, and sets his worn, brown cowboy boots on the black pavement. Cody removes his sunglasses and lets his eyes adjust to the bright sun gleaming off a dozen restored beauties in the lot. "Hope I get to take a couple of those babies for a spin."

"Not a chance." The voice drones from inside the first garage hanger. Cody steps in and sees two legs sticking out from under a race car. "You can look, but you can't touch."

"Hello? Are you talking to me?"

"Hand me a nine-sixteenths box end, would ya?"

"Ah . . . Joe?" Cody tries to see who's under there.

"Left side, top drawer."

Cody finds the wrench in the toolbox along the wall.

"Set it in my palm right here."

Cody obeys. The hand grips the tool and disappears.

"You must be Cody, am I right?"

"That's right."

"Joe." The hand comes out again with the nine-sixteenths. "Grab me the next size up, will ya?"

"You got a nice ride here. Yours?" Cody exchanges the smaller tool for the larger one and hands it to Joe.

"It sure is. And I'd like to keep it that way. From what I hear and what I see, you might have some trouble doing that."

"Hey, 'rubbing is racing,' right?"

Cody hears Joe tightening a bolt under the car. The instrument appears again, and Cody takes it. Joe scoots his legs up and slides his body until he's out from under the vehicle. He looks at Cody, studying him as he wipes the grease off his hands.

Joe rises and stands a full head taller than Cody. Formidable. Wowsers. Joe lets a long awkward moment pass between them. Cody is about to break the silence, when —

"No. It isn't. And don't ever quote *Days of Thunder* to me."

Cody's confidence macerates. He judged the benevolence of the situation too soon. And purely based on looks. Classic book-by-its-cover mistake.

Joe checks his watch and, seeing the time, grabs his jacket. "We can take my truck. The old Ford out there. Is that what you're gonna wear?"

"I . . . I guess so. Why?"

"Help me load that go-kart into the back."

Cody looks around for the kart, completely confused as to what's about to go down. Go-karts? Are they going to a derby race?

"Hurry now. We don't want to be late."

"Late for what?"

"It's Sunday. Church."

"Church?"

"Yeah. Steeple. Choir. Pastor. You know church, right? Please tell me I don't have to explain this concept, or we have more work to do than I was led to believe."

Cody does know. When he was a kid, his parents took him to Sunday school. That lasted until junior high, when he and Martin Schmidt would sneak out and wander around town for an hour. He had dabbled in churchgoing off and on with various girlfriends he was trying to impress. But no. Well, Sundays were race days. Besides, he preferred to keep his faith life, what little there was, private — and separate — from his race life.

Joe steps behind an unfinished, kid-size go-kart and starts to push. "Cody. I could use some help here. Let's go."

"Joe. There's one thing you should know about me. I don't do church."

"You do now." Joe deflects Cody's insistent look as he jostles the kart through the garage. "Consider it part of a well-balanced rehabilitation program. Otherwise, we don't have a deal." Joe is headed for a collision with a tire-changing machine when Cody hustles after him, grabbing the wheel to steer the kart out of harm's way.

Welcome to race car purgatory.

CHAPTER SIX:
SHE SHOULD

Amber pulls her minivan into a spot at the far end of the parking lot of Clarksville Community Church so she can avoid making contact with any of the worshippers arriving there. In her rearview mirror she sees the happy attendees, her old friends, greeting Karena, who stands outside the doors passing out bulletins as they enter. Joyful faces. Perfect and pain-free. A cruel reminder of what her life used to be. She turns away.

Bree opens the sliding door and hops out.

"I'll see you after work, okay?"

"I wish you would stay for church," Bree says.

"Can't. Rosie would kill me."

"Bye, Mom." Bree uses all her might to close the door. She sprints toward the church when Amber realizes the crazy crispies are still sitting on the passenger seat.

Amber jumps out. "Bree! Wait! Your snack!"

Bree spins around and sees her mother holding the silver pan. She runs back for it.

"Thanks! Mom . . . will you try to come next week?" Bree's eyes plead with Amber.

"We'll see." The excuse is wearing thin. But Bree accepts the answer and takes off again, spying Hannah, her Sunday school teacher, across the parking lot.

Amber turns to get back into her van when a car pulls up alongside hers. She recognizes it immediately. Her best friend, Bridgette.

"You can't hide from me, Amber Hill," says Bridgette, springing out of the driver's seat, looking as radiant as ever. She dashes to Amber's side and wraps her arms around her in a huge hug. "I'm so glad you made it to church."

"Bridge, I'm in my uniform, silly."

Bridgette steps back and checks her out. "Oh yeah. I was so excited to see you that I didn't even notice. How come you haven't returned my calls? I've been worried about you."

"I'm fine. Good. Just really busy."

"I miss you."

"I miss you, too."

"We should do a girls' night out. Or in.

Or coffee. Or a movie. Or something. We need to catch up, girl."

Bridgette's warmth flows over Amber. She wants to take it all in — that infectious joy that Bridgette so naturally exudes. If she even had just a sliver of it . . . But all she can muster is: "Yeah. I don't have a whole lot new to share."

"You don't have to. We'll just hang out. No pressure."

Amber had always found it impossible to resist Bridgette's sense of fun. Until Darren was killed. Two years ago tomorrow. Now, she can't seem to get past that wall she's built around herself.

"There's someone special I want to introduce you to."

"Oh. You've got another new one?"

"Not just *a* new one, *the* one. Bryan Cartright."

"Really. *The* one?" It takes Amber by surprise. What else has she been missing?

"We're starting to look at rings."

"Wow. Bridge. That's fast. When did you meet?"

"Bryan and I met about a year ago."

Amber feels somewhat betrayed, but mostly guilty. "I'm sorry I haven't had a chance to meet him yet."

"Yeah. I really hope you can. Soon. I want

50

you to get to know him."

"Yeah. I know I've been a bit unreachable. I'm sure if there was a problem with him, Karena would have let me know right away."

"She would. And she approves one hundred percent. But it doesn't feel as real without you being part of the mix."

Amber takes it in, wishing she could give more. Everything about her old life seems so unreachable. She goes for the door handle.

"I'd better get going. I'm already late."

"I know what tomorrow is, Amber. Even though it's been two years, I would never forget." Bridgette lowers her voice. "I was hoping that's why you were back at church."

"I can't, Bridge. Okay?"

"Okay. But . . . You shouldn't be alone."

"I won't be. I'll be with a diner full of people." Amber's joke falls flat. "I promise I'll give you a call and we can set something up."

"Sure." Amber's promise rings hollow, and Bridgette's shrug tells Amber she's not fooling her bestie.

"Thanks for remembering," Amber manages.

"I'm here for you, Amber. Always."

Bridgette heads toward the church. Amber

51

watches for a moment, catching Karena's glance across the parking lot. Karena smiles and waves warmly at Amber. She returns the wave with a sad smile and gets into her van. Her eye finds the foreclosure letter on the passenger seat, and her gut tightens. What would happen if she just tossed it? Pretended she never got it? Would it all go away?

Dismissing it, Amber pulls out of the church parking lot. Now officially very late, Amber turns off the main road to take the shortcut to Rosie's. It leads right past the cemetery where they laid Darren's body. She knows she should stop. She knows she should bring Bree. There are a lot of things "she should." She should be a better friend. She should be singing in the church choir right now. She should be happily married.

CHAPTER SEVEN:
DAZZLE ME

Cody checks his watch. They're a half hour early. To church. Who gets to church early? Joe maneuvers them down the center aisle, selecting a seat in the third pew from the front.

"We're sitting here? Right up front?"

"Yes. We are." Joe lets Cody slide in first.

Cody glances around. Other than the little old lady in the back and a few straggling choir members shuffling out of the choir loft, no one else is present. Cody tries to get comfortable in the stiff wooden bench. He slips his phone out of his pocket and starts to check his e-mail. Before he can click on his text app, Joe's hand swipes his phone out of his hands.

"Hey!"

"Guess it *has* been a while since you've been in church." Joe tucks the phone into his jacket pocket. "No cell phones."

"Joe. The service hasn't even started.

Lemme at least text my mom to let her know I made it here okay."

"Your mom? Really? Come on. I know I look young, but I wasn't born yesterday."

Cody chuckles.

"She really *is* my mom."

"No girlfriend?"

"I'm single."

"Just wait till that gets out around here."

"Yeah, well, don't help it along."

Cody looks up as a woman crosses the front of the church and places her Bible and a sweater on the front pew.

"Karena. Good morning," Joe calls out.

Karena looks up. "Joe. Hey. Good to see you. How was your week?"

"Blessed."

"Not as blessed as mine."

Cody finds the exchange odd. *Is this how folks in Clarksville greet each other? Joe better not expect those words to come outta me. There is nothing blessed about how my week went.*

"Karena, this is Cody Jackson. Cody, Karena Williams. The pastor's wife."

"Oh sure. We've been expecting you. Welcome. Nice to have you here." Karena reaches over the pew to shake Cody's hand.

"Ma'am. Nice to meet you." Cody stands

54

politely. *Does the whole town know about me?*

"Pastor Williams and I would like to have you over for dinner. Get to know you a little," says Karena.

"You would? Ah, sure. Better check with Joe to make sure I can fit it into my busy churchgoing schedule." He shoots Joe a teasing look.

Cody notices a few more families trickle in. Karena hustles off to welcome the new arrivals and is soon replaced by a young man wheeling into the handicap spot next to Joe.

"Nelson, my man." Joe leans over and hugs him. "This is Cody Jackson."

"Welcome to Clarksville."

"Thanks." Cody notices a small, unusual-looking cross hanging around his neck.

"Hey, I saw that last race of yours. What a crash, man. Can't believe you're sitting right here after that one."

"Yeah. So you're a fan?"

"I am. I am. Got into it more after I got stuck in this chair."

He's not sure if he should ask. "I can take you out in the car sometime. If you'd like."

"I sure would."

"You seem to like taking your life in your hands, don't you, Nelson?" Joe jokes. Nel-

55

son punches him playfully as three females slide into the pew in front of them.

"Now, this is a trio of trouble right here. Ladies, please meet Cody Jackson. He's new to Clarksville."

"Ladies. Nice to meet you." Cody nods his head in their direction, making eye contact with the oldest one.

"I'm Bridgette."

"Hannah. Sunday school teacher. And part-time babysitter." She looks at Bree.

"I'm Breeanne Hill." She shakes Cody's hand with a confidence that catches his attention. "Bree for short."

"Nice to meet you, Bree for short." Cody holds his gaze on her for a moment while he shakes her hand. She has a sweet and determined face; but worry, or maybe a shade of gloom, lurks beneath her expression. He wonders what her story is. And where are her parents?

Cody banters with them as they fire questions his way.

Yes, he's training with Joe.

No, he's not new to the sport. He's been doing this for about five years.

Who's his corporate sponsor? Well. Ah. That's complicated.

Yes, he does like racing.

Yes, he does have his own car. *Sort of.*

No, he doesn't know how long he'll be in Clarksville.

And no, Joe, he doesn't have a girlfriend.

Thanks for pointing that out after I told you not to.

And . . . Oh, hey, *changing the subject,* where can he get a good burger around here? Rosie's. Rosie's Diner out on old M37. *Didn't I pass that on the way in?* His stomach growls as the piano starts a prelude. *As soon as church is over . . .*

The pastor steps out from a side door, and the hushed chatter ceases. Cody's milquetoast image of the pastor from his youth is blown out of the water. This guy is impressive. Three-piece tailored suit. Perfect hair. White smile. And the physique of a football player. Respectable. Very.

Joe leans over to Cody and whispers, "That's Pastor Williams. He's been the rock of this church for about twelve years." Cody nods. "Great guy. You'll love him. Used to play football."

There is nothing diluted about this Goliath of the faith. *Now, let's see what he has to say. Bring it, Pastor Williams. Dazzle me. Or at least keep me from falling asleep.*

Pastor Williams steps up to the pulpit and opens the service with a quiet prayer. But Cody keeps his eyes open, locked on the hulk in the suit saying his prayers in a soft, low whisper. Like he's talking to an injured bird. Cody feels himself nodding off in the trance of the pastor's soothing tone.

"Amen!"

"Amen!" the congregation echoes.

Cody's eyes snap open.

Pastor Williams removes himself from the pulpit. He takes the three steps down from the altar until he's level with the people. He spends time engaging with his congregation, his eyes meeting every eye in the room. When he comes to Cody, he smiles, locking his gaze on him.

"What happens when the plans you thought God had for your life don't pan out?"

His deep voice thunders through the sanctuary.

Why is he looking at me? This has got to be some sort of setup. Joe did this. How else would the pastor know exactly what I'm dealing with here? On the exact day I arrive?

Cody slouches in the pew. *Total setup.*

"A lot of people blame God. They give up on God. Stop praying. Stop reading His word. Stop going to His church. It was once said that America will become great again when her churches are full. Do you see all those empty seats around you?"

58

Cody looks to the side. Half-filled pews. Behind him. The back seven rows completely empty. *Probably home watching the race. Where I should be.*

"Those are missing brothers and sisters. Love calls us to bring them home."

Ahead of him, Cody sees Karena and Bridgette nodding to the pastor's words in tandem. Hannah has her arm around Bree. *Seriously, does the kid not have a mom or dad? But who else would force her to go to church?*

"They need to know that God is not done with them. That He has not abandoned them. God wants them to come back to Him."

To do what? Sit in a boring old church?

"And if they are willing to turn to Him with just the tiniest seed of faith, He will show them that nothing is impossible."

Can God help me go fast and win races? 'Cause that's the impossible task I'm facing right now.

Pastor Williams scans the congregation, landing on Cody again. Cody tries to dodge his look.

"Today we find ourselves standing at the precipice of a defining time for our faith and our nation. Each and every one of you needs to put God's love into action, planting that seed of faith."

I have faith that Gibbs is going to get me back on the circuit. That's where I'm planting my trust.

"Who can you pray for today? Right now. Who can you invite back into the fold? Who needs your help and your love today? Who needs the peace and hope that only God can provide?"

The room is so quiet that Cody barely dares exhale. While he's trying to breathe shallowly, his stomach belts out a loud growl. Again. And draws a quick glance and a little giggle from Bree.

"Sorry," he mouths, pointing at his belly and shrugging. Bree smiles and hands him a hard candy from her tote bag.

"Thanks!" Cody mouths again, and pops the candy into his mouth.

The pastor steps back behind the pulpit as the choir files up to the front.

Okay, Joe. I hear you. Part one of your plan worked. I wasn't exactly dazzled, but I didn't fall asleep. And, Joe, I'm puttin' my time in here, but you'd better show me something shiny on the track.

CHAPTER EIGHT:
DIRECTOR OF
YOUTH OUTREACH

After the service, Cody follows Joe down the basement hallway of the church. "Is this where they serve the punch and cookies?"

"So you *have* been to church before." Joe grins. "In the all-purpose room. But first, there are a few little folks I want you to meet." Joe and Cody slip into the back of a Sunday school classroom, where a dozen squirmy kids are seated at a round table in deep concentration as they paint four-inch terra-cotta pots. Cody sees Bree slathering on pink tempera paint.

Cody recognizes Hannah at the front of the classroom. Behind her there's a whiteboard with handwritten words scribed in black marker:

If you have faith the size of a mustard seed, you will say to this mountain, "Move from here to there," and it will move. Nothing will be impossible for you.

That sounds vaguely familiar. Like I learned that verse sometime during my kid life.

The smell of the paint and the musty basement carpet take Cody right back to his Sunday school days. He was probably about Bree's age when he "accepted Jesus into his heart." His teacher had congratulated him on making the most important decision of his life. She said his whole life would be different from then on. Funny thing. She was right. His life became very different. His parents divorced. He had to move cities with his mom and change schools. His grades went down. He started to skip school and hang out at the racetrack. *Well, eventually that did turn out to be for the better. So, who knows? Maybe the whole Jesus thing did work.* Or maybe he had just stumbled into a way to survive on his own.

"What are we doing in here, Joe?"

"Hold your horses." Joe shushes him with a pursed look.

"David, why don't you read the verse for the day?" Hannah says to a boy with a cropped haircut and black-rimmed glasses who's filling his pot with loose soil.

"B-b-but my s-s-stutter . . ."

"It's okay, we don't mind," Bree tells him.

"Go ahead, David. Just take your time," says Hannah.

62

David presses his index finger to where the verse starts on the page. " 'Truly I t-t-tell you. If you have faith as s-s-s-small as a mustard s-s-s-seed, you can s-say to this mount-t-t-tain, 'M-move from here to there,' and it will m-m-move. N-n-nothing will b-b-b-be impossible for you.' " He has a relieved look on his face as he finishes.

"Excellent job, David. Thank you," says Hannah.

The students go back to work on their pots. Hannah holds something up between two pinched fingers.

"Can anyone see what I'm holding?"

The kids look up and shake their heads. Hannah unfolds her hand, and Cody finds himself craning his neck to get a glimpse of her palm as she shows each child what she has.

"This is a mustard seed. It comes from one of the biggest, strongest trees in the world. A mustard tree! But look how tiny it is at the beginning. That's a pretty powerful seed, huh?"

Scattered nods.

Mustard comes from that little thing? Huh, interesting.

"So what Jesus was saying in Matthew seventeen, verse twenty, is that even if our faith is small, like this seed, it can move mountains."

That sounds a little far-fetched. Why are Sunday school teachers always bringing up crazy ideas like this and expecting vulnerable little kids to make sense of them?

"A mountain is like a problem that you have in your life," says Hannah.

I'm sensing a theme here today. Coincidence? Thinly veiled, Joe.

"All you need to do is ask God to help you with that problem. And believe that He will."

Bree looks up. "Can He help my mom, too?"

"He sure can, Bree." Hannah begins passing out the seeds. "Even the tiniest bit of faith can make a difference in the lives of your family and friends. Because your faith can lead others to God."

The kids carefully tuck their seeds into the soil. Hannah comes around with a watering can and soaks each seed.

"Hannah, that was a beautiful lesson," says Joe. "Can I make a quick announcement?"

"Of course, Joe." Hannah motions him to the front of the room. "Let's all say good morning to Uncle Joe."

"Good morning, Uncle Joe!" the kids belt out.

Uncle Joe? Are you kidding me?

"Good morning, everyone. I want you to meet Mr. Cody Jackson."

"Let's give him a warm welcome," says Hannah.

They'd better not start calling me —

"Good morning, Uncle Cody!" the kids yell at the top of their lungs.

"Hey, kids," Cody returns in a lilting tone.

"Uncle Cody's the new director of our youth outreach program," says Joe.

"The what?" Cody turns to Joe, his jaw dropping.

"And his first project will be helping to build go-karts for the Clarksville Community Church go-kart derby," Joe announces.

The kids break into cheers.

"He'll be giving test drives in the parking lot after Sunday school."

"Sounds like fun, huh, guys?" Hannah says.

"Yeah!"

"Let's thank them."

A round of "Thanks, Uncle Joe! Thanks, Uncle Cody!"

Cody gives the kids a halfhearted wave and exits the room trailing behind Joe. "Joe. I don't know the first thing about go-karts. Or kids. This is a recipe for disaster."

Joe cuts into the all-purpose room. "You still want those cookies?"

"And when am I supposed to train? Huh? I didn't come to Clarksville to build go-karts!"

Joe points Cody to the cookie table at the center of the all-purpose room. "They're homemade. Try the chocolate-chip peanut butter before they're all gone." Joe spies a friend waving to him from a table at the edge of the room, leaving Cody abandoned.

He stands there for a second, trying to hold his own. Then he nervously heads to the cookie table. There's one chocolate-chip peanut butter left. Should he take the last one? Is that polite? It looks all soft and gooey in the middle. Just a little under-cooked. He likes them that way.

"Go ahead. It's all yours," a female voice coos behind him.

Cody turns to find a gaggle of eligible women descending on their prey.

CHAPTER NINE:
AN OFFER SHE CAN REFUSE

Patti steps into Rosie's Diner and feels a pleasant nostalgia. She spies Rosie at a table, taking an order, and notes that she looks exactly the way she did twenty years ago when she gave Patti a job. Patti's husband had run out on her and Darren, and she needed to get back on her feet. Rosie's big heart and successful diner had saved Patti during those first few years when she was learning how to be a single parent. Patti waitressed for Rosie until her MyWay independent beauty business was earning enough to keep her afloat. Rosie was also her first MyWay customer. She had purchased the entire skin-care collection and let Patti host beauty parties at the diner on her days off. Rosie had long ago stopped buying beauty products, but Patti periodically gifted Rosie with her favorite creams and makeup. A small token of her gratitude for her help during those lean years.

"How many in your party today, ma'am?" the hostess asks, flying up to the front and grabbing a stack of menus.

"Oh, just me."

The hostess leads Patti to a two-top and sets down a plastic menu. "Strawberry pancakes and the Reuben sandwich are on special today. Coffee?"

"Yes. Just coffee, please." The hostess nods and heads to the kitchen. Rosie swings by with an armload of dirty dishes.

"Patti Hill. You're a sight for sore eyes." She leans in and lops a free arm around Patti's shoulder. Patti leans in for the hug. "You gotta come around here more. I miss you, hon."

"Rosie. I miss you, too. Place looks the same."

"And so do you. Not a year older than when you worked here. Those beauty products really work, don't they?"

Patti reaches into her bag and hands Rosie a small MyWay box. "It's a new eye shadow cream called Candied Peaches. Part of our spring line. I think it'll look beautiful with your skin tone."

Rosie looks at the box and slips it into her apron pocket. "You know I love these little treasures. Thank you. So what can I get you to eat?"

"Nothing. Just came from brunch with the ladies." Patti scans the diner. "Actually, I came to see Amber."

"Well, sure, hon. She's working the back section today, but I'll send her out."

"Is she working out for you?"

"For the most part. She's a little distracted sometimes, but she's a hard worker. Never misses a shift."

"I'm worried she's having trouble making ends meet."

"Well, I don't know about that. She doesn't share that stuff with me, and I'm not one to pry."

"Now, we both know that's not true," jokes Patti.

"I suppose I walked right into that one. Look, you and Amber are different people. But you've been in similar situations, and you know these things take time."

"She doesn't have the same drive that I did."

"Amber's been wounded differently. But give her a chance. She'll find her way." Rosie's wise smile sends Patti a small measure of reassurance. "How about you? How have you been?"

"I'm okay. Sorry I haven't been in more. It's been . . ." A small lump in her throat stops her.

"Aw, hon. Don't you fret about it. I knew you'd be back when you were ready." Rosie pats her shoulder. "I'm just glad you're here now."

Patti glances over at a picture of Darren in his 101st Airborne cap that hangs behind the counter next to a couple of other young, local faces in uniform.

"It's good to see you." Patti manages a small smile.

"Look, I'm gonna get you a piece of lemon meringue on the house and tell Amber you're here." Rosie gives her a wink, and Patti feels a small degree better.

"Thank you, Rosie. I'd like that."

Patti's nerves twitch, and she distracts herself by adding another layer of gloss to her already expertly painted lips. When she looks up from her pocket mirror, Amber is standing there with a coffeepot.

"Hi, Patti. You wanted coffee?"

"Yes. Please." Amber turns the coffee mug over, and the hot liquid splashes onto the saucer. "It's nice to see you, Amber." She tries to be chipper, but her tone conveys the chip on her shoulder. "A shame I have to come all the way down here to do it."

"Anything to eat?"

Patti quickly assesses how to melt through Amber's icy wall.

"Rosie's bringing me a piece of pie." Patti seals her lip gloss into her sleek gray My-Way makeup bag. "So, how are you?"

"I'm doing fine." Amber stands there, pot at her hip. "Cream and sugar?"

"No, black. Thanks."

"I've got a ton of tables in back, so if there's nothing else . . ."

Patti dives in. "I guess I'm just surprised to find you working today."

"Why?"

"Amber, it's just . . . tomorrow of all days. I thought maybe . . . we could . . ."

"It's the end of my shift, and I've got a lot to catch up on." Amber's jaw sets. "Rosie needs me."

"Have you taken Bree to visit Darren's grave?"

Amber pauses, her cheeks flushing. Patti has hit a nerve.

"If she asks, I'll take her," Amber says.

"She's nine. You have to do these things for her. You set the tone."

"Patti, I'm not going to do something that might upset her."

"It doesn't have to be an upsetting moment." Patti reels it in, wanting to keep Amber engaged. "So, how *is* Bree doing?"

"She's fine."

"Is she at home with a sitter?"

71

"No, she's at church."

"I see." Patti puts on a pleasant smile. "You know, I'd really like to spend more time with my granddaughter. I'd be happy to watch her sometimes . . . when you work."

"She likes going to Sunday school. And after that, Hannah watches her."

"Oh, I see." Patti drops the saleswoman attempt as frustration takes over. "It just seems to me that Bree could benefit from a more stable home environment."

"And that's what I'm giving her." As Amber raises her voice, nearby diners start to stare. Patti smiles back to dissuade their looks.

"By working seven days a week?" Patti lowers her tone.

"I don't really have a choice right now."

"It seems to me that with Darren's death gratuity payment, you shouldn't have to work so much."

Rosie swings by with a piece of lemon meringue and sets it in front of Patti.

"Everything okay here?" Patti catches Rosie's concerned look.

"This looks delicious, Rosie," says Patti. "Thanks for the pie."

"Amber, I'll check on your tables for ya," Rosie says, and disappears before Amber can protest.

"Amber, have you mismanaged the gratuity money?" Patti gets right to the point.

"You don't have any faith in me. Never have." Amber starts to turn.

"I'm sorry. I didn't come here to pick a fight." Patti hands Amber a small MyWay cosmetics box. "I came to make you an offer."

Amber opens it and pulls out the products. Patti doesn't like the strange look that follows.

"Eye shadow and lip gloss?"

"It's more than that. I want to help you set up your own MyWay franchise."

"I don't understand."

"I think you'd make a great MyWay beauty consultant." Amber's dumbfounded expression lingers, making Patti uncomfortable. "You can make stable money as an independent consultant. You'll be able to quit working here and stay home with Bree when she needs you."

"That may have worked for you, but I'm not interested."

Amber puts the products back into the box and slides it back to Patti.

"Then what's your long-term plan, Amber? Because I sure hope it doesn't include slinging burgers and fries for Rosie for the next twenty years." Patti meant no ill will against Rosie and all she had done for her, but Rosie was a businesswoman, and she had turned Patti into one, too. Patti could do the same for Amber. If she would just let her.

"I've got things under control," Amber says.

"It doesn't appear so. You look haggard and run-down. Where does Bree fit into all this?" Patti is beyond treading carefully. She swallows, trying hard not to unleash her full anger.

"We may have our differences, but I think we can agree that Bree is the most important thing in the world to both of us."

Amber seems unaffected as she stares at Patti, who shoves the cosmetics back into Amber's hands as she rises from the table.

"Do yourself and your daughter a favor. Think a little harder about your future." Patti drops a couple of dollars on the table. "Someday you'll thank me."

Patti walks briskly out, leaving the pie as she catches Rosie's disapproving eye. She wants to wipe that sanctimonious look right off Rosie's brow. Sometimes it takes a little tough love.

Rosie never had to prod Patti like this. Patti needed no goading when it was time to step it up for Darren's best interests. Darren had always come first. And MyWay beauty consulting was Darren's ticket to the college education Patti never had. And then came Amber. Senior year of high school. Three months after graduation, a wedding. And that following June, beautiful Bree. Two months later, Darren enlisted in order to support them.

Amber had messed up Patti's plans for Darren once; and now she was doing it again with her only grandbaby.

Patti storms across the parking lot to her car. She needs the comfort of her couch. From there she will find a way around this. There's always a way. She just needed to figure it out.

CHAPTER TEN:
RACING FOR GLORY

Cody follows Joe across the church parking lot to Joe's old Ford pickup.

"So are we doing some track time this afternoon or what?" Cody reaches for the passenger-side door.

"Wait a minute. Slow down. We're not leaving just yet."

"We're not?" Cody turns to see Joe removing the tarp from the bed of the pickup.

He leans over the side of the bed and sees the kid-size go-kart with the words "Racing for Glory" emblazed in gold paint on the side.

"The name of the Clarksville church derby car team," says Joe. "Gimme a hand."

Seriously? "We're doing this now?"

"Yup. Kids'll be out any second. I want you to show them the ropes. Okay?"

Do I really have a choice?

"Joe, I've never even driven one of these things, and you expect me to teach a bunch of kids?"

"This is not optional, by the way. This is part of your training," says Joe.

Submission has never been Cody's strong suit, but he's curious to see where Joe's unorthodox training methods are taking him.

As if on cue, kids stream out through the front doors of the church and circle around Joe and his kart, bombarding him with questions and excitement.

"Okay, who wants to take a spin?" says Joe.

Every hand shoots up. Kids start to push their way to the kart. *Must be at least twenty of 'em. Great. We're gonna be here all afternoon.*

"Back up. Ease up. You'll all get a turn," Cody tells them, holding up his hands to push the crowd back. "Line up along the sidewalk."

And do what? I don't know how to deal with kids. They're smelly. And they say really inappropriate things at all the wrong times. Cody steps forward, looking at the unruly bunch. "Um . . . All right, everyone. Away from the kart. On the sidewalk. Um, I'm gonna need it boy girl boy girl, shortest to tallest, down the line."

Joe gives him a puzzled look. Cody shrugs.

Makes sense to me. He starts moving bodies like chess pieces until he's satisfied with the equal gender order. He places Bree and David next to each other, since they're the same height.

"Okay. They're all ready, Joe." Cody steps back and folds his arms across his chest. "Now what?"

"Well. Now. Fire up the kart," Joe says, reaching into his truck for a few helmets.

Cody goes around to the rear of the kart, primes the choke on the lawn mower–size engine, and pulls the starter cord. The go-kart fires up, and the kids go crazy with shouts and cheers.

Doesn't take much to entertain these country bumpkins.

"You." Cody points to a wide-eyed boy at the front of the line. "You're first."

The boy steps up. Cody gets him into the kart and shows him how to use the gas and brake. The kid catches on quickly, and Cody sends him to circle the parking lot.

When he returns, the kids in line cheer. The boy loses concentration and almost runs over Cody. Cody grabs the steering wheel. "Foot off the pedals!" He pulls him over to the side and wheels him to the start line. Joe helps the driver out of the kart and starts removing his safety gear.

"Next driver!" Cody calls out, noticing a minivan pulling into the far end of the parking lot. A woman in a pink waitress uniform gets out and stands near the van to watch. She catches his eye. Cody smiles. It takes a moment before a small smile forms and then quickly disappears. *Does she know she's late for church?*

"You going to punch in and coach up our next driver?" says Joe.

Cody jolts back to Joe, who follows his gaze. "Don't even think about it."

"What?"

"She's outta your league."

"How do you know?"

"That's Bree's mom. Amber. And she's had a rough go of it."

"What happened?" Cody glances at Joe's stern jawline.

"She lost her husband in Afghanistan. And she doesn't need your shenanigans in her life right now."

"You don't think much of me, do you?"

"Focus on your training."

"I will. When it starts."

"It already has."

Bree steps up, next in line, grinning ear to ear. Joe hands her the helmet. "She's all yours. I've gotta take a pit stop inside." Joe heads off, leaving Cody with Bree.

79

"You ever driven one of these before?"
Cody asks. Bree shakes her head. "Okay,
hop in. Grab the steering wheel."

He helps Bree into the kart. "There are
two pedals on the floor. Right is gas. Makes
it go. Left is brake. Makes it stop."

Bree nods.

"Which one brakes?"

"Left."

"Which one goes?"

"Right."

"You got it. Give it a little gas and steer
around the cones. Okay?"

Bree takes off, flying expertly across the
parking lot. *Wow, another Danica Patrick in
the making.* He can see her smile growing
bigger as she eases around the second turn.
This is an altogether different Bree than the
one he met this morning. That gloomy face
is gone. *She feels free.* Cody knows the feeling well. It's the thing that keeps him coming back to the track.

Cody glances over at the minivan. Lady in
pink is back in the driver's seat. Cody can
see her head resting against the headrest on
the driver's side. *Wonder why she isn't out
here watching her daughter.*

David sidles up to Cody as Bree coasts to
a stop. Cody helps her out of the car.

"You did great out there, Bree." She takes

off her helmet and hands it to David.

"Are you g-going to help us b-build our own g-go-karts?" says David.

"Looks like that's going to be part of my sentence."

"Were you in prison?" asks David.

"Do you know David's uncle?" asks Bree.

"He's d-doing a sentence in J-Jackson."

"We pray for him."

Cody changes lanes fast.

"Okay, here you go, David hop in." He checks David's helmet. It's snug.

"Is it a m-m-manual or an a-automatic?" David slides right into place and buckles the seat belt.

"Automatic. Right gas. Left brake."

"Okay. I got this."

"You sure?"

"Yeah, I c-c-cut the grass at home with a riding m-m-mower."

"You do? My dad would have never let me do that at your age."

"Oh, I d-d-don't have a d-d-dad."

Open mouth. Insert foot. "All right. Ready?" Cody gives the kart a push. "Gas!"

David zips off. *Another natural.* Cody and Bree watch him take a lap.

"Does it cost anything?" Bree asks.

"Does what cost anything?"

"Building the go-kart?"

81

"Oh, uh, I don't think so. This is my first day, so . . ."

"How fast do they go?"

"Fast enough." Cody keeps his eyes on the parking lot. "David! Eyes on the road!"

David rounds the last turn and swings out too wide. "Pull it in! Pull it in, David!" The steering wheel gets away from him and his kart beelines for Joe's truck.

"Foot on the brake! Hard!"

David does the opposite. The kart lurches forward just a few seconds from T-boning Joe's antique Ford. At just that moment, Joe exits the church and sees his aquamarine beauty about to be rammed.

"Braaaaaaake!" *Gotta save that beautiful Ford!* Cody dives after David's kart.

David throws his hands up off the wheel and covers his eyes.

"Grab that kart, Jackson!" yells Joe, running across the parking lot.

Cody leaps into action, grabbing the back of the kart and using all his weight to stop it. The kart drags to a stop, its nose lightly grazing the vintage Ford's fender. Cody cuts the choke and the engine sputters out.

"David, you okay?" Cody asks, coming around to help him out. David gets out of the kart on shaky legs. "Hey, you okay, buddy?"

David nods.

"I thought you said you could drive a riding mower."

"It doesn't go *this* fast."

"How bad is it?" Cody can't look. Joe rolls back the kart to inspect a three-inch scrape on his fender.

"Nothing to cry over. You can buff and paint that in the morning." Joe pushes the kart toward the start line. "Next rider!"

I can buff and paint? When do I get to drive? Cody is not some hired hand. He's not here to help with all Joe's little pet projects. He's here to drive.

"I know what you're thinking. And the answer is soon enough."

Joe heads inside the church, leaving Cody with seventeen more eager and impatient drivers.

CHAPTER ELEVEN: THE LITTLE MUSTARD SEED

How dare Patti waltz into Amber's life — after being absent for almost two years — and pretend that beauty products are the solution to all her problems! Amber sits wearily at the kitchen table, still dressed in her waitress uniform, fuming over her mother-in-law's surprise visit to Rosie's. Become a cosmetics saleslady? Get real, Patti. And why exactly does she think Amber would be a successful salesperson for anything related to makeup? Amber's lucky if she has enough time to slap on loose powder and a few strokes of mascara. For Pete's sake, she still owns the same eye shadow compact she bought for her wedding. Besides, MyWay is expensive. She can hardly feel right about promoting products she herself can't afford. Drugstore-brand facial cleanser and a five-dollar bottle of moisturizer work just fine.

Amber tries to lay her angst aside as she

pages through the Sunday paper a customer left behind at Rosie's. She flips through until she finds the classified ads in the back and scans down the columns, trolling for something promising.

Patti's stunt keeps distracting Amber's thoughts. Glancing up, she sees the MyWay starter kit Patti had forced on her. Eye shadow and lip gloss? No, thanks.

Truth is . . . Patti hit a sore spot. Amber does need a better-paying job. She shoves her newspaper at the box and flips it off the table, out of her line of sight. It lands on the floor with a soft *thwunk.* The little act of aggression somehow makes her feel slightly better. And also slightly ungrateful.

Amber folds up the newspaper, revealing the real enemy. The foreclosure envelope. She hasn't had the courage to open it all day. Now here it sits, like a ticking time bomb waiting to explode her life. Time to dismantle.

Amber slits the envelope open with her nail and begins to read. The letter is from Mr. Jim Wellington, CEO and bank president. Her loan is in default. Her house is going into foreclosure. This is her first notice to vacate the property within thirty days.

It's way worse than she imagined. Her

heart races. There must be a mistake or a loophole. Had she really fallen *that far* behind in payments? It was only the last two months that she missed. Maybe this was just a bank formality. Maybe all she needs to do is catch up. Surely she can find the money somewhere. She'll head over in the morning and convince this Wellington to help find her another option.

"What's that?" Bree asks, bouncing in and seeing the discarded items sprawled across the dining room floor. "What happened here?"

Amber looks up from the letter but doesn't reply. Bree joins her, setting a four-inch clay pot painted pink and rimmed in green on the table. She then bends over and picks up the box, placing it next to her mother.

"Isn't this the stuff Glam-ma sells?"

"Glam-ma?"

"Yeah. *Grandma* and *glamorous.* Glam-ma. Get it?"

"I get it." Amber marvels for a second at Bree's ingenuity. And she's right. Patti is beautiful and glamorous and successful and confident. Everything that Amber is not. Bree definitely inherited Patti's glamour and spunk. Amber feels a twinge of guilt that Patti and Bree haven't seen much of each other. It hasn't been intentional. But neither has exactly reached out, either. So there. The phone rings both ways. Bree busily applies the MyWay lip gloss and puckers her lips.

"Can I have this?"

"No. It's going back to Grandma."

"Glam-ma!"

"Go wipe it off."

Bree heads into the kitchen, and after a moment Amber hears the water running. What is she doing in there? Amber circles a couple of job possibilities she'll look into in the morning. Hospitality manager, Dunsbrook Inn. Cook, Clarksville Elementary. Nursing-home staff. Must have CNA. Amber's always wanted to be a nurse. She wonders how much schooling she would need to get her CNA certificate. Also where the money would come from to pay for it.

Bree scurries back in with a cup of water and carefully adds a drizzle to her pink terra-cotta pot.

"So, how was church today?" Amber mutters with her head still in the paper.

"Great. We met this new guy at church named Cody. And he and Uncle Joe are gonna help us make go-karts."

"Yeah, I think I saw you guys when I came to pick you up."

"Did you see David hit Uncle Joe's truck?"

she asked excitedly.

"He did?"

"Yeah. When it was David's turn, the brake broke on the kart, but he didn't know it and he almost hit Joe's . . ." In her excitement, Bree tips over the cup of water, and it spills onto the table and all over Amber's newspaper.

"Bree, c'mon. Watch what you're doing." Amber sends Bree a sharp look.

"Sorry, Mom." Bree tries to mop up the water with her shirtsleeve.

"No, don't. I got it." Amber dashes into the laundry room off the kitchen and grabs a towel, returning quickly to soak up the water, which drips into a puddle below the table.

"What is that thing in there, anyway?"

"This is my mustard seed. We planted it in Sunday school."

"A mustard seed? Why not a bean or marigold?"

"Because Jesus says if you have a little faith, this tiny seed can turn into the biggest tree in the world."

Amber looks at Bree, unsure. Bree soldiers on.

"And in science class I learned that plants like to be talked to so they'll grow."

"They do, huh?"

"I think he needs a name."

"He? It's a he?"

"Yeah. And I can't just call him 'Hey, seed.' " Bree scrunches up her nose in thought. "Matthew! Matt for short."

"Why Matt?"

"Because of the Bible verse. Matthew seventeen."

"I see." Amber wishes she had even an ounce of Bree's humble, unwavering faith. Even when Bree learned that Daddy wasn't coming home, her first question was "Is he with Jesus in heaven?"

"Where do you think we should keep him? He needs lots of light."

"Honey, don't get your hopes up. Some seeds just don't grow where we live."

But Bree is undaunted. "Mom, this one will."

Amber gives in to her persistence. "Put him in your room. Your windows have southern exposure. It's the best sun in the house."

And with that, Bree scoops up Matt and darts for the stairs. Amber can hear her footsteps ascend the wooden staircase and pad into her room, above the dining room.

What is she going to tell this child when, two weeks from now, there's nothing but dry dirt staring back at her? What was Hannah thinking?

CHAPTER TWELVE:
EVERYTHING SHE CAN

Amber waits in the plush, tranquil lobby of First National Bank in downtown Clarksville, clutching her purse and foreclosure notice as her foot taps anxiously beneath her. It doesn't take long before she's summoned into the tinted-glass office of Jim Wellington, a half-bald, pasty man with the wit of an accountant. She knows the type. Spends his days behind a desk and his weekends unwinding in his lakeside condo doing crosswords with his wife and walking his yippy Yorkshire terrier.

Amber takes a seat in a velveteen armchair opposite Jim's dark walnut desk, sparsely topped with a computer, several stacks of paperwork, and a single silver-framed family photo. Not a paper is askew. He takes his thick fountain pen between his thumb and forefinger, using it like a pointer as he goes through Amber's file.

Amber's nerves are on edge, and adrenaline courses through her slight, thin form. The concerned expression on Jim's face does not escape her. She rubs her palms together in an attempt to dry the sweat from them.

"What caused you to fall behind in your payments, Mrs. Hill?" Jim begins.

"Well, I never meant to get behind, actually." Connecting her thoughts to her words feels like stirring molasses. "I'm not sure what happened. But I want to make it right."

"I appreciate your willingness. Why don't you tell me a little bit about your personal accounting process."

"Okay. Basically, I pay all my bills the old-fashioned way. I write checks and mail them."

"That's perfectly fine. I always encourage my clients to do what works for them." This puts Amber more at ease. "So, how do you budget for your bills?"

"Budget? Well, I just pay the bills off when I get them in the mail. But I wait until the end of each week. So I pay off whatever has come that week."

Jim nods and purses his lips. Amber can tell this is the wrong answer.

"And what happens when there's not enough money in the account to pay all the week's bills?"

"Well, I write the check and mail it a couple of days later."

"After you've deposited more money?"

"Sometimes. Not always. I'm not great at keeping track."

"Mrs. Hill, it's a reactive, rather than pro-active, system you're working there. And it's the reason why you missed the last three house payments."

Amber nods. "I'm willing to make adjustments."

"That's good to hear. I'd like for you to make an appointment with my assistant and financial adviser, Kendra Drake. She can help you fine-tune your budget. Would you be willing to do that?"

"Yes. Of course. Will that help me keep my house?"

"It'll be a start. But I'll be honest, I'm not sure this is a salvageable situation without some significant outside help."

"What are you saying?"

"The only way you can stall this process is if you can come up with the missing payments, plus this current month's payment."

Amber pauses. At a loss. That's a lot of money. More money than she makes in a month.

"Can you draw from your savings?"

"I don't . . . have any," she admits. "I can

try to pick up more shifts." It's probably not enough, but it's all her brain can come up with on the spot.

"Mrs. Hill, may I ask you something rather personal?"

Amber nods.

"Did you receive a death gratuity check from the military?"

"I did." Amber nods again, glancing down at her lap. She knows what's coming. She'll need to give an account of the hundred grand she received from the government.

"I'm assuming by your expression that you no longer have that money?"

"That check wasn't the safety net it was made out to be."

Jim shifts uncomfortably in his seat. "I'm listening."

"When Darren was deployed . . . it was tough to make ends meet. His electrician salary was cut in half when he left. I had to put a lot on our credit cards. Throw in a transmission for the car, a new roof, the water heater going out . . . I just got really behind. I used the check to pay everything off. I thought it was the responsible thing to do."

Jim nods.

Amber senses his desire to offer solutions. "What else can I do here?"

"Have you considered perhaps renting out a room or two in your home?"

"Get a roommate?"

"Yes. Splitting costs might make it more affordable for you."

"I don't know. It doesn't feel safe to me."

"People do it all the time. Ask for referrals. Establish a trial period — say, thirty days."

"You make it sound so easy. I'm not sure I'm ready to share our space."

"It's just a suggestion. But if it's not for you, then you need to be willing to let the house go."

"I was thinking about getting a different job. You wouldn't happen to have any referrals, would you?"

"I wish I did. Have you noticed all the empty shop windows downtown? Clarksville has been hit pretty hard since the recession. A lot of our companies moved out years ago. Even though the rest of the country is back on track, we're still suffering from a depleted economy. However, from time to time, things do land on my desk. It helps if I have an idea of what kind of job you'd like, or what other goals you have in mind for yourself."

"I guess I . . . I haven't ever really thought about it. I just always . . . My plan was to be a wife and mother."

"And those are very important and worthy professions, Mrs. Hill. But sometimes life throws us into situations that nudge us to adjust our plans."

Amber holds back tears and forces herself to keep a stoic look on her face. She can't let Jim Wellington see her falter, even if she has to feign confidence with every ounce of her being.

"Are there other skills you can draw on? Hobbies? Interests? Things you've always wanted to try?"

"I don't really know what else I'm good at." Why does it sound so weak now that all her hopes and dreams and plans were tied up in Darren? "I was thinking nursing assistant."

"That's a good goal. The library offers free career counseling and skills evaluation. Why not start there?"

Amber nods. "If I have time."

"Mrs. Hill, I don't mean to speak harshly or to scare you, but you don't have the luxury of waiting. You should have come to me when we served you the first notice. Let me explain what's about to happen now. If you miss the next payment, there are only two options: you can short-sale your home, or the bank —"

But all Amber hears is . . . "Sell our home? I can't sell our home."

"Then the bank will be forced to take possession. I'm very sorry, Mrs. Hill."

"Is there anything else I should know?"

"I think we've covered everything." Jim shuffles the papers together and slides them neatly back into their file.

"What else can I do? Please, I'm willing to try. I just need a little more time." Amber's facade drops. She doesn't dare move. Or breathe. Or blink. This man holds her life in the balance.

"The best I can offer is a two-week reprieve before we move into the next phase of the foreclosure."

"What does that mean, exactly?" A smidgen of hope arises in Amber.

"It means you have two more weeks to come up with the money to save your house."

"Okay. I see. Well, I can work with that." She manages a tight smile as she rises from the velvet armchair. "Thank you for your time, Mr. Wellington."

"In the meantime, I would ask you to please consider other options for your future."

Amber flees from Jim's office, across the lobby floor, and down the steps into the street. She has no idea how she's going to pull this off.

CHAPTER THIRTEEN: SINGLE AND TRYING TO GET AHEAD

The next morning, Amber drops Bree off at school a half hour early, where she finds the door is still locked and she has to wait another fifteen minutes until the janitor unlocks it. From there she rushes to Rosie's, only to arrive a half hour late for her morning shift. Can't win.

Dashing into the front of the diner, she's relieved to see Rosie hovering in the kitchen, scolding the cook for not ordering enough rye bread. She sneaks in behind the front register, punches in, and then exchanges her coat for an apron. She just finishes cinching the apron around her waist when Rosie's voice summons her from the counter.

"Glad you could make it in this morning."

Rosie cruises up, overloaded with a tray of piping-hot pancake platters.

"I'm so sorry, Rosie. I had to bring Bree

to school a half hour early, and the door was still locked."

"Save it," Rosie snaps. "Grab the coffeepot and follow me."

Amber trails behind Rosie to table twelve, where six hungry fishermen are eagerly anticipating the Rosie special — two eggs, two slices of bacon, and a tall stack of her famous pancakes.

"Morning rush starts at seven. I need you here by six thirty." Rosie distributes the plates as Amber fills coffee mugs. "Anything else I can get you, boys?" The men shake their heads, already several bites in. Amber trails Rosie back to the kitchen.

"Did you have a chance to think about that shift-manager position?"

"How about you try being on time for the job you have first?" Rosie nods toward the cash register, where a line of seven customers has formed.

Rosie heads back toward the cooler, leaving Amber to tend to the exiting customers.

Amber speeds through the line, surprised to see that the last customer is her old friend Monica Stevens. She met Monica shortly after she and Darren were married. Darren's best friend, Frank, was dating her at the time. They went out as couples almost once a week until Monica and Frank split right before Monica's sophomore year of college. The friendship couldn't survive the long distance, and Monica and Amber lost touch, their paths going separate ways — Amber's to motherhood and Monica's to corporate climbing.

"Amber, hey. I didn't know you worked here."

"Yeah. About six months now."

"It's been a while since I've been to Rosie's. Had to meet a client here for breakfast."

"Oh. Glad you came in. What are you up to these days?"

"Just made junior partner at Perkins and Standale. So, now, technically, Perkins, Standale, and Stevens."

She looks incredibly put together. Like a model right out of *Style* magazine. Silk shirt. Coach bag. Long, dark, glossy hair. And a MyWay face that would make Patti drool. Amber is suddenly aware of her dowdy, barefaced appearance and her faded pink smock and ponytail.

"Congratulations."

"And best of all, it came with a huge promotion. So I bought a condo, over on the lake." Monica says it with such emphasis that Amber is tempted to applaud.

"I'm not surprised at all. You were always

a go-getter."

"Well, successful maybe, but still single." Monica forms those burgundy-matted lips into a playful pout.

The word "single" jolts Amber. Unmarried or widowed — they both fall into the same category. Age twenty-eight and completely alone.

Monica leans in. "Let me tell you, though — I'd better be married by the time I'm thirty."

Amber nods.

"Hey, how's Bree doing?" Monica hands Amber her check and a hundred-dollar bill.

"She's good. Good. Growing like a weed." Amber opens the register and struggles to do the math on $100 minus $26.72. *Why does Rosie insist on keeping this vintage cash register that doesn't compute the change?*

"Just round up to forty and keep the rest for a tip." Monica helps her out graciously.

"Monica, that's too much."

"It's fine."

"Thank you." She makes change and puts the remaining cash in the tip jar on the counter.

"Hey, you should bring Bree by sometime, and we'll go out on the boat."

"That sounds great." Monica hands her a business card. MONICA STEVENS, ESQUIRE,

PERKINS, STANDALE & STEVENS.

"Give my assistant a call, and she'll get something scheduled."

Assistant? Wow. "Sure." *What would it be like to be so busy that one needs an assistant to manage it all? She probably takes care of Monica's dry cleaning and walks her dog, too. Just like in the movies.*

"Good to see you, Amber."

Rosie swings by with an armload of dirty dishes.

"Amber, table seven needs coffee refills, and thirteen is asking for a high chair."

Amber exhales. "Got it."

"See you soon," says Monica, slinging her designer handbag over her shoulder and swishing out the door, leaving a trail of exotic, earthy-smelling perfume. Something Patti would sell.

Amber grabs a high chair from behind the cash register and tucks it under one arm. She heads for the coffee station, only to find both pots sitting empty on the burner. Behind. Why does she always feel like she's two steps behind? Monica's visit had certainly highlighted that fact . . . in *spades*.

The breakfast rush empties around ten, and the restaurant quiets to a single, elderly man sipping coffee and doing the daily crossword in a corner booth. As Amber refills his coffee, he doesn't even look up. She returns the coffeepot to the burner and takes to cleaning the countertop. She sprays disinfectant on a clean rag and wipes down the napkin holders until they shine like mirrors; the salt and pepper shakers stand like soldiers guarding either side. Rosie likes the place to sparkle.

Amber wipes the nozzles of a row of ketchup bottles she's collected. Rosie, brow moist with sweat, pads out from the kitchen. She grabs the last chocolate muffin from the cake display, peeling back the liner.

"Looks good in here, kid," Rosie says, taking a bite of the muffin.

"Thanks, Rosie. I'm trying to make up for earlier."

"I know you are." Rosie splits off a chunk of muffin and holds it out to Amber. "You want some?"

"Nah, you enjoy it."

"There's a stack of pancakes in a box in the fridge. Take it home for you and Bree."

"Thanks, Rosie." Amber begins to place a sanitized ketchup bottle on each table.

"It's not that I don't think you're capable of being a shift manager," Rosie says after a moment. "You are."

"But you won't do it because . . . ?"

Rosie motions for Amber to take a seat next to her at the counter. Amber saunters over but refuses to sit.

"You're not ready, kid. Your head's somewhere else."

"My head's exactly where it should be."

"And tell me, where's that?"

"Trying to find a way to get ahead."

Rosie takes a sip of milk. "These things take time. Don't beat yourself up."

"I'm out of time, Rosie."

"How's that?" Rosie cocks her head in Amber's direction.

Amber clams up. *She can sense my desperation.* She can't let Rosie know about the foreclosure or her bottomed-out bank account. She doesn't want the entire town labeling her "that poor war widow."

"Never mind."

"Is there anything I can do? As a friend," Rosie says.

"How 'bout another shift or two?"

"You're already working seven days a week."

"Right. So what's another few extra hours if I'm already here?"

"When are you gonna squeeze in time to spend with that delightful daughter of yours?"

Amber turns as a customer enters and

takes a booth.

"Let me worry about that, Rosie."

"Hon, I know what you make, and it's not a treasure chest, but it's a livable wage. Is there something else going on?"

"No, I'm fine." Amber fills a glass with ice and water and grabs a menu.

"And Bree?"

"She's fine."

She can feel the burn of Rosie's concerned look following her as she hustles off to greet a new diner. "Welcome to Rosie's. Right this way."

CHAPTER FOURTEEN: TRAINING WHEELS

Cody finishes buffing out the scrape on Joe's vintage Ford as Joe drives another car into the stall next to him. *Don't tell me he's gonna ask for help on that one, too.*

"This one needs a new oil filter," Joe says, getting out of the driver's seat. "And when that's done, you can get started tearing the engine out of that old racer outside."

"Joe. When am I gonna race? It's been three weeks since I've been in the seat." Cody tosses the buffing rag aside. He goes over to Joe as he pops the hood on the newly arrived car.

"From what Gibbs told me, and from what I've seen on your reels, you need to learn a little patience. So we're gonna work on that first."

"He sent me down here to cool off?"

"If you were my driver, I would've just fired you. The right driving attitude comes from inside. Otherwise, it's always crash and burn." Joe pulls the dipstick. "It's low. Grab me a couple quarts of 10W-30."

"I think maybe you just needed a free hand." *There, I said it.*

"Who fixes your cars after you crash them?"

"My crew." *What does this guy really know about racing?* Cody hands Joe two quarts of oil from the shelf.

"Do you know how much work and expense goes into that?"

Cody shrugs. "Gibbs foots the bill."

"Gibbs told me your sponsor pulled out. That money tree's dried up, son."

"What?"

"Oh yeah. It's way worse than you thought, isn't it?"

Am I gonna race again? "What does that mean for my . . . future?"

"Gibbs sees something in you. I don't know what. But he's working out a plan to find you a new sponsor. On the condition I can get you to change your attitude."

"Look, Joe, I'm a solid driver. I just need to get in the car."

"You need direction. A lot of it."

"I'm open to any tips you have."

"Tips? Oh, no. You want tips, read a book." Joe shakes his head. "Here's the plan. We're gonna start from scratch. You're gonna tear that car apart and put it back together as many times as I say. I want you to respect how every inch of your car functions. I want it to sparkle and shine. And I don't care how long it takes. Do you understand?"

Cody nods. *This guy's crazy.*

"The proper response is 'Yes, sir.' "

"Yes, sir," Cody mumbles.

"And when we're on the track, you'll do exactly what I say, when I say it. Got it?"

"Yes, sir."

"You're lacking precision and patience. You keep those two words at the forefront of your mind. Got it?"

"Yes, sir."

"Good. Now with that attitude, you just may have the tiniest chance at being a winner someday."

Joe starts to walk away. "Oh, and fix the brakes on the green go-kart. I'll be back after lunch."

He leaves. Cody stands alone in the garage, facing the raw truth of his situation for the first time. *This is way worse than I thought.*

Cody turns to his race car. "We're never gonna get back to Indy with Joe on our tail."

CHAPTER FIFTEEN:
GIRLS' NIGHT IN

Amber picks up Bree from her friend David's house and arrives home exhausted from her busy weekend shift. She sends Bree upstairs to play in her room for a while so she can get some cleaning and laundry done. Bree offers no resistance as Amber follows her upstairs to her bedroom. She slips right into her bed with an armload of books. Amber goes through the upstairs, picking up dirty clothes. By the time she returns to Bree's room, she's napping peacefully.

Amber tiptoes back downstairs with her basket full of wash and heads to the laundry room off the kitchen. She's always loved this space. It calms her and reminds her of the times she and Darren held conversations and laughed as they folded laundry.

Amber stands in front of a mountain of clean laundry she has neglected to put away for several weeks. She slowly pulls piece after piece, folding each one methodically, lost in the task. She remembers one of their last conversations before Darren deployed. It was about the house. Darren had gone over a list of everything she would need to know about the upkeep while he was gone. The toolbox. The power tools. Fuse box switches. Water heater. Lawn maintenance. Gutter cleaning. Heating and cooling. How to fix minor plumbing issues. At the end of the list he had scribbled a name and number. A handyman. Her plan B should things get over her head.

Well, here she is. *Way* over her head. And no handyman is going to fix this mess.

"Mom?" Bree's voice shoots up behind her. Amber jumps. "Mom!"

"You're up." She turns slightly to find Bree with her hands on her hips.

"Do you have one of Dad's patches?"

"Probably. What for?"

"For my go-kart."

"Your what?" Amber stacks a pile of towels in a laundry basket to bring upstairs to refresh the bathroom linens.

"The go-kart club? At church."

"It's a club now?" Did she know this?

"I guess. Cody's running it. Remember?"

Oh, that's right. This new guy. Uncle Joe's friend.

"Uh. Does that cost anything?"

"No."

"There might be one in the photo album. Why don't you check?"

The doorbell rings, startling Amber again. Odd. She can't remember the last time anyone came to the door in the past few months. After Darren's funeral, streams of mourners and friends had graced her front porch. But within two weeks, the doorbell grew quiet, the front porch emptied, and the house went so still that Amber couldn't stand being there all day in the empty space while Bree was at school. She put on music, went for walks, ran errands — but always came back to that depressing silence. After a year went by, she started looking for a job. Rosie finally had an opening six months ago. It was sweet relief to leave the solitude of their house for hours each day and be surrounded with people and noise. At first, she looked forward to even the most mundane tasks, like cleaning ketchup bottles. When that wore off, she relished spending time with the people who came through the diner doors. Hearing about the minute events of their lives somehow alleviated her pain during those hours away. And when she was at home, she noticed that the house no longer tortured her. She softened into its memories. As long as she was there with Bree, it became tolerable . . . in small doses.

"Mom!"

The doorbell rings again, and Amber hurries over. Bree is standing by the door.

"Why didn't you let them in?"

"You said to never answer the door."

"You're right. But these are friends."

Through the stained-glass window of the door she can make out two familiar figures. Amber flings the door open.

"Ladies. What a surprise."

"We took a chance. You're not busy, are you?" asks Bridgette.

" 'Cause we're way past due for another girls' night in," adds Karena.

Amber takes one look at the covered casserole dish in Bridgette's arms.

"Is that . . . ?" Bree's eyes go wide.

"Baked ziti!" says Bridgette.

"Get in here, girls!" Amber ushers them inside.

Bree quickly helps Amber set the table, and the four of them sit down for a satisfying meal. The baked ziti dish empties quickly. After Bree stuffs her face with a second helping, Amber sees Bree's sleepy eyes coming on.

Food coma kicking in, thinks Amber. *Poor*

thing acts like she's been starved. And she has been — starved for a good home-cooked meal, for sure. Amber promises herself she'll try to do better.

"Okay, kiddo, go get ready for bed — pjs, teeth."

"No, I don't wanna . . ."

"Say thank you to Karena and Bridgette."

Bree goes over and gives them each a hug. Amber leads her to the stairs, and Bree puts up no fight as she lifts her tired legs up the steps.

"Mom, will you sing for me tonight?"

"Not tonight, Bree."

"Please? Just one song," her little voice pleads. Amber glances at Karena and Bridgette, who shoot a hopeful look at each other. Amber seems to consider it for a second.

"Get ready for bed. I'll come tuck you in in a few minutes."

"You never wanna sing to me."

"Bed. Now." Amber uses her mom voice. Hopes dashed, Bree trudges up, and they soon hear her heavy steps reach the top of the stairs. Amber turns back to the table. An awkward pause.

"Bridge, that was *so* good. Thank you."

"Sorry we didn't leave you any leftovers this week," says Karena. Amber forks one last bite. "We need to do this more often."

"I agree," says Amber. "I've missed this."

"And we miss you, Amber," says Bridgette.

"I meant your cooking," Amber teases. She detects something in the air shift between her friends.

"Why won't you sing for your daughter?" Karena asks.

"Karena. Come on. That's Bree's way of stalling at bedtime."

"I'm not so sure about that," Karena says gently. "I think she misses hearing you sing."

"And when are we going to hear that beautiful voice of yours again in choir?" asks Bridgette.

"The choir needs your help. We're a disaster without you," says Karena.

"Ladies, was the pasta just a ploy to get me to come back to church?" Amber grins.

"Busted," says Karena.

"Ziti evangelism," says Bridgette.

"I'll be your first convert." Amber stands and starts clearing the dishes.

Bridgette gets up to help. "Sit down, lady. You deserve a break. You do this all week."

Amber surrenders her dirty plates to Bridgette, who takes them to the kitchen.

"Okay, choir aside. What are the chances we're gonna see you back at church?" asked Karena.

"Did the pastor put you up to this?"

"I'm asking because I . . . we care about you."

"What does church have to do with my life right now?"

"You gotta make time for it. Your life will be better, I promise," says Bridgette, returning for the empty ziti dish.

"Look, I'm just not ready."

"God doesn't expect ready. He just wants you to show up so He can love you."

"We know you're still hurting. It's exactly at times like these when we need to lean on our faith," says Karena.

Something in Amber breaks. "I tried putting my faith in Him. And where has that left me?"

"Oh, Amber, God's still with you, blessing you every step of the way," says Karena.

"Really? Where? My husband was a blessing. Where is he right now?"

"I know it doesn't always feel like He's there," says Bridgette softly.

"You're right. It doesn't feel like it at all. It feels a lot better if I just stay away. At least He can't hurt us anymore."

"God didn't do this. Suffering and death are not a part of His will for us," says Karena.

"He allowed this to happen. He could

have protected Darren." Amber swallows the lump in her throat, but it refuses to go down.

"He's hurting right along with you. And He wants to join you in your suffering. He wants you to come to Him," says Karena. "He can restore you."

Amber knows Karena means well, but at the moment, it just sounds like she's delivering one of her husband's sermons. "I'm not ready to trust him with our lives again."

"Amber, don't forsake Him or His people," Karena pleads. "We're here for you."

Amber stiffens and rubs her index finger and thumb along the sides of her throat, trying to smooth out the lump. "I appreciate all that you've done. I really do, but I've got this."

"I'm sorry. We didn't come here to upset you," says Bridgette.

Amber takes the casserole dish from Bridgette and tries to regain her composure. She has to let them know that she hasn't lost her sense of humor. She's okay. Really.

"Here's the deal. I'm not running from God. But if God wants me, He knows where to find me: in my kitchen . . . making this sinful baked ziti. Bridge, you gotta get me this recipe!"

She whisks off to the kitchen sink to soak

the pan and give them a moment to change the conversation.

CHAPTER SIXTEEN: NELSON'S SECRET

Sunday-night doldrums have settled in on Patti as she pads through her five-bedroom Victorian. Every creak in the floorboards reminds her how hollow the home is, and she can't stand to be here another minute. She texts her brunch friends, but everyone's either out or not answering. Impatient to change her mood, Patti grabs her coat and keys. She needs comfort food. Rosie's roast beef potpie.

When Patti arrives at 8:00 p.m., the crowds are gone. She takes a seat at the counter. Rosie approaches with a fresh pot of coffee.

"Sit down and join me for a cup of coffee," she tells Rosie, who is glad to see her. She hands off a few straggling patrons to Mickey, her night shifter.

"I will. But first, you want me to get you something to eat?"

"My usual," says Patti.

119

"Coming up." After a moment, Rosie returns with a heaping beef potpie. Patti breathes in the aroma of the piping-hot dish. "You'd better bring me a to-go box right off the bat, because if I don't section off at least half of this, I'm gonna eat the whole thing and regret it in the morning."

"Oh, you skinny little twig. You could use a few extra pounds," Rosie teases, taking a stool next to her.

The diner doorbell dings, alerting Rosie that she has another customer. Patti shifts her glance to the open door. Her eyes travel down to a wheelchair rolling in. The young man in the chair stops at the cashier's stand.

"I feel like I know that guy," says Patti.

"Him?"

"Has he ever been in here before?"

"I've never seen him," says Rosie.

"Sure? You know everyone around here."

"So do you."

"Apparently not." Patti studies him.

"Anywhere you like," Rosie hollers and slides off her stool. "I got this one, Mickey," she calls into the kitchen, catching Mickey scarfing down a french fry hot off the deep fryer.

"I'll get his story. Stay put." Rosie waddles behind the counter for a pitcher of water and some fresh napkins as she helps the man find an accessible booth near the front.

From her perch at the counter, Patti has a safe view to study the guy without his knowing. He's young, early twenties, baby-face skin that wears an aged expression. He's seen things he shouldn't have. Things he can't erase from memory. He wears a denim jacket with patches. She can't quite make out what they say, but judging by the shape of them, she'd guess they were probably military.

He acts nervous, his eyes darting toward the door and around the restaurant. He picks up the menu Rosie left and peers at it in brief spurts, shifting his gaze back and forth to the door.

He just doesn't seem settled. She searches her memory. Where has she seen him before? Nothing registers. Was he a friend of Darren's? Or maybe a son of one of her clients? Rosie approaches him, and Patti leans in to eavesdrop.

"What can I get you tonight?" Rosie touches his shoulder as she leans over to pour him a glass of water. The guy jumps, his elbow bumping the water pitcher and knocking it out of Rosie's grip. It bounces off the table and crashes to the floor.

"Oh, I'm sorry. I . . ." he says.

"Don't worry at all. I didn't mean to

startle you," says Rosie, reaching over him with a rag to mop up the table. "Something to drink?"

"Just water. Thanks."

"I'll bring a new pitcher." Patti can't see if the guy took to it or not. "Need a minute to look over the menu?"

"Yeah, yeah," he answers softly, and takes off his coat.

"Roast beef potpie's on special tonight. Comes with mashed potatoes or french fries. And a piece of pie. Apple. Cherry. Chocolate custard. Or lemon meringue."

"Thanks. Yeah, I'll have that. With cherry pie."

"You got it." Rosie scribbles down the order.

Then he does something that takes Patti by surprise. Using one arm, he presses down on the armrest of his wheelchair and actually tries to stand up, reaching with the other arm toward a coat hook on the post next to his table. She can't keep her eyes off him as he struggles on shaky legs. He extends his arm, eyes lasered on his goal. He comes within an inch of the peg and misses, sinking back down into his chair with a thud.

"I can hang that for you," says Rosie, reaching out to help him.

"No. No. I'm fine. Forget it." He lays the jacket on his lap.

Rosie gives Patti a quick glance. Patti nods, encouraging her to get more from him.

"I'm Rosie, by the way." She reaches out her hand to shake, but he doesn't take it.

"Private Nelson . . . I mean, Mike. I'm Mike."

"So you were in the military?"

"I was." He leaves it at that.

"Which branch, hon?"

"101st Airborne."

Nelson looks around the room again, this time catching Patti's stare. She quickly turns her gaze to her plate. *That's it. He was in Darren's unit!*

"Seems like this wheelchair isn't a permanent thing," Rosie says.

"I hope not."

"Good boy. You keep doing what you need to do to get outta that thing."

"Yes, ma'am. I'll keep trying."

Rosie starts to step away.

"Is, um . . . is Amber working tonight?"

At Amber's name, Patti looks over.

"No, hon. She isn't." Rosie slips away and makes herself busy behind the counter.

Patti slips from her stool, taking this opportunity to hustle up to Nelson.

123

"Hello, sir. I want to introduce myself. I'm Patti Hill."

He gives her a blank stare, and she's about to respond when he cuts her off.

"Oh yeah. Yeah. Darren's mom. I recognize you from the Facebook pics. Nice to meet you, ma'am." Nelson sits a little taller. Patti shakes his hand.

"I overheard and I . . . You knew Darren? You were in his unit, right?"

"Yes. I got transferred to Darren's unit."

"You did? When?"

"About a month before . . ." He trails off and jerks his glance toward the door, then back to his menu.

Patti tries to hide her growing awkwardness. "I can relay a message to Amber if you like. Or . . ."

"Thank you, ma'am, but, um, I . . . it's just something I need to do in person." There's a pain behind Nelson's eyes that she knows he isn't going to share with her. "You understand?"

No, I don't understand! I don't understand why my son's life was cut short!

"I do. I understand." Patti deflates as she backs away. "Well, enjoy your dinner. And thank you for your service." It sounds so rote, but she has to offer something.

"Mrs. Hill . . . He was a hero."

Patti looks back at his sincere eyes.

"I hope you know that."

"Thank you," she says in barely a whisper.

"Here's your potpie," says Rosie, returning with the savory steaming pastry. She sets it on the counter at Patti's spot and goes to greet a new customer.

Patti has to leave. Now. She drifts back to the counter and slides a twenty under her cup. As she crosses the parking lot to her car, she looks back to see Nelson hunched over the table, scooping up his meal, the secret of Darren's demise just simmering there at the table inside Rosie's Diner.

Chapter Seventeen: The Patch

When Amber pads upstairs to bed, she sees that Bree's light is still on, and pokes her head in. Bree is fast asleep under a pile of covers, her little arm draped over a book. As she draws closer, Amber recognizes that the family photo album is open to a page from Darren's graduation from army boot camp. Bree has removed the 101st Airborne patch. It lies on the pillow next to her cheek.

Amber sets the patch on the nightstand and slips the photo album from under Bree's arm. She gives her a little kiss on the forehead, tucking her arms under the covers. Amber takes a moment with the album, sitting on the edge of Bree's bed. She stares at Darren's picture.

He has a serious face turned up by a small smile. At six feet, Darren's lean, strong build filled out his dress uniform. Handsome. Very handsome. Darren always had exceptional athletic abilities. With state records in football, track, and wrestling, he earned multiple full-ride college scholarship offers. But it was the army's offer that interested him the most.

Darren's drive to be a part of the 101st Airborne stemmed from his thrill-seeking nature. He was cut from the cloth of the 101st, born to their mission to be called into action when the need was immediate and extreme. On their first date, at age seventeen, Amber had asked Darren what he wanted to do with his life. His eyes lit up. Without hesitation he said, "I want to be in the 101st Airborne."

She had had no idea what that meant.

Darren didn't hesitate to tell her everything he had been reading and learning — the division's history, commanders, and missions. They were organized on August 16, 1942, and are based in Fort Campbell, Kentucky. They were the first Allied soldiers to land in occupied France during World War II. It was in Vietnam that they began their helicopter missions.

Amber had been impressed, of course. Mostly about the fact that Darren was so convinced of his future path. She hadn't a clue what she wanted to do when she grew up. He told her that his mother didn't support his dream and was pushing him to go to college. As they fell in love, Amber easily slipped into being a part of Darren's dream. It made her feel protected, safe, and a part of something bigger than her sheltered life with her grandparents. Amber told him that he needed to follow his heart or he'd never be happy. He would live to regret it. And if Darren's mother wouldn't support him, she would — 101 percent.

By the time they tied the knot, Darren was headed to Fort Campbell instead of college, and Amber was no stranger to Patti's disapproval. Darren had done his best to try to convince Patti that one day, down the line, he would get more education. But there was too much adventure to be had before settling down. Patti couldn't see that her son would never be a desk-dwelling paper pusher.

He was depth and soul, a Screaming Eagle.

Chapter Eighteen:
The Screaming Eagle

Cody paces between the workstations, passing out hammers, nails, and wood glue, hoping the kids don't sense his nervousness. First day of Racing for Glory, and Joe has the audacity to leave him here alone while he runs errands. *I don't know what to do with these kids.*

Cody does a quick mental inventory of the five who have already settled into their workstations. *I thought Bree was supposed to come. And her stuttering friend from Sunday school.*

Cody rechecks the go-kart instruction manual that Joe left for him. He can hardly make heads or tails of the technical mumbo jumbo. *Fake it till you make it.*

"Hey, are we gonna start soon?" asks a redheaded kid with a crew cut.

"Okay, kids, let's get started." He glances at the first set of steps. "We're going to take the bottom and side cutouts that Joe made for us and lay them a hundred eighty degrees in orientation. Then we're going to glue the outer two boards at a ninety-degree angle to the bottom board and clamp them together."

What? Seriously, this thing reads like an engineer wrote it.

He looks up. Five bewildered faces stare back at him. *Exactly how I feel.*

Cody tosses the manual aside. "Okay. Watch me." He picks up a board. "Take the bottom board and lie it flat on your workstation. We're gonna glue the side boards to it."

The kids nod, but most have a hard time lifting the heavy plywood.

"Okay, I'll be right around to help."

Cody quickly circulates to each workstation. Soon the go-karts take shape. Cody shows each kid how to hammer nails into the sides to reinforce the glue job. "Pair up and help each other. One holds the kart steady. One hammers. Watch your fingers. And the fingers of your partner. I am not trained in first aid."

He gets a couple of concerned looks but brushes them off as he consults the manual for the next step. *Just gotta stay one step ahead of them.*

"Are we too late?"

Cody looks up from the cryptic instructions to see Bree lighting up the garage with her smile. David stands next to her, a little out of breath, his backpack slung over one shoulder.

"Hey, guys. Glad you could make it. Those two stations have your names on them." Cody points to two empty workbenches set up along the perimeter.

Cody notices Bree's pink sneakers as she leads David to their places.

"W-w-w-what are we gonna do today?" David asks.

"Well, we're putting together the frame of the kart."

Cody shows them how to assemble the three pieces of wood to form a base. He holds the sides while Bree and David take turns hammering.

"Okay, you guys, now we need to glue every joint to make sure they're nice and strong."

More bewildered stares from the small sea of faces.

"What's a joint?" asks the redheaded kid.

"Where the two pieces come together," says Bree.

"That's right, Bree," says Cody. "Basically, just make sure there are no holes anywhere along the bottom."

The kids squeeze glue bottles like frosting tubes over their karts, and the glue begins to puddle on the workbenches and the floor. Before Cody can prevent it, one of the kids steps in it and traipses across the floor, creating a gooey trail.

"Whoa, easy. You're stepping in it. Shoes off!" Cody tosses rags to the offender and to each workstation. "Mop up the glue, or Joe will kill me."

As if on cue, Joe appears holding several bags of supplies. He takes one look at the place and shakes his head. "Gone for twenty minutes. Take these, will you?"

Cody lifts the bags from his arms and leans in to whisper, "I don't know what I'm doing here, Joe."

"You got that right, Captain Obvious. Why'd you give them each a bottle of glue?"

"They need it for the kart. Isn't that . . ."

Joe shames him with a look. "That's why I put out those Styrofoam bowls."

"Oh. I thought those were for their snacks or something."

"No. You put a little glue in those and then they use those sponge brushes I set next to each one to spread it on the kart."

How on earth was I supposed to figure that out?

"Let's help them clean up the glue and

132

clamp the seams so the karts dry nice and snug, and then I think we've done enough for today."

"Good plan." Cody heads over to Bree and David, who are still hammering their side panels on. "You guys want a little help?"

David readily gives up the hammer.

"I'm good," says Bree. "Almost done."

Cody puts an extra hand on the kart to steady it. Bree confidently lines up a nail and drives it into the wood. "Nice skill, Bree."

"Thanks. My dad taught me. We made a birdhouse one time."

"That's a father who sounds pretty amazing."

"He was," says Bree, lining up another nail.

Cody pours a small amount of glue in their Styrofoam bowl and hands David a sponge brush. "You want to smooth the glue over the seams. Fill in the gaps. Okay? Slow and precise. Don't wanna glob the glue all over the place."

David nods and dips his brush into the glue and paints it on his kart exactly on the mark. No muss. No fuss.

"Like this?"

"Yeah, that's perfect, David. Nice work." David glances up at Cody with a grateful smile. And it dawns on him. Patience. Precision. David has it down. And he's only nine.

These kids don't have fathers to show them how make go-karts. Or come watch them race. Or tell them "great job." There's a lot more going on here than I realized.

"So have you two started to think about what you're going to name your karts?" says Cody.

"G-g-g-goose G-g-glider!" stutters David.

Cody nods. "I like it. Has a smooth sound. Bree, what about you?"

Bree nods. "Yep." She dips her brush into the glue and carefully applies a layer.

"Are you going to tell us?" says Cody.

"I'm going to show you." Bree sets the brush in the bowl and digs her hand into her jeans pockets for something. She holds it out for Cody and David to see.

"It's this."

Cody looks at the black patch in her palms. It contains a white eagle head and the word "Airborne" across the top in yellow in all caps.

"The Screaming Eagle," says Bree.

"I like that. What's the significance of the patch?"

"It was my dad's. He was 101st Airborne. What do you think?"

"This was your dad's?"

Bree nods. Cody notices that Joe is standing off to the side, glancing from Cody to the patch. *Cody Jackson. Role model. Never woulda put that title by my name before.*

"I think your dad would've loved it."

"I want to paint this logo on the hood," says Bree.

"Okay. We can do that. Right, Joe?"

"Not a problem," says Joe.

"What color?" asks Cody.

"I like pink. But camo. Pink camo."

Cody looks to Joe and gets the nod.

"You got it."

As Bree starts to fill in the other seam of her kart, David pitches in to help.

"Big responsibility here, huh?" Joe says. "But I think you're up for it."

Cody nods. "I think so."

CHAPTER NINETEEN:
NO FOOD IN THE HOUSE

Patti is very pleased with herself when her plan B works. She's able to get Rosie to tell her Amber's work schedule. Armed with the information, she calls Amber and offers to pick Bree up from school on the two afternoons a week when Amber has to work the dinner shift. Amber politely agrees. She suspects Amber is just thin on options and energy.

Today is the first day of their arrangement, and Patti arrives at Bree's school a few minutes later than she would have liked after getting caught up with a new MyWay consultant on the phone and losing all track of the time. She doesn't find Bree waiting outside, so she parks the car and heads into the school building.

After a few wrong turns, Patti finds Bree's classroom. A few straggling kids are getting help from the teacher on homework. But no sign of Bree.

"Excuse me, I'm here for Breeanne Hill. Am I in the right classroom?" she asks the teacher.

"Oh, and you are . . . ?" says the lanky brunette in skinny jeans, a tunic, and a wispy neck scarf.

"Patricia Hill, Bree's grandmother."

"Of course. But Bree left about twenty minutes ago. With David Pipoly. They were going to Joe's Auto."

"That's odd. She knew I was picking her up. I don't understand." Patti was getting a touch nervous. Amber hadn't said anything about a David Pipoly or Joe's.

"Maybe she thought you meant pick her up at Joe's Auto?"

"What's going on at Joe's?"

"Racing for Glory."

Patti gives her a befuddled look.

"It's a kids' go-kart club. Sponsored by Clarksville Community Church. Joe runs it out of his garage."

"Oh. I see. And Bree's a part of this?"

"From what I understand."

"Thank you," Patti says, rushing out the door.

She drives the four blocks to Joe's.

Inside Joe's garage, half a dozen boys and girls are pounding and painting wooden go-karts at various stations set up around the

137

garage. In one corner, Joe shows a boy how to drive a nail into the plywood. He misses and almost whacks Joe in the gut.

Patti searches the little faces but doesn't see her granddaughter at any of the karts. Her worry changes to unease. What if Bree never made it to Joe's?

"Can I help you?" A man's voice calls to her from the other side of the stall. Patti turns to see a handsome stranger in greasy jeans.

"Ah, yes. I'm here to pick up Bree Hill. I'm her . . ."

"Glam-ma! What are you doing here?"

Bree pops out from behind her kart in the back and bounces up with a huge hug for Patti. Patti instantly breathes a sigh of relief.

"Bree, your Mom didn't tell me you were going to be at Joe's. I went to school first . . ."

"Grandma, Cody and I are building a go-kart!"

Cody? Who's Cody? Didn't her teacher say David? And what will her mother think about her pink shirt being stained with grease and paint?

"That's nice, honey. Which one is he?"

The greasy hunk who greeted her just a second ago smiles sheepishly and grabs a rag to wipe his hands.

"Ma'am. Cody Jackson. Pleased to meet you."

She shakes his hand and smiles indulgently, not sure how she feels about her granddaughter being with a bunch of grease monkeys. She glances around and sees a couple more girls in the mix. Her mind eases a little, but she still wonders what on earth has possessed her granddaughter to build a go-kart.

"Oh. Patti Hill. Nice to meet you. How long have you been working for Joe?"

"Cody's a race car driver, Grandma."

"Oh, that sounds . . . dangerous," says Patti, with an eye to Cody.

"Guess Mom's working late?" asks Bree.

"Yeah, it's her dinner shift at Rosie's. Looks like I've got you all to myself tonight." Patti sends Bree a warm smile.

"Rosie's out on old Thirty-seven?" Cody asks.

"It's the only Rosie's I know of."

"They have great pancakes," Bree chimes in.

"I'll have to stop in and try them," says Cody.

"Do you know Amber?" Patti can't keep the air of suspicion out of her voice.

"Not yet. But if she's as great as her daughter, I'd sure like to." Cody unleashes a broad smile on Patti. Despite his good looks, an edge of disaster radiates from him. He's exactly the type Amber would be attracted to. His build and looks resemble Darren's. Patti is certain he's a bit of a wild card.

"Bree, grab your things. Let's go."

Bree finds her backpack and waves goodbye to David, who's putting a base layer of paint on his kart. Bree gives Cody a fist bump.

"See you tomorrow, Cody. Bye, David!"

Patti sees a small hand wave from behind a kart-in-progress.

"Nice to meet you." Patti throws the insincere pleasantry to Cody as she takes Bree's hand and leads her out of the garage. She doesn't trust how friendly he's being with Bree. Her mind leaps to the assumption that he might eventually use Bree to attract Amber. And Amber just might fall for it. She's in that vulnerable place where a man might easily slip in and fill the void.

Once at Amber's, Patti settles Bree at the kitchen table to do her homework.

"You hungry?" Patti asks Bree.

"Starving. Do you know how to make baked ziti?"

"Is that what you want?"

Bree nods. Patti searches the pantry for the right ingredients and quickly becomes disappointed by the lack of food.

"Grandma, do you know how to do percentages?" says Bree, squirming at the table over a math worksheet.

"I use them all the time. You need some help?"

"Yes, please."

"Your mom sure doesn't keep much in the house, does she?"

"Sometimes she brings home leftovers from the restaurant."

Patti opens the fridge. Little scraps of this and that — moldy cheese, expired sausage links, wilted broccoli — nothing she can make a meal from. She tosses the bad food in the trash.

"How about pizza?" Patti reaches for her phone.

"Grandma, what number is twenty-five percent of two hundred?" Bree looks up, frustrated from her math paper.

Patti grabs two apples and a knife. She begins to slice up the first apple.

"Okay, this apple is one hundred percent." She quarters the apple. "Now how much is each piece?"

"Twenty-five," says Bree confidently.

"Good. Now let's take this other apple

and" — she quarters that one — "how much is each?"

"Same. Twenty-five percent."

"Good. So what is twenty-five and twenty-five?"

Bree takes two slices and suddenly sees the answer. "Fifty!"

"Perfect!" Patti says, and Bree scribbles down the correct answer on her sheet as she pops a slice of apple into her mouth.

"Cheese and pepperoni okay?"

Bree nods with her mouth full of fruit.

As Patti dials the Pizza Ranch, she sees the unopened MyWay cosmetics box on the kitchen counter, tucked behind some plastic containers left out for recycling.

"Yes, I'd like to place an order for delivery. Patti Hill. Oh, hi, Caroline. I thought I recognized your voice. Yes, I have more Butter Biscuit eye shadow. Stop by the house tomorrow. Medium. Pepperoni and cheese only. Thanks."

She hangs up. Caroline has been a client for five years, drawing in the entire female side of her family and half the Pizza Ranch customers. And she's just one of many examples of how deep Patti's MyWay empire extends into Clarksville. She would gladly let Amber dip into the pool if she would only have half an ounce of humility and common sense.

Chapter Twenty:
Take a Deep Breath

Amber's mood reflects the gray, early-spring skies and the drizzly mist that clings to the air and mats her hair as she rushes from the parking lot into Rosie's. Anxious thoughts whir through her mind. How to pay off the mortgage? The gas? The electric? The water? And then . . . what's left over. Only seven days until Jim Wellington can't stop the foreclosure. She needs to prove to Rosie she's worthy of the promotion.

"He came in here asking for you," says Rosie as she sets a stack of dirty dishes in the bin under the counter where Amber fills syrup jars.

She cocks her head in Rosie's direction. "Who's that?"

"That nice-looking fella with the lonely face."

"Rosie, you just described the entire Monday-morning senior men's coffee klatch."

Rosie chuckles. "Like that sense of humor poking through." Rosie nods discreetly to the handicapped table by the front door. "Him. The one in the wheelchair. The young guy."

"I don't know." But Amber knows exactly who Rosie's talking about. She had seen pictures of Nelson on Darren's Facebook page. And she had met him once or twice on Skype calls between her and Darren. Amber grabs a bag of sugar packets and moves around to each table, restocking the containers.

"How do you know him?"

"He's been coming in here lately, asking for you. Tells me he was in Darren's unit. I don't think he's going to be in that wheelchair for long," Rosie says, wiping off the countertop.

"Oh? What do you mean?"

"He tried to stand and hang up his coat."

"I thought he was paralyzed."

"I did, too. But there he was, trying to balance on those skinny chicken legs."

"And you didn't ask?"

"I tried to help him, but he wouldn't have it. And after that, I wasn't going to pry."

Amber has often wondered about Nelson's story and what he knows about the events surrounding Darren's death. But she's been afraid to ask. Rather, afraid that knowing may rip open old wounds barely healed. And who needs deeper scars? Not her.

The bell on Rosie's Diner door dings and a handsome young man saunters in, catching Amber's eye as she fills the last container with sugar packets. "Take a seat anywhere you like. I'll be right with you." The guy smiles at her like he knows her. He grabs a stool at the end of the counter.

Amber moves around to the counter, reaching for her notepad and a pen in her apron pocket. "Hi there. What can I get you to start?" Amber looks up at the man sitting in front of her, and her stomach makes a quick flutter. The same feeling she had in high school when she first met Darren. What's happening? This feels weird. Not right.

"Hi. Coffee. Black. Please." She recognizes something comforting and familiar in his warm smile and soft brown eyes. She catches herself staring.

"Cream and sugar?" Amber glances at his place setting. No mug.

"Nope. Black."

"Oh. Yeah, you said that. Sorry." She reaches behind her for a coffee mug and saucer and places it in front of him. "You want to see a menu?"

"I hear you have great pancakes."

Amber walks to the coffee station and grabs a fresh pot. "We're famous for them." She fills his mug and returns the pot.

"I'm Cody Jackson, by the way. I saw you at church — well, I mean . . ." He extends a hand awkwardly. Amber gives him a look, like his name sounds familiar but she can't quite place it. "Cody Jackson? I know your daughter, Bree."

"Oh, you're the go-kart builder."

"Actually, I'm a race car driver by trade. I'm here working with Joe for a bit."

"Training. I get it." Amber knows all about Joe's past racing successes and that from time to time he'll take on rookies or troubled drivers and train them for Gibbs's team. Cody doesn't act like a rookie. Not with all that swagger. "Well, nice to meet you. I'm Amber. And welcome to Clarksville." She hands him a menu.

"No need. I'll do the pancakes."

"Short or tall stack?"

"Tall. I'm starving."

"Joe has you working hard, doesn't he?"

"He does. He does. Sounds like you know something about that old geezer."

Amber smiles. "I've known Joe for about nine years. And if Gibbs sent you down here to train with Joe, you must have some potential."

"I'd like to think so."

"And you must be one of Gibbs's problem children." His smile frosts. She pricked his ego. Oh boy. "Don't worry. If anyone can whip a racer into shape, it's Joe."

"He has a rather unorthodox way of going about it," says Cody.

The bell dings at the front door. Amber glances up to see two families enter.

"Bacon or sausage with those pancakes?"

"Bacon."

She scribbles down his order.

"You got it. Anything else?" Amber motions for the waiting parties to occupy the two booths along the window.

"Well, yes, I was . . . I was wondering if we could maybe grab some coffee sometime."

Flutters again. Did he just ask her out?

"Oh, ah . . . I'm not really . . . I can't right now."

"Nothing fancy. Super casual."

"That's really nice, but I . . ." Amber freezes midsentence. Until this moment she has not given dating a single thought. And she's not sure how she feels about it.

"Look, I'm new in town, I just thought it would be nice to get to know someone. You

148

know, other than Joe. And a bunch of kids. Maybe Friday?"

The cook's bell dings from the kitchen, saving her. "Hold that thought. I've got to get that." She rushes off, leaving him hanging. It's unfair. Awkward. But she panicked. Amber grabs the order from the kitchen window as she floods with a variety of mixed feelings. Discomfort. Insecurity. Excitement. She puts Cody's order in, drops off a few menus to the newcomers, and forces herself to return to Cody's spot with more coffee.

"Cody. I'm flattered by the ask. I really am. And I wish I could say yes. But it's just not a great time for me." She blurts it out and sees Cody struggling with the disappointment. "I hope you can understand."

"Of course. Yeah. Just thought I'd ask." She can't help notice the way his brown eyes turn down at the corners. No hiding his disappointment.

"Thanks. Pancakes'll be right up." Amber leaves Cody adrift in her wake.

Entering the kitchen and out of his view, Amber takes a deep breath. So this is the next step. Of course it is. Did she expect to remain single forever? It's natural to move on. And oh, those beautiful brown eyes. And he's so kind. But . . . but she is so unprepared. So very, very unprepared. And if he's working with Joe, that means he's a project. One she probably couldn't — or shouldn't — take on right now.

"Your cakes are up!" the cook shouts.

Amber swipes the hot plate from the heating rack in the order window. She can't seem to keep those flutters down.

CHAPTER TWENTY-ONE:
WHERE'S THE
LEATHER COUCH?

It's the little things Patti notices first. The corner where Amber used to house her four-hundred-dollar KitchenAid mixer is bare. A collective bridal shower gift from the ladies at church. Opening the cupboards, she finds that mismatched thrift-store CorningWare dishes now replace the gorgeous Kate Spade service for eight that Amber and Darren had received piece by piece from their wedding registry. She searches further. What else is missing?

The wine goblets are gone. The three-hundred-dollar food processor. Amber's professional knife set. Gone.

Patti wanders through the kitchen to the laundry room. Darren had purchased a brand-new stackable washer and dryer for their second anniversary. Both gone. A rusty goldenrod washer now stands next to an off-white dryer with a dent in the door. Secondhand replacements. This is oddly disturbing.

She continues her tour through the house. In every room the furniture and décor has been replaced or pared down. Amber, who has always had good taste and a crafty style, has done a great job of making the place feel homey, but it's clearly a secondhand home. And there's only one reason Patti can think why. Amber's broke. And bartering.

Patti stops in the living room to marvel at the thick, dark-stained wood trim, the tall-paned windows, and the stone fireplace. She loves this room. She was so satisfied with Amber when Amber picked this home, a Victorian with craftsman styling, very much like Patti's own four-story, five-bedroom Victorian. She has spent every Christmas Eve with them around this fireplace since they were married. Excepting the last two years, of course.

When Darren and Amber bought this house, an idea had sprung into Patti's mind to send them a generous housewarming gift. She had just earned a bonus from MyWay and wanted to spoil her only children. Putting aside her worry that Amber would think her mother-in-law was stepping on toes by picking out furniture, Patti ordered them the gorgeous chocolate-brown leather couch and matching armchairs she had seen at

Crate and Barrel. A perfect blend of Darren's masculine taste and Amber's preference for streamlined classics.

When she went over to see it for the first time, she found Amber sunk into the rich, soft cushions with Bree cuddled up asleep in her arms. Any residual trepidation about stepping on toes was quickly put to rest as Amber declared, "I love it! Bree falls right to sleep as soon as we sit down."

Patti now glances around the room, her eyes searching. Where's the leather couch? All three pieces are completely missing from the living room. In their place are a rust-colored woven wool couch and two mismatched chairs with stains on the seat cushions. Patti yanks a throw blanket from the couch to find it's covering a six-inch tear along the back. That was a five-thousand-dollar furniture set. What happened to it?

Shock and despair sink into Patti's gut. Just how bad are Amber's bills? And just how little is she earning at Rosie's?

"*Grandma?* Are you coming up?" Bree's voice calls to her from the top of the stairs.

Patti finds Bree leaning over her desk poking her finger into the soil of her mustard-seed pot.

"Does it need some water, peanut?"

"No. But he feels cold."

"Oh. He?" Patti enters and sits on the edge of Bree's bed.

"His name's Matt." Bree goes to her dresser and pulls out a cable-knit gray sweater. She brings it to the desk and tucks the pot inside the sweater, wrapping the sleeves together to form a little cocoon.

"There you go. That'll warm you up." She then adjusts her lamp over the pot. "That should help, too."

"You plan to leave that light on all night?" Patti is tickled by Bree's little routine.

"Can I? Teacher says plants need light and heat to sprout."

"I don't see the harm." Unless it raises Amber's electric bill.

Bree wanders to the side of her bed and kneels to pray.

"Hi, God. Please say hi to my dad, up in heaven, and help my mom feel better. I really miss hearing her sing. And please make Matt grow. Amen."

Patti unfolds her hands and smiles at Bree. "That was a lovely prayer."

"Do you pray, Grandma?"

The question startles Patti. Prayer, in her opinion, is unhelpful, unnecessary, and a waste of time. "I believe in friends, family, a

154

positive attitude, and good old-fashioned elbow grease."

"What's elbow grease?"

"Hard work," says Patti. "Nothing is impossible with a good dose of hard work."

"Jesus says nothing is impossible with faith the size of a mustard seed."

"I see." Patti isn't sure where to go with that. She believes in being a good person, but she never had much space or tolerance in her life for religion. It boxes a person in. Too many rules to follow. And too many hypocrites following them.

"How come I never see you at church, Grandma?"

"I go to brunch on Sundays with my girlfriends."

Bree gives her a look that lets Patti know that not an acceptable answer.

"What time is brunch?"

"Eleven thirty."

"Church is over by eleven. You could come to church with me first if you want and then go to brunch."

"Thank you for the offer. I'll think about it." *Bree has it all figured out, doesn't she? Hard to resist such an earnest offer. Hate to have to disappoint her.*

It's not the first time Patti has been asked this question. There was one other time in her life. When Darren was in high school. He was a sophomore and dating a girl who invited him to an after-school Bible study organized by the young-adults ministry of Clarksville Community Church. He started going to impress the girl, but after a while a friendship ensued with the youth pastor. Within no time, that pastor had sunk his hooks deep into Darren and convinced him that he was full of sin and unworthy of doing anything good without God. Patti had called it propaganda. Darren was a good son with a good heart. Darren disagreed and said that everyone is born into sin and needs reconciliation with God through Jesus Christ. He wanted to become a Christian.

Patti was no atheist. She believed in some higher being. A God, perhaps. Jesus — well, he seemed more mythical. She was quite sure she didn't have need for either on a day-to-day basis. As evidenced by her bank account, she was doing pretty well on her own.

After a few months, Darren and the girl broke up. Patti was somewhat relieved and felt assured that Darren would stop going to church. However, within a couple weeks, Darren announced he was going to be baptized and live his life for God. He had said things to her like: "Finding my purpose in serving my Savior." "Letting Jesus take over my heart." "Choosing the path of righteousness."

Darren's Godspeak sounded cultish, but as they talked more, Patti saw that perhaps being a Christian wasn't so awful. It meant that Darren promised he wasn't going to drink alcohol, do drugs, or fool around sexually. Patti was definitely on board with all of that, and she gave her consent.

Darren invited her to come to church and be a part of his baptism ceremony. Patti agreed to attend. The people seemed nice enough. But the ceremony was odd and creepy. All this talk about being born again. It was kind of gross. And exactly how is being reborn physically possible? The pastor's message was about getting rid of old wineskins and replacing them with new ones. None of it made sense. She felt uncomfortable the entire service as she lingered in the background. After the three-hour service, Darren celebrated with his new "Christian brothers and sisters."

That's when it clicked. Darren had always wanted siblings. She rationalized that somehow this God club satiated that longing. And truthfully, they seemed to be good influences. Darren could definitely do worse. So much worse. The Christian cult seemed like a good compromise. At least she wouldn't have to worry about getting those 2:00 a.m. police calls like her friend Bethany. The things those kids put her through.

No. Patti didn't go back to church after that. And she sure wouldn't be starting now. Even at the bequest of her beloved grand-daughter.

"Did you brush your teeth?" Patti asks Bree. Bree smiles exaggeratedly at her, bearing all her teeth. "They look clean to me."

Patti gets up from her seat on the corner of the bed. She pats it. Bree's signal to jump in.

Patti swoops in for a kiss. "Good night, peanut. I love you."

"I love you, too." And with that, Bree slides under the covers. Patti tucks her in with another hug and turns off the light.

"No, no, wait. Keep it on."

"Sorry. I forgot." Patti turns the light back on. She looks down at the fallow pot swaddled expectantly in the sweater. "Sweet dreams, honey."

Patti hopes they will be about her father.

She heads down the wooden staircase to the living room to wait for Amber on the musty, scratchy, threadbare couch. As Amber rids her life of so many familiar things, Patti wonders if Bree will start to forget details about her dad. That, coupled with the fact that Amber won't even take Bree to her daddy's gravesite . . .

Amber may be too stubborn to accept help from Patti, but she's not going to let the memory of Darren slip away from Bree.

CHAPTER TWENTY-TWO:
MY DAUGHTER'S FUTURE

Amber drags herself to the parking lot shortly after eleven thirty and gets into her minivan. It takes a few turns of the ignition before the engine revs up and she can put it into gear. It's bad. It's been bad. For months. But she keeps nursing it along as the repair slides lower and lower on her list of financial priorities.

Amber drives home with the windows down and the radio cranked so she can stay awake. She flips through the channels, landing on an obnoxious voice barking out a commercial.

"Apply now! Get paid now! Bad Credit? No Credit? Come on down to Perfect Payday. At Perfect Payday, we don't care about your credit score. Get a cash advance today!" The voice grates on her, and she's about to change the channel. But then something causes her to pause. "We're open twenty-four hours a day, seven days a week.

On the corner of Maple and Fifth. No application required. No waiting period. Walk out with cash in hand!"

She takes in the information. Considering. Is it really that easy? What's the catch? And just how much could she borrow?

"Hurry down to Perfect Payday! Cashiers are waiting for you now!"

Amber quickly changes the dial to a country station. "Bless the Broken Road" by Rascal Flatts is playing, and it brings a small, tired smile to her lips.

Her fingertips tap to the beat on the steering wheel. The song seems to offer her a moment of relief. After a few measures, she finds herself mouthing the words. Little notes escape from her lips. Deep inside her, the music finds a pulse . . . and a very tiny piece of her heart stitches itself back together.

Amber manages to stay awake for the twenty-five-minute drive home. She pulls the minivan through the dimly lit alley in back of her house and crawls her vehicle into the attached garage at the rear. She trudges through the back door leading into the kitchen and tosses her purse on the counter. She sees Patti's purse lying on the table. For a brief second she forgets that

Bree has been with Patti all night.

As if on cue, Patti enters the kitchen, looking put together and fresh, even at midnight. How does she do it? MyWay beauty products, no doubt she'd say.

"Hi, Amber."

"Patti. So sorry I'm late. Cleanup took forever. And then I stayed to prep for the a.m. shift."

"I remember those days. Done at midnight. Back at seven."

Sarcasm? I'm in no mood.

"Was Bree good for you?"

"A perfect angel."

"Thank you for coming over."

To Amber's relief, Patti gathers her purse.

"I'm happy to. I'll plan to pick her up again on Thursday."

"Yeah. Great. Bree will love that."

Patti starts for the back door, then pauses. Amber can feel Patti's mind working something up.

"Where's your leather furniture set?"

Amber braces herself. *Now? We're going to do this at midnight in my kitchen?* "It's gone."

"I can see that. Why?"

"It just felt like too much for us."

"Bree loved that couch."

"We don't need such large pieces of

furniture now that it's only the two of us."

Amber stands her ground, but she can see Patti isn't through.

"And where's your formal dining room set?"

"Reduce. Reuse. Recycle. Nothing wrong with that."

"It was a good, solid piece."

"For what? We're not exactly hosting dinner parties over here."

"You might in the future."

"The future's so far off."

"How are you going to pull yourself together?"

"Patti, you know what? I'm tired. I want to go to bed."

"When will you give some thought to your and your daughter's future? I'm just wondering what your plan is."

"Please, Patti. Not now."

"Your daughter needs more food in this house."

With that, Patti shows herself out.

Why is this all happening? Why is God punishing me over and over and over? Can't I just get a break? And why does Patti have this knack for always catching me at my lowest? Darren would be appalled at the condition of her life.

Her stomach growls. In her efforts to show

Rosie what a hard worker she is, she forgot to take a dinner break. A hunger pain sends her to the pantry. She unscrews the lid of an empty peanut butter jar. The cracker box contains a single stale cracker. A can of kidney beans. A package of noodles. Oh, wow. Patti's not kidding. Amber tries to remember the last time she went grocery shopping for more than bread, milk, and eggs. When was the last time they sat down together for a meal that she made in this kitchen with ingredients that didn't come out of a can, jar, or box?

Amber collapses at the kitchen table. Her gaze lands on the MyWay bag she stuffed into a corner under the kitchen cabinet. She's convinced it's taunting her. She pictures herself, plain-faced Amber Hill, peddling powders and perfumes. Hosting makeup parties for wrinkly old ladies. Strutting around town in heels. For a second she sees it the way Darren would, and it makes her giggle. Darren would be ROFL to find Amber wearing a MyWay badge and dutifully acting as heir to Patti's beauty empire. He admired his mother to the moon and back, but never missed an opportunity to razz her about being the town beauty queen. She could sell her wares to a fan at one of Darren's football games or a cashier at a

McDonald's drive-through. And she had. The woman had the grace, finesse, and the persuasion of a diplomat. Her gumption was so annoying.

Patti Hill has no idea what Amber is going through. Think about her daughter's future! Please. Only every single minute of every single day. But all that worrying did nothing to fill her bank account.

Bree's future. If she's so worried about Bree's future, why doesn't she . . .

A funny thought flashes in Amber's mind. Maybe Patti could groom Bree for her lipstick legacy? She almost laughs out loud at the thought. She imagines Patti getting Bree all dolled up in a frilly tulle dress and eyeliner like one of those beauty-pageant toddlers to tote her wares. Beauty for everyone at every age and stage.

She must be delirious with hunger.

The image melts from her mind, and she sits with her sullenness.

What good did it do to plan? Or worry? Or stress?

Or hope?

Tomorrow is never a guarantee. That, she had learned.

Chapter Twenty-Three: Geometry Comes in Handy

Finally, a day at the track. About friggin' time, Joe.

Cody looks down at his calloused, grease-stained hands as he slides his gloves on. He shoves his fingers to the tips, stretching the leather that has shrunk from lack of use. Or maybe it's that his fingers are so swollen from the repair work. Whatever. Doesn't matter. He's on the track again.

He clenches his gloved hands around the wheel. His finger joints ache, as does most of his body from rolling around the garage floor on a creeper and being hunched under the hood of a car all day. Sometimes well into the evening.

He draws in a deep breath as he revs the engine and turns his wheels out of the pits and onto the track. The accelerator goes to the floor. *Speed. Sweet, sweet speed!*

The calm of the early morning is shattered as Cody thunders his car down the frontstretch. Warm-up lap. Then two more.

Not as smooth as the Indy track. A little off camber entering turn three.

He'll have to compensate by picking a higher line and cutting sharper as he exits turn four.

"Okay, Joe, ready for a timed run," he says into his headset.

"Roger, ready when you are," the reply comes back.

Cody blasts by Joe and the crew like lightning. *Nothing like an empty track and a full tank of gas!*

"Feels bumpy on that third turn. Any way around that?" Cody zips past them, completing the lap, and lets up on the accelerator, coasting the car into turn one.

"Not a bad lap there, Cody. Do another one just like it. But this time, when you set up for turn four, I want you to push the apex of the turn as late as possible. Hold your line high and delay that entry point," says Joe through the headset.

"What? Too many words, Joe."

Cody rips open the throttle and moves from the second turn down the backstretch into turn three. He sets his gaze to line up with the top of the track near turn four. If he can hit that point and swing into the curve, he'll be able to get the smoothest turn at the greatest possible speed.

"Point the car at the latest possible geometric apex point . . ."

"Joe, I failed geometry. You're not making sense to me." Cody pushes the gas pedal to its limit as he takes the frontstretch again.

"Great. Now I've gotta teach you basic math skills on top of everything else?"

"Please, no. I'll do more engines. Anything. Just don't hand me one of those protractor thingies."

He sails into turn four and feels his back tires bow slightly to the right. Just another inch and he'll be fishtailing to the rails. He barely comes out of the curve. Right on the edge of crash and control. *That beautiful edge. Can't teach that. It's in the gut.*

Cody slows as he passes the pits and waves to Joe with a smirk. Joe tips his hat. *Good ole Joe.*

"Lemme explain it to you like you're a five-year-old."

"Now you're speaking at my level." Cody can hear the pit crew laughing through the headset.

"When you get ready to come up to a turn, point the nose of your car up to set your line about a foot higher than you've been doing, and at the last possible moment, when it feels like you're just about to go straight into the rails, cut that curve. The momentum will swing you through the turn. It's called setting the exit trajectory."

"Ah . . . yeah, yeah, I'll try to set that up on the next lap." *Isn't that what I'm doing?*

"Do you understand what I'm asking?"

Why can't he see that's exactly what I'm doing? "Yes, sir."

Cody screams down the backstretch and lifts his foot off the gas pedal for a second as he coasts past the pit crew again and gives Joe the signal.

"This is the one."

"Okay. We got you on the clock. Make it count. With patience and precision."

Cody makes the approach on turn one, easing into it.

"You're soft on that one," Joe informs. "Make it up on the stretches."

Cody overcompensates, flooring it down the backstretch toward turn three. He sets his apex and aims. His foot slams down on the gas. He should be able to slingshot around the corner and gain the extra seconds he lost on the first.

"You're coming in too hot!" Joe screams at him through the earpiece. "Slow it!"

"What? You want me to slow down?" *That doesn't make sense! I need the momentum!*

"Yes! You won't be able to come out of it!"

Yes, I will. He doesn't know what he's talking about. Gotta keep it on the edge.

Cody hits the curve too fast, and his car starts to slide out of the edge. He works ferociously to straighten it out, fishtailing to maintain control. He struggles to avoid the rails, but he loses the edges entirely. His bumper scrapes the rail and bounces the car into a spin. He doughnuts multiple times down the track toward turn four. Cody eventually manages to steer himself out of it as he skids to a stop on the grassy infield. No other sounds can get through the ringing in his ears.

He tries the door handle. Won't budge. The ringing comes in waves now. Between the waves he can detect blurs of sound.

"Cody? Hey. Cody?" He recognizes the pit crew's muffled voices. They slowly come into focus through his protective eyewear. His brain stops whirling, and he releases his safety harness and helmet. *I'm okay. I'm good. Intact.*

The pit crew helps Cody climb out of the window. *The car. Is it — ?*

Once his eyes adjust to the sunlight, he's afraid to look. *Thank God!* The car's in one piece. *Whew. Dent in the rear bumper? That's an easy fix.*

Wait. Am I in one piece? He shakes out each appendage. *Yup. I'm all here.*

"Whew! That was a thrill, huh, Joe?" Cody yells, to compensate for his intermittent hearing.

He looks over to where Joe is pacing back and forth a few feet from the car. *If Joe were a cartoon character, there'd be steam billowing from his ears.*

"Hey, Joe, good news! No damage to the car!" Cody strides over confidently. "You can breathe again."

Joe turns his reddened face to Cody. "Cody, you cannot make that sharp a turn at increased speeds. I'm telling you, you will spin out every single time. And that's irresponsible and dangerous."

"I was trying to use the momentum as a catapult. Gain speed. Gain time." His full hearing begins to return.

"No. You need to learn when to press the pedal and when to let off. Calculate each turn and each pass for maximum velocity — and safety."

"That's what I was doing, right?"

"You were riding on the edge." *How could he know that?* "I'm not stupid, Cody. I've been training drivers since you were in diapers."

"I don't get you, Joe. And I don't get how you think slowing down is the way to win a race."

"I told you that you need to listen to me when you're on the track. When I say go slow, you don't hit the gas. I have the bigger picture here. I can help you. But only if you listen."

"You're not the one out there, Joe. The track's uneven . . . and this car is a piece of —"

"It's not the car." Joe eyes him. Cody glances away.

"I'm just saying . . . if Gibbs can get me a better sponsor, then I can get a better-performing car that can take the turns faster."

"A better sponsor? Based on this report card? What fantasy world are you living in?"

"So I'm stuck here until you pass me onto the next grade?"

Joe nods. "*If* I pass you! And only when you get all As."

"I told you I failed geometry!" *This is impossible!* Cody throws his helmet against the inside wall. He turns and sees Joe staring at him. Cody locks eyes with the old geezer.

"Racing for Glory tomorrow afternoon. Don't forget," Joe says calmly, and then waits for Cody's response.

"Yes, sir." *Don't worry, old man. I'll be there. But not because of you.*

CHAPTER TWENTY-FOUR: BLUE-COLLAR ATTITUDE

"I've promoted Mickey to day manager." Rosie's painful words bounce around Amber's brain as she grabs her apron and starts clearing the back three booths, stacking dirty plates in the gray plastic dish bin. She sets the last one down hard, sending a crack through the center. It slides off the uneven stack and shatters a water glass. She can feel Rosie glaring at her from the kitchen. She doesn't care. Rosie has made herself crystal clear. At this rate, Amber will never climb out of debt in this dead-end dive. She needs to strategize her next steps.

Monica comes to mind. A desk job may not have been Darren's speed, but Amber is sure she could be happy punching in on a nine-to-fiver in a quiet, professional office. It would definitely beat smelling like grease every day. She could rake in a steady paycheck. And she wouldn't need to pawn Bree off on babysitters or her grandma.

After work, still wearing her uniform, Amber makes a split-second decision to stop at Monica's firm, Perkins, Standale & Stevens.

Her pink smock and white tennis shoes immediately stick out in the sea of dark suits and skirts. The lobby's vast marble floor and high ceilings echo conversations that filter in and out of offices down the hall and on the second level of the open-concept, modern structure. She spots the receptionist station and heads toward a blond bob in her early twenties. She wears a headset and smoothly transitions between several calls at once. She glances up at Amber with a professional but insincere smile.

"May I help you?" says the bob.

"Ah, yes. I want to see Monica Stevens." Amber's eyes follow a pair of attorneys whishing through the lobby in a heated conversation.

"And you are . . . ?"

"Amber Hill."

"And what time is your appointment?"

"No, I . . . we're friends and . . ."

"One moment please." The bob puts her finger up at Amber and takes a call. "I'm sorry, he's not in right now, let me transfer you to his assistant." The bob presses a series of numbers on the keypad and looks back at Amber without missing a beat.

"When is she expecting you?" The bob smiles politely.

"No, I didn't make an appointment. I'm a friend."

"Your name again?"

"Amber Hill."

"Okay. A minute please." The bob dials a number while simultaneously typing out an e-mail message. "I'm not getting her assistant. Let me try her direct line."

Amber nods, suddenly super aware of her bare white legs sticking out of her skirt. After a moment, the bob shakes her head.

"Her voice mail picked up. She must be in a meeting or out of her office. You're welcome to take a seat and wait. I can try again in five minutes. Or, if you like, call in later and make an appointment to see her." The reception line rings, and the bob answers. "Perkins, Standale, and Stevens. How may I direct your call?" Amber stands there feeling more and more out of place. The bob transfers the call and looks up at Amber, waiting for her decision.

"I'll just call later. Thank you." Amber turns to go just as Monica clicks into the lobby in her three-inch black patent leather heels, overloaded with a shoulder bag of files.

"Monica. Hey."

"Amber. Hello. How are you?" She barely slows down. "What are you doing here?"

"I actually came to see you."

"Oh. Well. I wish you would have called first. I'm on my way to a partner meeting."

"Yeah. Sorry. I was on my way home from work and just swung by."

"Hey, we still need to get together. Call me. Okay?" Monica continues across the lobby. Amber trails her.

"Yeah. I will." Amber realizes her opportunity is slipping away. "Hey, I know you're busy, but I was wondering if you ever have any positions open here."

Monica stops short of the hallway she's about to enter. She turns and looks at Amber as though she let out a fart in church. She motions for Amber to step closer.

"Um. Sometimes. But correct me if I'm wrong — you don't have a college degree, do you?"

"No. Why? Is that a problem?"

"It's a basic requirement for application."

"Even for that job?" Amber gestures slightly toward the bob.

"Rebecca's working on her master's in criminology."

"To answer phones?"

"She's applied to be an FBI intel agent. This is just a fill-in job until her application goes through."

"Great. Then you'll need someone to replace her."

"Yes, I guess we will. But you're missing the point."

"Monica, please, you know I'm a fast learner." Amber's voice has moved into the danger zone, and things are going downhill fast. But she can't let it go.

"Look, Amber, on-the-job training and high-net-worth clients are not a good mix. I wish I could help you, but I can't."

Amber's blood pressure rises. She thinks fast. "I'm really good with people."

"But you have no office experience."

"Everybody has to start somewhere. I can smile and press buttons. How hard can it be?" She darts a look at the bob.

"Harder than it looks. It's a super fast-paced environment."

"So's waitressing."

"At Rosie's? Come on."

"You try working full-time and raising a kid. Alone." Monica has officially crossed Amber's insult tolerance line. She has no idea. She works just as hard as Monica!

Monica pulls Amber into the hall where their voices won't echo.

"I'm really sorry about everything that's happened in your life. I really am. I wish things could have turned out differently. And I'm here for you as a friend. But there's nothing I can do for you at the firm. I hope you can understand."

"Just give me a chance to prove myself," Amber begs. She can't help it. She needs this plan to work.

"I don't make the hiring decisions."

"Your name is on the door." Now Amber's just angry. Monica's not being fair with her. They were close once. Didn't that friendship count for anything?

"That doesn't mean I can just go hiring all my friends. Look, a bit of advice. If you want to work in a white-collar world, you need to shed that blue-collar attitude."

Amber has had it. "Friend? You disappeared after the funeral just like everyone else."

"I called. I tried. I felt like you shut me out. I wanted to be there for you. But you acted like you wanted to be left alone. So finally, I did." Monica's mobile rings. She fishes it out of her shoulder bag.

Amber is stung by her words. Had she really done that? Monica actually sounded hurt.

Monica draws in a breath as the phone

rings again. She checks the caller ID and lowers her voice to address Amber. "I have to take this."

Amber stands shell-shocked as Monica presses the phone to her ear and disappears down the hallway.

Amber can feel the stares at her back. She turns and is met with several sets of eyes, including the bob's. Oh yeah. They've heard it all. She shoulders her purse and begins her walk of shame through the lobby. She should have called first. But even so, with friends like Monica, who needs enemies?

CHAPTER TWENTY-FIVE:
BEAUTIFUL AGAIN

Patti has a standing date with the wives and widows of the Disabled American Veterans, Clarksville chapter, for Beauty Saturday, which she hosts on the second Saturday of each month with her best friend and My-Way associate, Kim. Although the focus is on giving back rather than making sales, Patti and Kim have both amassed a handful of new clients from the wives and widows of Beauty Saturdays. Every woman wants to look and feel beautiful, especially during times of distress and uncertainty.

But even more important than gaining new business is the fact that Patti has made some deep friendships, and seeing these women has become the highlight of her month. For Patti, it has become a way to connect with others who have lost loved ones in war, and it's been the single most healing thing she has done since Darren's death, even more so than her Sunday-morning ladies' brunch. She is able to express things to these women, and they to her, that can be understood only in the language of loss.

One of her favorite women is Paula, a more recent widow of forty-five with sixteen-year-old twins. When she started coming to Beauty Saturdays, her complexion was as dull and gray as her mood. She allowed Patti to give her a rejuvenating facial, but afterward she expressed nothing more than a flat thank-you. Patti took no offense.

The following week, she gave Paula a follow-up call and left a voice mail. A day before Beauty Saturday, Patti phoned again and left a message. "I hope you enjoyed the facial. Would love to see you again tomorrow. I just got a new shade of eye shadow in, and I think it would look gorgeous on you."

Paula took the sales bait and showed up at the meeting. Patti gave her a complete makeover and sent her home with the eye shadow, which did much to brighten Paula's eyes and made her look less tired. Patti's kindness and persistence soon took effect on Paula. When Patti made her follow-up call several days later, Paula answered right away and was gushing. She shared how she left Beauty Saturday and went to pick up some groceries. While she was at the store, four people commented on how pretty she looked. At home, her sons asked her what she had done differently to herself. They said she looked happier. Paula kept the makeup on when she went out for dinner that evening with a girlfriend, and a man dining alone stopped by to introduce himself and asked for her phone number. She was flattered but declined.

Paula was hooked. After she had spent almost a year in mourning, a subtle application of makeup had lifted her morale and stabilized her confidence.

Paula showed up month after month, an eager student as Patti taught her makeup techniques. She started to open up and share her story. Slowly and over time. Eventually Paula noticed the 101st Airborne patch sewn into Patti's makeup bag and asked her about it. Patti, slowly and over time, shared Darren's story — at least, what she knew of it. Paula had understood her grief and frustration with the fact that she didn't know all the details of Darren's fatal accident. And sometimes, they just sat with each other. Neither one speaking. Letting the silence knit them and their pain together.

■ ■ ■ ■

Today is beauty Saturday, and Patti searches the room for Paula among the thirty or so guests who have shown up. She's not surprised to find her near the welcome table, chatting with several new faces. Since Paula's confidence returned, she is always recruiting new wives and widows to the group. Paula has become quite the hostess and evangelist for Beauty Saturdays. Because of this, she and Patti don't talk as much as they did at first. Today, however, Patti feels down and wishes she could have a few minutes of Paula's time.

Kim agrees to lead the meeting, and Patti hangs out near the beauty display table in the back of the room. The presentation format is simple and well received. It begins with a warm welcome and a brief explanation of the MyWay company and what Patti and Kim have done to support the DAV. From here Kim launches into the topic of the morning, which ranges from skin care basics to treating acne-prone skin to assisting aging skin to better nail and hair care, or tips on when to use professional aesthetician services. Then comes a live beauty-technique demo using several volunteers from the group. Kim ends the morning by promoting seasonal products, handing out door prizes, and scheduling complimentary makeover appointments for the following week.

Patti stands at the back of the room, while up front the group is engaged in Kim's presentation on the benefits of laser therapy to remove age spots, moles, and fine veins on the face. Patti's thoughts begin to wander.

"You look far away," whispers Paula, nudging her from the side with a warm smile.

Patti gives her a hug and whispers back, "It's good to see you. How are you?"

"I'm fine. What's going on? I know that look."

"Bit of a troubling week." There's no use sugarcoating anything in front of Paula.

"Come with me." Paula takes her by the arm, and they slip out of the ballroom into the lobby of the hotel. Once seated comfortably on a couch in a private corner of the lobby, Patti lets her guard down.

"Did you get some bad news?" Paula starts.

"Not exactly good news. I don't know what to make of it."

"Start from the beginning."

"It's about Amber. She's let me into her life a little more lately."

"That sounds positive."

"Yes. It should be. But I'm getting a close-up look at her situation, and it's pretty scary."

"Is she in trouble?" Paula is always ready to lend a hand now that she's come out from under her dark cloud.

"I think she's in very grave trouble. But she doesn't see it. Or won't admit it. Or doesn't care."

"I'm sure she cares. She may just be feeling overwhelmed."

"She certainly doesn't want my help."

"A very natural reaction to what she's been through. And how things are between you. Just try not to take it personally."

"But she's sinking. Fast. And taking Bree down with her."

"Tell me what you're seeing, Patti."

"She works seven days a week for pennies. She's sold everything of value in her home. She barely ever spends time with Bree. The child has no food in the house. And Bree's running around town without any supervision. It's borderline neglect. I have half a mind to call child services!"

"Don't do that. It'll only add salt to her wounds."

"I know. I won't really." Patti sighs in desperation. "But what else can I do right now?"

"Keep being there for her. For Bree. Grief has its own timetable."

"And she'll be on welfare and food stamps before she knows what hit her. I even offered to set her up with a MyWay franchise. She wouldn't even consider it. How foolish is that?"

"That was a beautiful and generous offer, Patti. I'm sure deep down she knows you care."

"I'm not so sure. Amber's very stubborn."

"Which means she's got the fight in her. That's a good sign."

"I don't know how much more I can take," says Patti.

"I know it's hard to watch. I can only imagine how I must have looked with my life spiraling down after Mark's death. No one could do anything that made a difference."

"But you came here. And you kept coming. You turned your life around."

"But I had to make that choice. And Amber has to do the same. She has to find her way out of this."

Patti hears the wisdom in Paula's words. But it's hard to swallow.

"I never thought I could live again. Didn't even think I wanted to. Until you showed me I could be beautiful." Paula enfolds Patti in a hug. "Don't give up on Amber."

CHAPTER TWENTY-SIX: CREDIT CARD AND ID, PLEASE

Today is the deadline to stop the foreclosure proceedings. Jim Wellington will be expecting Amber to deliver the sum by five.

No credit. Bad credit. Cash now.

The radio announcer's words plant themselves in Amber's mind. On rewind and replay.

Cash now.

Cash now.

She needs cash. Now!

Amber weighs the decision during her entire day shift at Rosie's.

Perfect Payday will be a one-time-only event, she promises herself. It's just until she can land a better job.

Amber parks her minivan near the front door of Perfect Payday and takes a deep breath before heading in with her arms clutched around her purse.

"How much do you want to borrow?" asks the hipster clerk with four visible arm tattoos and a man bun. He removes one earbud from his ear and cracks open the glass partition.

"Eight hundred."

He doesn't even bat an eye as he gives her a hardened stare. "Credit card and ID, please."

Amber removes the items from her purse. The clerk punches her information into his computer, and a form spits out of his printer.

"This is what we call an 'unsecured loan.' It's a thirty-eight percent APR that starts accruing today."

"When is the loan due?" Amber's voice cracks.

"Two weeks." He hands Amber a pen.

She picks it up and scrolls a shaky signature.

The clerk slides eight one-hundred-dollar bills across the counter along with her payment agreement. Amber glances over it, pausing at the paragraphs of fine print.

"It says here you'll take me to court if I fail to pay?"

"That's right. If we don't see you back here in two weeks, we have the right to petition the court to step in and garnish your wages, Amber." He points to her name tag fastened to the lapel of her pink waitress smock. "You work at Rosie's?"

Amber smirks. "Yeah."

"Cool. They have killer pancakes."

Amber nods. There are not enough pan-cakes in the world to save her house right now.

"You still wanna go through with it?"

Amber meets his questioning look as the pit in her stomach grows.

She nods again.

The hipster slides the money through the glass partition.

Amber slips the cash into her purse.

"Here's your paperwork." He hands her a copy of the loan agreement. "Two weeks."

Without a word or glance, Amber rushes out.

CHAPTER TWENTY-SEVEN: NO SHORTCUTS

Amber takes the bank steps two at a time, rushing past Kendra Drake. *Wasn't she supposed to provide me with some sort of financial consultation?* She doubts the pampered millennial, who still lives at home with the safety net of her parents, can teach her any new budget tricks she hasn't already tried. And failed at. Kendra tries to stop her as Amber barrels by, straight to Jim Wellington's office. Only to find the door closed. *No. No. No!* She still has four minutes. Through the frosted glass, Amber sees Jim's shadow moving inside the office. She raps on the window.

"Mr. Wellington? It's Amber Hill!"

After a moment his silhouette moves to the door. He opens it and Amber bursts in, shoving an envelope at him.

"Here. Is this enough to stop the foreclosure?"

Mr. Wellington takes the envelope. "Come

in, please." He closes his office door after her. "Please have a seat, Mrs. Hill."

"No, I can't stay long. I have to pick up Bree. I just need to know if my house is okay."

Mr. Wellington opens the envelope and does a quick eye count of the contents. "This is a good start. It catches you up to only one missed payment. But that leaves a full payment and another due in two weeks."

"How much total?"

"Sixteen hundred to catch you up and officially cease the foreclosure process."

Amber swallows hard. She doesn't want to lie. "I'll try."

"But can you maintain this kind of payment schedule? That's what I'm most concerned about, Mrs. Hill."

"Let me worry about that."

"As your lender, it's my legal duty to worry. And I know you never set an appointment with Kendra. Have you taken any steps at all to explore your future?"

Amber senses that Jim knows she's holding something back. He's probably seen it a hundred times before. Desperation stinks like a chicken coop.

"Mrs. Hill. I know how you came up with this. There are no shortcuts in your situation."

Amber's caught. Jim pauses.

"How are you gonna cover all these expenses plus another loan?"

Shamed like a little child, Amber has no answer. But the fight has a stubborn hold on her.

"That house is the only home our family has ever known. Darren and I spent our weekends together remodeling every square inch. It's the only home Bree knows. I'm not letting it go."

Amber removes herself from Jim's office, beelining for the exit. She can hear the perky Kendra Drake chirping at her as she flees. "Mrs. Hill? Um . . . when would be a good time to . . . ah, schedule you for a financial consul—"

The door closes on the "tation," and Amber hurries down the sidewalk toward her minivan. There is absolutely nothing she wants to discuss with Kendra. How on earth could that chipper young thing, who has never stepped foot out of Clarksville, possibly understand the depths of what she's been through as a young widow? Life is not a balance sheet you can adjust for a positive net result.

CHAPTER TWENTY-EIGHT: IS IT SAFE?

Amber immediately heads to Bree's school to pick her up from after-school day care, racked by the nagging thought that she still has no food in the house and no money to buy any. She'll stop by Rosie's and pick up some leftover chicken dumplings. Bree loves those.

She arrives at Bree's classroom excited to tell her about their dumpling-dinner plans, only to find the door locked. Odd. She checks the time. 5:23 p.m. After-school day care goes until six. Where is everyone?

Amber begins to hunt down the halls toward the principal's office and runs into Bree's teacher.

"Ms. Bultema. Hi, I was wondering if you've seen Bree. She's supposed to be at after-school care."

"And you are?" Amber stops dead in her tracks. Did she really just ask that?

"Amber Hill. Bree's mom. You don't

remember me?"

"Oh, of course. I'm so sorry. I guess it's been a while."

Amber realizes she isn't a regular visitor to the school, but still. Shouldn't the teacher remember who she is?

"I think the last time I was supposed to see you was October. For parent-teacher conferences," Ms. Bultema explains.

"Really?" Amber had fallen asleep on the couch after work and missed the appointment.

"Bree's at Joe's."

"The auto shop?"

"Yes. She goes there on Wednesdays for that go-kart club."

"Right. I guess I got my days mixed up." She must think Amber is a total twit not to know where her own daughter is.

"It happens. Hey, stop by the classroom some afternoon when you can. I love to have parents get involved."

"I'll try." Amber weighs the offer. Is she being sincere, or is there an underlying guilt trip? But hey, since she's not getting Mom of the Year awards, why worry about it? If she can show up at home with chicken dumplings, that's a win.

Amber hoofs it out of the school and down the block to Joe's Auto.

She enters Joe's garage to find a hive of activity. At least half a dozen kids are working on go-karts in various states of completion. Some paint, some drill, some fasten tires. The garage echoes with chatter and laughter. Such a stark difference from the somberness of their home life.

Amber finds Bree in the middle of the hustle and bustle, intensely tending to her own go-kart. The excitement in the air is infectious, and soon Amber is feeling lighter. She notices right away that Bree also has a carefree look about her as she sands the plywood side of her vehicle.

"Hey, kids. Ten more minutes and we're gonna wrap things up." Cody's voice projects from the back of the garage. Amber catches a glimpse of him bending over to grease the steering rod of Bree's friend David's kart. She recognizes him from Rosie's and the failed date attempt, and hopes things won't be uneasy.

Wanting to watch Bree for a few minutes undetected, Amber steps into the corner of the garage, out of Bree's eyeline. It's so rare she has a moment to see what her daughter is really like when she's not in her mother's presence. She is careful not to rush her project, stopping every few seconds to check the smoothness of the wood. It's a very tender and loving approach to this inanimate object.

"Hey, Amber. Great to see you again. Whatcha doing hiding back here?" Cody's smile melts away any lingering awkwardness from their diner encounter.

"Hi, Cody. Just watching Bree. I've never seen her so engaged in something."

"She loves that kart. She'll be so excited to show you. Here, come on over." Cody starts to lead her, but Amber puts a hand on his arm to stop him.

"In a minute. I like seeing her like this." Bree shows off her work to a couple of other admirers. Amber savors her daughter just being a kid.

"She's a hard worker," Cody says.

"I'm a little surprised, actually. Bree mentioned this kart thing, but I didn't really understand what it involved."

"You signed the parental release form, right?"

"Well, yes, but I just kinda . . . skimmed it."

Cody playfully shames her with a look. "Busted."

"Hey, I trust Joe. So . . ."

"I get it."

"Well, tell me about it. Looks like quite a little assembly line you have going here."

"Yeah. I wasn't so sure when Joe told me about it, but it's pretty fun, actually."

"So how does it work?"

"Well, Joe and I end up doing most of the construction. But the kids do the designing and painting. And then, you know, we race them."

"Racing? Really?"

"I set up a course out here in front of Joe's. I'll teach them a few track basics and turning techniques."

"Oh. Wow. Sounds very professional. Is it dangerous?"

"There's the occasional bumper-car incident." Amber's concerned look prompts Cody to expand. "But the motors on the karts only go about five miles per hour. So the kids never really get up enough speed to do any damage if they hit anything. Or each other. Plus, I set up old tires around the edge of the track."

"And they wear helmets?"

"Always. Safety first," he reassures her.

"Mom! Come see, come see!" She's been spotted. Amber turns to see Bree's eager face popping up from her kart. She wipes sawdust off her forehead.

Amber walks around to Bree's kart, and Bree excitedly pulls her mother to the logo sketched on the hood. It grabs Amber's attention immediately. This is why Bree is so absorbed. Amber bends down and traces a finger over the Screaming Eagle. A shadow remnant of the man she loved.

"So that's why you needed the patch?" Amber smiles at Bree. "Wow, this is really cool."

"Thanks. I'm all done sanding. Do you want to help me paint?" Bree hands her a paintbrush, and Amber dips it into the primer. Amber begins to paint a bare spot on the side.

"Cody says to put it on nice and thick."

"Oh. Okay." Amber goes to dip the brush in the can again, and Cody claps his hands.

"All right, gang! That's it for today. Let's get this place spick-and-span. You know what to do."

"Aw, we just got started." Bree's face drops.

"I'll help you clean up. How 'bout that?" Bree nods and shows her mother to the sink, where they wash all the brushes and paint trays. Bree gives the brushes a thorough rinse. She shows Amber where to hang them to dry. Amber is impressed at her level of responsibility. They make their way back to the kart. Bree places the clean paint trays on a nearby shelf.

"So, what made you want to put Daddy's

logo on your kart?"

"I just like it."

"Is that how you remember him?" The question slips out before she realizes. Up until now, Amber has been cautious of asking Bree about her memories of Darren. Mostly because it brought to the surface her own pain. And she hates breaking down in front of Bree.

"Yeah. I like to picture him in his uniform." Bree's simple answer delivers an element of comfort to Amber that she didn't expect. "It's kinda like he's right there with me."

Amber nods and blurts out, "Okay, kiddo. Is there anything else we need to do before we head home?"

Bree looks around. "Nope. We're done."

"Okay, well, I parked at the school, so we need to walk . . ."

"Actually, can I walk home with David?" Amber is suddenly aware of a whole new level of independence that wasn't there just two weeks ago. Did all this stem from the go-karts?

"Um. Sure. See you at home for dinner."

Bree joins David and the other kids who trickle out of the garage to waiting parents. Amber gathers her purse and heads for the door. Cody joins her.

"So, what do you think?"

"I think she's growing up too fast," Amber jokes.

"She's a great kid."

"It's nice to see her happy. She doesn't always show me that side at home." That's not what I mean. "I'm not a bad parent. I just . . . it's harder being a single mom than I imagined."

"You must be doing a great job. She's really taken ownership of her kart."

Of course she has. It's her connection to Darren. "Thanks for doing this. It's a good thing."

They walk a few paces. Then: "You deserve to be happy, too, you know."

Amber stops and turns to him. *What?* Cody can read the question on her face.

"I mean . . . life's not all about work, work, work."

"Okay. I guess not." *Where is he going with this?*

"I know you already said no — and I respect that and all — but . . . I don't mean to be pushy — that's the last thing I'd ever want to do. . . ."

That flutter surfaces for a second. Is he trying to . . . ?

"So I heard about this really great musician playing at Harry's Coffee tomorrow night. Want to check it out?"

More flutters. He's really not backing down. The idea doesn't fill her with dread like it did at first. A night out might be a nice reprieve. Flutters again. "Yes. Sounds like fun."

"Okay. Great." Amber can almost hear the sigh of relief from him as his shoulders drop.

"Great." Should she offer another response?

"Pick you up around six thirty?"

"Okay." *What do I do next? What's the protocol? It's been, like, ten years since anyone asked me out on a first date.*

"All right."

"I'll see you tomorrow, then."

"See you tomorrow."

Amber slips out of the garage, the last to leave except for Cody. She heads off down the block to her minivan, still parked at the elementary school. The flutter melts away, replaced by that growing pit that feels like her stomach is going to eat itself. Different from hunger pains. Apprehension. Her face tenses as she walks.

What makes her think she's anywhere near ready to add one more element to her life? Or Bree's?

The pit turns to gnawing.

She prays Rosie has a couple of leftover dumplings.

CHAPTER TWENTY-NINE: PRE-DATE JITTERS

Cody

Cody slams the hood of a 1984 Buick LeSabre as he checks the clock hanging between the stall doors of Joe's garage. Six o'clock on the nose. *If I quit now, I'll have just enough time to wash up, clean out the passenger side of my car — okay, maybe the whole car — and then try not to freak out. It's a cup of coffee. It's not like trying to hit the apex of a turn at eighty miles per hour and not spin out. I got this.*

Cody clocks out and heads into the office, where Joe is working the books at his desk.

"Joe, I gotta head out on time today, okay?" Cody heads for the door in the corner that houses what passes for a bathroom at Joe's Auto. He flips on the single-bulb light mounted above a mottled mirror and keeps the door open a crack to air out the musty odor.

"What's the status on the LeSabre?" Joe

calls from his desk.

"Was down two quarts of oil. Added that. Fixed the leak in the transmission line. And the brakes are worn. Need to replace 'em."

"I'll call the owner in the morning and give 'em a quote on new brakes."

Cody grabs his duffel bag from under the cracked pedestal sink and takes out a few toiletries. He washes his hands and face under an anorexic flow of ice-cold water from the faucet. "You really need to get a new faucet, Joe. When was this thing installed? 1967?"

"Sixty-eight."

"Guess they didn't have hot water back then, either, did they?" He smiles at his own joke.

"What are you doing in there? Taking a bath?"

"Getting ready."

"Ready for what?"

"Date." *Not that it's any of your business, old man. I'm entitled to a little bit of a private life during this jail sentence.*

"Who's this date with?"

The door flings open, startling Cody. He sees Joe's distorted image glaring back at him in the warped mirror.

"Amber Hill."

"What did I tell you about that girl?"

"Oh, don't get your knickers in a bunch. It's just coffee."

"It better be."

Cody slaps water on his face and rubs it off with a paper towel. He digs into his bag and comes up with a comb. Joe is still staring at him, concern furrowing his brow. "What? I can't have a little fun? My personal life is not part of the Gibbs deal."

Joe leans against the door frame. "No, I know. You are. But if I offer you a little advice, will you listen?"

"What do you got?"

"Cody, this is important."

"Even more important than the apex?" Cody grins at Joe as he exchanges his dirty T-shirt for a dressier shirt crumpled in his bag.

"I've known Amber since she married Darren. They were really in love, and they made a great couple. Darren was a lot like you in spirit. Adventurous. High-strung. Ready to take on the world. And he did. And Amber never stood in his way. But it cost her and Bree greatly."

Cody shakes out his shirt, trying to smooth the wrinkles. "I'm grateful for his sacrifice, and he sounds amazing — downright intimidating, actually. But she said yes to the date. So . . . I'm not exactly sure how this applies to me."

"Amber's had a big loss in her life. She may be lonely and looking for companionship. That's only natural. But I don't want you taking advantage of that. She's not ready for a long-term relationship. There's a heap of trouble still brewing in her."

"You make it sound like I'm heading into a train wreck." Cody buttons his shirt up halfway, frowning at his unkempt shirt in the mirror. "You think if I put on my leather jacket over this, it'll hide the wrinkles?" He turns to Joe for approval and finds Joe shaking his head at him. "No good, huh? You don't have an iron, by any chance?"

"Cody. I'm worried you'll be a distraction."

"I think she *needs* a distraction . . . from all that sadness. And maybe you need to stop feeling sorry for her." Cody slips out of his work shoes and into a pair of cowboy boots.

"I want nothing but the best for Amber and Bree." *So do I, old man.* "But you're not it right now."

"Whoa . . . first of all, you don't know that. And second, slow your horses. This is just a cup of coffee."

"I know what coffee can lead to. I was young once."

"When was that? When you installed this faucet?" Cody's chuckle is quickly silenced by Joe's stony look. "Joe, look, I haven't had a date in over two years. It's been all track time for me. I'd like to settle down someday. Find that one true love. I've got to start somewhere. And Amber seems . . ."

"Amber is everything she seems right now. Sweet. Vulnerable. Fragile. Don't play around with her heart. Don't lead her on. And don't think you can fix her. Got it? Be a friend. That's it. End of story."

"Friends. Got it." Cody uncaps his deodorant stick and rubs it under his arms.

Joe shakes his head. "You're gonna need to do more than that to impress her. Come here."

Cody follows Joe back to his desk. He removes something and throws it at Cody.

"Put this on."

A small bottle of cologne lands in Cody's grip.

Amber must really be something if Joe's getting this defensive over her. I think it's going to be a great night.

Amber

Amber answers the door in a complete panic. She's still in her robe and slippers, with hot rollers tumbling from her hair and mascara smudged in dark circles under her eyes. Hannah's shocked look tells her everything she needs to know. Disaster!

Bree, who is partially hidden behind her mother, sticks her head out and pleads with the paralyzed Hannah. "Can you get Bridgette? We need a little help here!"

Amber nods, a curler dropping out of her hair.

Hannah turns around and dashes down the steps. *"Bridgette!"*

Amber and Bree follow her out onto the front porch.

A car just pulling away from the house screeches to a halt. Backs up. Parks. The ignition turns off, and within a second Bridgette jumps out of the car and dashes up the walk. She takes one look at the bedraggled Amber and shrieks.

"Bad, huh?" Amber asks.

"Get inside! Get inside!" Bridgette ushers them all through the front door.

"He'll be here in thirty minutes," says Amber.

"Okay, deep breaths. We're in triage mode, people. Hannah. Bree. I need a washcloth, Q-tips, hair spray, and a drier sheet. Go! Go!"

Hannah rushes upstairs, with Bree leading the way.

Bridgette sees the MyWay starter kit on the dining table. "What's that?"

"A bribe."

But Bridgette is already unloading its contents.

"This shade is perfect for you."

"I'm not using that stuff," says Amber.

"Upstairs, lady. Let's go!"

Bridgette takes Amber by the shoulders and pushes her toward the stairs.

6:27 p.m.
Amber slips into her dress and jean jacket. She turns to Bridgette for a final look. Bridgette applies a touch of MyWay lip gloss to Amber's lips. She steps back to let a transformed Amber take a look at herself in the full-length mirror. Hannah and Bree admire from the bed.

"You look great, Mom!"

"Thanks to Bridgette." Amber makes a small bow in appreciation.

"And thanks to MyWay," Bridgette teases.

"Don't start." Amber waves a finger.

"You look really beautiful, Mrs. Hill," says Hannah.

Amber smiles. "Thanks, Hannah."

Hannah hugs Amber and takes Bree's hand. "Let's go see if we can find a snack in the kitchen."

They take off. Amber can't take her eyes off the image she sees in the mirror.

"It's showtime. He should be here any second," says Bridgette.

"You do great work, Bridge."

She hasn't been this done up since Darren took her out for a fancy dinner before he left on his last tour. The afternoon before the date, Amber had used a gift certificate and splurged on a facial and makeup application at the spa downtown. The treatment made her feel and look radiant. And Darren couldn't keep his eyes off her all night.

She's sure she doesn't like that glow tonight. But it is a miraculous transformation.

"You really pulled this off. Thank you."

"That's what I'm here for. You did the same for me. Sort of. Remember our winter formal?" Bridgette lets out a bellowing laugh.

"Junior year? Oh, do I." Amber groans. Bridgette will never, ever let her live it down.

"Those highlights you gave me the night before. Oh my goodness. What a wreck."

"I was going for honey tones."

"More like headlight yellow streaked unevenly on the top of my head."

"You pulled it off, though. And Regina

Carpenter wanted to know who had done your hair so she could go in and get the same look."

"She even took a picture of me to show her hairdresser!" Bridgette is almost in tears. "But my hair was the least of my worries. I was too embarrassed to tell Matt I was allergic to that daisy corsage."

"And your eyes got all swollen!" Amber says.

"And my mascara was down to my neck after we iced them in the banquet-hall kitchen."

"And then Matt, that rat, took off after the dance with that other girl. What was her name?"

"Betsie!" recalls Bridgette.

"Yeah! Big-lips Bets!"

"And then she dumped him the next week. They deserved each other."

Amber feels a catharsis as the laughter sheds almost all anxiety from her body.

"It's so good to do this with you again." Amber hugs Bridgette.

"I've missed this," says Bridgette.

"I've missed you."

"You, too."

Amber turns serious as the memories seep in. "Winter formal. That was the night I first met Darren."

"It was, wasn't it? But he didn't go to our school."

"No. That senior, Amy, was dating him and invited him to our dance. She got really mad at me when he asked me to dance."

"Wow, there was a lot of boyfriend-girlfriend stealing going on that night," jokes Bridgette.

Amber gets quiet, and her eyes begin to flood. She blinks back the tears. "Nope. Not gonna cry."

"Better watch your mascara, there." Bridgette wipes a small smudge from under Amber's left eye.

"I don't know if I should be doing this."

"It's just coffee."

"No. It's not that. It's just — Somehow it feels . . . disloyal."

"Amber. Look at me."

Bridgette turns Amber's face to hers.

"First, it's been two years. Not that I'm putting a time limit on your grief. But . . . it's okay to have a little fun. Got it?"

Amber nods. Bridgette's not quite sure she believes her, though.

"And second, it's just coffee. You know? Bitter black beverage with excessive jitter levels."

"Coffee," Amber says, with a distance in her voice. An image of Darren and her dancing plants itself in her memory, threatening to sour her mood and change her mind about the date.

The doorbell rings downstairs. And she snaps back to reality.

CHAPTER THIRTY:
OFF-LIST SHOPPING

Patti pushes a shopping cart through the grocery store aisle as she carefully selects only the items from the shelves that are on her weekly grocery list. A big believer in eating organic, natural foods, Patti won't purchase anything that contains more than five ingredients. She shies away from canned, jarred, or boxed items, preferring to make her meals and snacks from scratch. Sure, it takes a little longer, but she enjoys the time in the kitchen. It relaxes her.

Patti wheels her cart, a cornucopia of fruits and vegetables, down the freezer aisle toward the checkout stand. Just as she's almost at the end of the row, the ice-cream display catches her attention. Patti's kryptonite.

She stops.

She plants herself in front of the glass door, a passageway to the frozen delights.

And then Patti gets a brilliant idea.

CHAPTER THIRTY-ONE:
OVERSHADOWED BY THE SHADOWBOX

"Mom! Cody's here!" Bree's little voice shouts up the stairs.

"Okay, okay," says Amber, halfway down the steps. She spies Bree at the bottom, smiling from ear to ear.

"I showed him to the living room. Was that okay?"

"Yes. Thank you, sweetie. And did you and Hannah find a snack?" Amber marvels at Bree's hospitality. *Good girl.* Reaching the bottom of the steps, she can smell popcorn cooking in the kitchen.

We don't have popcorn in the house. Ah, that Hannah. Of course, she brought a bag. Hannah thinks of everything.

"Bedtime at nine, okay? Don't forget to brush your teeth."

"I won't." Amber gives Bree a quick kiss and sends her to the kitchen.

"Bye, Cody!" Bree calls to him.

"Bye, Bree!" Cody's voice echoes back

from the living room.

Amber enters and finds him in front of the fireplace staring at Darren's medals in a shadowbox on the mantel. A Purple Heart. A Silver Star.

In his leather jacket, faded jeans, and side-tousled hair, Cody looks the complete opposite of Darren. For a second, Amber feels peculiar about this stranger occupying a living room that used to be hers and Darren's.

"Hi."

Cody spins around, startled by her stealthy entrance. "Hi. How are you?"

"I'm good. You?"

"Really good. You look really pretty."

Flutters. Amber smiles and stands there for a second, unsure what to say next. It takes a moment before she realizes that he just complimented her. "Oh. Thank you. Sorry, it's been so long since anyone said that to me. Bridgette is mostly to blame for all this." She does a nervous quarter twirl and then stops halfway through. "I don't know why I just did that," she twitters. More flutters.

Cody grins. "It was cute."

Cute? Ugh. Cute is so girlish. Is that how he sees me? She steps toward the mantel with a confident stride. "Are you ready to go?"

Cody glances back at the medals. "He

must have been an amazing man."

Amber sees the respect in Cody's eyes. "He was."

"Joe told me he died on patrol."

"That's right" is all Amber can muster. He better leave it at that.

"These medals have me pretty curious. Do you know what happened?"

Conflicting emotions shoot through her. "He died on patrol with his team. I've never really asked beyond that."

"I can only imagine." He lets a silent moment go by as they both stare at the medals, lost in thought. "I have the utmost respect for our military men and war heroes."

"Thank you." This is not how she imagined this date starting, Cody frozen in front of the mantel. "Well, shall we go?"

"Oh yeah. Of course."

She leads him to the front door, and at the last second he jogs a step ahead of her to open it. A good sign, she thinks. Darren would approve.

CHAPTER THIRTY-TWO: A BURGLAR WHO KNOCKS

Patti goes straight from the grocery story to Amber's house. She knocks once. Twice. Then a third time. She can see lights on and two shadows moving around inside. Why on earth are they not answering the door? The groceries are getting heavy in her arms. She knocks again. Louder. More forceful.

"Amber? It's Patti! Are you there?"

The door opens a crack. Bree's eyes peer around the corner.

"Grandma!" The door swings wide to reveal Bree and Hannah on the other side, wielding a rolling pin and a meat tenderizer.

"What are you doing with those?" Patti asks as she steps through the door, both arms cradling brown paper grocery bags.

"We thought you were a burglar." Bree giggles.

"A burglar who politely knocks three

times?" teases Patti.

"We were watching a scary movie, and I guess our imaginations ran away with us," Hannah explains innocently, closing the door behind Patti.

"And I'm guessing you're here to babysit, Hannah?"

"Yes, ma'am. Amber went to Harry's Coffee. She should be back in a couple of hours," says Hannah, dropping the meat mallet to her side.

"Oh, did she meet Bridgette there?"

"Cody picked her up," says Bree with a broad smile.

This information does not sit well with Patti, but she puts on a party face. No matter. She still gets to spend time with her granddaughter.

"I see. Well, I brought you a treat. Who wants an ice cream sundae?"

"Meeeeee!" Bree jumps up and down, circling her grandma in a wild frenzy. Hannah grabs one of the grocery bags and heads to the kitchen with Patti. Bree scurries in ahead of them.

As Patti unpacks the bags, Bree's eyes go wide. There are several gallons of different kinds of ice cream, chocolate *and* caramel sauce, maraschino cherries, whipped cream, M&M's, mini chocolate chips, and colored sprinkles.

"Grab the biggest bowls you can find."

"This is awesome!" says Bree, gloating over the pile of ingredients.

"One big, fat, sugar feast," Hannah says, scurrying to the cupboards for bowls. "Bree's never going to sleep now." Hannah passes a canny look to Patti, and they grin knowingly.

After carefully building their ice cream creations, Patti and the girls all squirm back in their seats on the sofa. Hannah unpauses the movie, and scary music fills the room. The tension on the screen and in the room grows. Patti cocks her head at the TV. It's an old black-and-white Alfred Hitchcock thriller. Is this what kids are into these days? And does Amber know Bree is watching this stuff? Patti wonders if she should put the kibosh on the program. But there's no profanity or sex or gratuitous violence — just suspense. A lot of it. She glances at Bree, who doesn't seem fazed. But will this give her nightmares?

From the screen, squeaky violin music intensifies.

Hannah squints one eye, afraid of what might happen next on-screen. "She shouldn't go down there!"

Bree slaps both hands over her eyes. "Why

is she going down there?"

"She should not go down there." Patti is fixed on the screen.

"We shouldn't be watching this," says Bree, removing a hand from one eye so she can shove a hug spoonful of ice cream into her gaping mouth.

"How can you ladies stand the suspense?"

"It's like a jack-in-the-box. You don't know when the *pop!* is coming, but you keep cranking the handle," says Hannah.

"I hate those things," says Patti.

They watch the movie to its end. As the credits roll, Hannah texts her mom to pick her up. Patti notices Bree's eyelids drooping sleepily as she struggles to stay awake.

"Bedtime, peanut. Head on up and get your jammies on while I see Hannah out. I'll be right up," says Patti, shooing Bree off the couch. Bree waddles to the stairs.

Hannah gets her things as Patti reaches into her purse and hands her a healthy sum.

"Oh, Mrs. Hill, you don't have to pay me. I'm doing this as a favor to help out Amber."

"That's very kind. But I insist. Put it away in your college fund. Education's not cheap these days."

"Thank you. I'll use it to buy Sunday school supplies. And thanks for the ice cream." Hannah heads out the door to her mother's waiting vehicle.

Patti climbs the stairs to Bree's room and finds her in her pjs at the windowsill, fiddling over Matt with a pair of earbuds.

"What are you doing, sweetie?" Patti comes up next to her and sees that Bree has the earbuds sunk into the soil next to a tiny green hump of a stem pushing its way through the topsoil.

"Matt loves music," she says.

"Oh, he does, huh? What kind?"

"Country, mostly. Rascal Flatts is his favorite."

"I see." Patti grins at her granddaughter. "He's got good taste, then. Looks like he's going to be a healthy little sprout."

"I told her Matt would grow. She didn't believe me."

"Who didn't?"

"Mom." Bree rearranges the gray sweater around the base of the pot. "But I have faith."

"Okay, kiddo. Bed."

"Good night, Matt. See you in the morning."

Patti pulls back the covers, expecting Bree to hop in. Instead, Bree pauses to kneel at the side of her bed, folds her hands, and lifts her eyes to the ceiling. "Hi, God. Thanks for Grandma and ice cream and

Hannah and scary movies. Please say hi to Daddy. Make Mom feel better. And help Matt to grow big and strong. Amen." Bree hops into bed, pulling the covers tight up to her neck.

Simple prayer. Simple faith. If that's what helps Bree get through this time in her life, then so be it. That, and scary movies. Patti tucks Bree in quietly, not wanting to disrupt the mood. "Good night, peanut. Love you," she whispers.

"Good night. It's fun having you here."

"It's fun being here. See you later." Patti kisses her on the cheek as Bree's weary eyes fall closed. She's asleep before Patti can turn off the light.

Patti pads downstairs, checking the time. It's almost ten. She expected Amber to be home by now. She cleans up the kitchen and washes the dishes. Ten fifteen. Patti goes through the house to turn off the extra lights and settles into one corner of the sofa with an afghan. She searches for a magazine to read and spies several in a basket on the end table. Extending her arm over the side of the couch, she reaches for one, inadvertently jostling the basket off the edge of the table. It topples over, the contents spilling across the floor. A small pile of mail slides out from in between the magazines. Patti scoops up the paperwork, noticing the envelopes are marked with overdue notices. Electric. Gas. Water and sewer. Credit card companies. She sifts through them, prying into the contents.

Suddenly, she spies a piece of mail that has fallen underneath the couch. As she picks it up, the letter slips from the envelope. Reading the first few sentences, Patti is flooded with disappointment and disbelief. What is going to happen to this little family?

CHAPTER THIRTY-THREE: SCRABBLE

Cody's firebird roars to a stop across the street from Harry's Coffee Shop, a Scrabble-themed coffeehouse that is a welcome addition to Clarksville's struggling downtown district, and the only place one can go for a coffee after the sidewalks roll up at 6:00 p.m.

"Sit tight," Cody tells Amber as he throws the muscle car into park.

Cody exits his car. Amber draws in a couple of deep breaths as he sails around to the other side to open her door. Amber steps out and faces the coffee shop full of people. Instant panic hits her. It hasn't crossed her mind that she would be seen in public with Cody. Not that it matters. She isn't doing anything wrong. But people talk. And they will surely start the gossip train about seeing widow Amber Hill on a date with Joe's prodigy project, Cody Jackson. It just adds another facet to this new life that she needs to adjust to.

Cody leads her across the street toward the front door. It's a cool but calm spring night, and Amber marvels at the beautiful glow of the soft lights on Harry's sign hanging above the storefront. It's like they're inviting her into some secret, new world that she has long been outside of.

She steps in. The earthy smell of coffee envelops her, and the solo guitar sounds lap over her in soothing waves, setting her senses at ease. Cody spots a table near the front with a Scrabble board. She finds nothing but friendly glances as they wind their way through the café.

Cody makes sure Amber is settled before he pulls his stool up to the table across from her.

"How good are you at Scrabble?" He grins, shuffling the leftover pieces from the previous café player around on the table to mix them up.

"I know some pretty big words," she teases. Cody sweeps the pieces off the board.

"But first . . . what can I get you to drink?"

"Just coffee." Bridgette's words flow out, reminding her to have fun.

"Cream and sugar?"

"Black."

"Hard-core. Like it. Okay, I'll be right back."

Amber nods and turns her gaze to the stage. She finds herself tuned in to the singer's clear, evocative voice. The musician, Micah Tyler, sure knows his way around a guitar. Listening to him perform gives Amber a sudden urge to pick up her own guitar. The last time she touched hers was just before she received *the news.* Since then it's been stashed away. In the corner of her bedroom. Under a layer of dust.

"Come thou fount of every blessing, tune my heart to sing thy grace."

Amber leans on Micah's music to pull out of the dour memory of days when she sang and played. Feels like a lifetime ago.

"Sing thy grace . . . sing thy grace . . ."

When was the last time she sang anything but complaints? Hard to find something praiseworthy nowadays. *This is the day that the Lord has made. Let us rejoice . . . and be glad in it.*

Glad for a dead-end job? A bucketful of debt? A boss who won't give her a promotion? A friend who shuns her? A house she may lose? A meddling mother-in-law?

"Streams of mercy never ceasing, call for songs of loudest praise."

Chord after chord blends together. She

still doesn't feel grateful, but she does feel tiny pieces of her heart fuse back together with the balm of Tyler's voice.

Cody returns with two coffees and a mile-high piece of chocolate cake. "Looked too good to resist," he says, handing her a fork and setting down the plate between them.

"That is a huge piece of cake!"

"You're not gonna tell me you're gluten-free or vegan or allergic to chocolate, are you?"

Amber laughs and dives her fork into the frosting. "Not. At. All."

They take stabs at the dessert, quickly bringing it to its doom.

So much for just coffee. Amber grins to herself, savoring the rich chocolate ganache center of the cake.

"You have a little chocolate right there above your lip," Cody tells her. Amber quickly licks it off. "You got it."

She takes it as a good sign that Cody is the kind of guy who isn't afraid of pointing out a little mess.

"Enjoying the music?"

"I am. Have you heard this guy play before?"

"Never. Joe told me he was coming through on a coffeehouse tour. I thought he'd be worth checking out. Nothing else to do around here."

"Good point. He's good. I like him." Amber sips her coffee. The song ends, and the café erupts in applause. Micah excuses himself offstage for a quick break. Piped-in background music falls over the room, mixed in with soft chatter from the other patrons. They sip their coffee for a while, alternating between silence and small talk. After a coffee refill and another set from Micah, Cody asks her, "Wanna play a game of Scrabble?"

"I sure do." Amber stacks her tiles in neat rows below the board. "Prepare to go up in flames!"

Cody winces.

"Oh, sorry. Bad choice of words."

"No, it's kinda funny, actually."

Amber places two tiles down on the board: L and S.

"So, what's your story? What was the straw that broke the camel's back?"

"I see you've been eavesdropping on the gossip at Rosie's Diner."

"Not at all. I just know that if you're work-ing with Joe, it's not by your choice."

Cody draws a few Scrabble letters and adds them to his tray.

"The last race I drove, I had a little fender bender. My car caught on fire."

"Was it your fault?"

"Maybe. But I still managed to finish the race. Even with the front half of the car in flames."

"Congratulations."

"Those weren't exactly the words Gibbs used."

"Ouch."

"Yeah, that was the last race where I actually crossed the finish line."

"Well, what's the main problem, then?" Amber's heard enough of Joe's racing stories to know that every driver has his Achilles' heel.

"Turns. I realize how dumb that must sound."

Amber cocks her head at him. "I don't follow."

"Joe says I take them too fast."

"And what's he doing to help you?"

"He keeps telling me patience, persistence. So far, I've spent more time building go-karts than turning laps." Amber senses the frustration in his voice.

"When do you think you'll get back out on the track?"

"My first race is next week." Cody adds a couple of letters to the board, spelling "CAR."

"Wow, 'CAR.' Five whole points." She

giggles. "Is that all you ever think about?"

"Can't help it. It's who I am."

Amber senses a touch of defensiveness.

"It's okay. I get it. Darren used to say the same thing about being a Screaming Eagle." She smiles and lets him know it's okay. "When you're passionate about something, it just comes out all over everything in your life."

"I heard you used to have that kind of passion for music, Ms. Church Choir Director."

Amber takes her turn at the game and her time formulating a response.

"At one time, church was the center of my life. I used to spend a lot of time there."

"And now? Why don't I see you there?"

"Busy. Working."

"Do you miss it?"

"I don't know. I guess I filled my time with other things and stopped seeing the point."

"That's an honest answer." Cody lays another tile on the board. "R."

"Bridgette told me you're a pretty good singer."

"Bridgette talks too much," says Amber, brushing it off. "How about you? I didn't peg you to be the churchy type."

"I wasn't the churchy type. Till coming here." Cody chuckles and lays an I up from the R. "But I guess it doesn't hurt. I drive a tin box around a track at two hundred miles per hour. Guess I could use a little more faith."

"Fair enough." Amber raises her coffee cup to her lips as Micah returns to the stage and applause trickles through the café. He strums a few chords to warm up. Amber's eyes instinctively go to his fingers.

"Some songs just get better with age. Feel free to join me on this one."

His fingers pluck out the first few bars, and he folds his voice into the lyrics of an old-fashioned hymn, "Blessed Assurance." Amber immediately recognizes the tune. She looks down at her letters and adds to her Scrabble word. E. S.

Cody watches her form the word "LESS."

Without knowing it, Amber is mouthing the words to the chorus. *This is my story, this is my song. Praising my Savior all the day long.* The tune flows effortlessly. A piece of her soul awakening. *"Praising my Savior all the day long."*

Cody is mesmerized by her as Amber gets lost in the chorus, a soft voice coming from her lips. After a moment, she looks up and realizes he's staring at her. Her lips purse.

"You should be up there onstage."

"What? Oh no. Sorry . . . I'm so embarrassed." She glances down at the Scrabble board. "Hey, it's your turn."

Cody takes a piece, examines it, and then places it on the Scrabble board to complete her word — "LESS" to "BLESS."

"Sometimes less is more." He looks up at her.

"Clever. Twenty-one points for you." She scribbles down the score on her napkin.

"Amber, can I ask you something?"

"Sure."

"This sorrow you're carrying around. Do you think God meant for you to have that?"

The question rocks her to the core. When she doesn't answer, Cody scrambles to re-phrase.

"I didn't express that right. I mean, it seems like both of our lives have really gotten thrown off track."

The pun is not lost on Amber, who unfurls a grin. "Agreed. And . . . what's your point?"

"Do you believe God is still blessing us despite everything that seems to be going wrong?"

"Is this a trick question?" Amber grows with unease.

"No. That's not what I'm . . . I just . . . When I look at my life right now, things might seem pretty desperate. I have no idea if I'll ever be asked back to race with Gibbs.

Which is my life's dream. And I should be upset. But all I can see is His blessing. Right in front of me." His gaze locks on to hers. "If I didn't come here, I would never have met you."

Amber is stunned into silence for a few moments. "I'm glad for you. And I'm sure Joe will help you make a comeback. But as for me, I think . . . I know that . . . It's been pretty impossible to see any blessings on my path the last couple of years." The painful pit in her stomach returns.

"Fair enough," Cody responds. "But I hope someday soon you can see things from my perspective."

Amber glances up to the stage, where Micah has moved on to a more upbeat song. It's been an interesting, wonderful, anxious, and refreshing evening all mixed into one brew of emotions. And she suddenly finds herself exhausted. Amber checks the time. It's getting late. She needs to be up early for work the next day. And the night can't get any better than it is right now. Better not to spoil a good thing.

Cody walks her out, and she finds the spring evening has taken on an unexpected chill. Amber cinches her jacket closed to keep warm. "Thank you for tonight. This was . . . fun."

"You don't sound too sure about that."

Amber smiles as they head across the street toward Cody's Firebird. "I'm sure. I kinda forgot what it feels like not to worry. For a few minutes, anyhow."

"Then, mission accomplished. And I hope we can have more worry-free times together." Cody walks her to the passenger door, where they come face-to-face. He folds her in to himself gently. She recognizes those eyes. The kind that lead to a kiss. Flutters dance in her stomach. He starts to lean in.

Amber pulls back. "Please . . . don't. I . . . I'm sorry. I'm just not ready."

"Sorry, I didn't mean to . . . misread the moment. My bad." Cody straightens up and takes an embarrassed step back.

"It's okay. Really." Amber turns with a furtive glance back at Harry's, glad to see that no one is looking out.

"Let me get the door for you." Cody leans around her to open the creaky Firebird. Amber ducks into her seat.

The drive to Amber's house takes less than ten minutes. When they arrive, Amber's gaze moves suspiciously to a familiar car parked across the street.

"So, can I call you soon?" Cody asks as

his Firebird growls to the curb.

"Yeah, that'd be fine." *What is* she *doing here?*

Amber flings her car door open a second before Cody has it in park. She slams the door and is halfway up the front walk before Cody is out of his car.

"Amber? Everything okay?" He calls from the sidewalk.

Not. At. All.

"Thanks again, Cody. Talk later." Amber shoots up the front steps and disappears inside.

CHAPTER THIRTY-FOUR: NONE OF YOUR BUSINESS

Amber dashes into the house and sees Patti sitting on the couch, the bills and foreclosure letters spread out on her lap.

"What are you doing here?" Amber tries to hold in her temper. "Where's Hannah?"

"She stayed for a while and then I sent her home. Don't worry. I paid her."

Amber sees Patti folding up the bank letter.

"Is that my mail?"

"This seems really bad, Amber."

"You're going through my mail?" Amber watches her in disbelief.

"Have you talked to the bank?" Patti shuffles the letters back into a pile and places them in the magazine basket.

"You aren't supposed to see this. You aren't even supposed to be here."

"But I have and I am. And I want to help you and Bree. Why can't you get that through that stubborn head of yours? You're

239

out of time, lady. And your power's going to be off by the end of the week."

"I'm making a payment tomorrow. Not that it's any of your business."

"What about the bank? That's a lot of money. I know you don't have it. But I would be happy to lend it to you if we could work out some sort of arrangement."

Amber doesn't like the sound of this. "Stop treating me like a charity case. I'm not one of your DAV widows."

"That's not at all what I'm suggesting. If you let me set you up with your own My-Way franchise, then, over time, you can pay me off with a percentage of the profits. It's business. Pure and simple."

Not this *again!* "Stop with the sales pitch already. I'm not selling that junk!" Amber blows right past the line.

"You're wearing *that junk* right now!"

Amber rubs the eye shadow off with her jacket sleeve.

"And that *junk,* as you call it, *was* and *is* my lifeline. And, had things worked out differently, it would have provided the kind of future I always dreamed about for Darren."

And there it is. Amber now knows without a doubt. Patti resents her.

"You always think you know what's best for everyone, don't you?"

"Amber, has it been explained to you what happens when the bank takes over your home? The cops show up at your door and kick you and all your stuff to the curb. Is that what you're waiting for?"

"That's not going to happen. I'm taking care of things."

"Sure you are." Patti stands up and brushes past Amber to get her coat from the hall closet.

"Don't treat me like I'm seventeen and trying to steal away your precious little boy." Amber knows it sounds catty, but the filter has long ago come off. She. Has. Had. It.

"So how was your date with Cody?" The snideness in Patti's tone sets her off even more.

"None of your business."

"I just find it interesting that while your life is spiraling downhill, you can find the time and energy to cultivate your love life. Seriously, Amber, get your priorities in line."

What did she just say? Oh no . . . not having it. "Patti. You need to leave. Now."

"I guess I always expected you to move on . . ."

"Get out." Amber stares her down until the latch on the front door clicks behind Patti. Amber rushes over and snaps the dead bolt into place. She storms into the living room and faces Darren's medals, anger raging inside. It takes everything in her being not to burst into tears or rip the living room to shreds. She's not sure which would make her feel better.

Amber hears Patti's ignition turn over. The engine disappears into the night. The image Patti has put in her head haunts her. Would Jim Wellington really kick them out of their home?

Her muscles begin to quake. In half a second she's a pile on the floor. Melting into the stale-smelling, rust-colored, garage-sale sofa that replaced the leather one, Amber gives in to her weakened state. Tomorrow she'll find a solution and prove Patti wrong. She is not getting thrown out of her and Darren's home.

CHAPTER THIRTY-FIVE: HOT WHEELS

Should I text her this morning? Yes. I should. Especially after that weird exit.

8:12 a.m. pops up on his cell phone screen.

"Cody? That you?" Joe's voice booms from the garage.

Crap. No time. Late already.

"The date went great, in case you're wondering," Cody shouts from the office as he clocks in for the day.

"Glad to hear it. Now, get in here."

"I was the perfect gentleman."

"I doubt that!"

"And she was the perfect lady." Cody grabs his work shoes from behind the counter and slips them on.

"I don't doubt that!"

"She even rejected my attempt at a kiss." He finds his work coat hanging on a coat-rack next to the bathroom door.

"What happened to just friends?"

"That was your rule. Not mine."

"Forget it. I don't want the gory details," Joe shouts back. Cody chuckles to himself. *Knew that would rile him up.*

"Are we doing the brake job on the LeSabre today?" Cody steps into the garage.

"*You* are," says Joe, looking up from a strange project atop Cody's race car.

"Whoa! That's some hobby you got going there!" Over in the far stall, Joe puts the finishing touches on an elaborate Hot Wheels racetrack cascading over the top of Cody's race car. "So this is what you do after hours, huh, Joe?"

"Thought you might enjoy some extra track time. Pick your car." Joe hands him a box of cars, and Cody digs in.

"I'm gonna have a hard time fitting into one of these." Cody grins as he snatches a 1967 Firebird.

"Take it easy! Some of those are classics."

Cody sets the car gingerly in his palm. "Which one did you pick?"

Joe holds up a yellow Camaro. "Never lost a race."

"You will today."

"Don't bet on it."

Cody sets his car on the left side of the double track in the slingshot device rigged to launch the cars up and over the steep race car terrain onto the roof. Joe places his car next to Cody's.

Cody pulls his slingshot back as far as it will go, then inches it back a few millimeters more. It's stretched to the limit. Out of the corner of his eyes, he sees Joe pull his back with less force. *That car's never gonna make it.*

"Ready?" says Joe.

Cody nods.

"Set."

Cody locks his eyes on the track.

"Go!"

He and Joe release their cars simultaneously.

The pair of Hot Wheels rockets over the hood of Cody's race car. Cody's Firebird is half a foot ahead of Joe's Camaro as it climbs up the windshield into the first turn. *Got you beat outta the stacks, old man! Take that!* He watches as Joe's pathetic car follows smoothly behind in a steady trajectory. *Is it even gonna make it up the incline of the windshield?*

He glances up ahead to his Firebird as it gains speed on the decline and heads into the first curve. But it's coming in too hot . . . It jumps the track, flies over the edge, through the air, and crashes to the cement floor.

Cody glances back in time to see Joe's yellow Camaro make the turn with expert precision. It sails through the loop and speeds back down the windshield, over the hood, and into Joe's waiting hand.

Cody ducks down to rescue his Firebird from the ground. He finds it in pieces. "Oh no! Don't look, Joe."

"Lemme guess — yet another busted-up race car."

"I'm sure I can find another one for you on eBay."

"You bet you will."

Cody cups the mangled car in his hand. *Wonder how much this is gonna set me back?*

"Now explain to me what just happened," says Joe.

Well, isn't it obvious? "I was trying to beat you, Joe."

"How? What was your strategy?"

"Punch it into the turn to —"

"And how'd that work out for you?"

"Going slow has never won me anything."

"Fast hasn't, either. It's costing you. Why can't you get that into your brain? While you still have one."

Cody looks down at the shattered '67 Firebird in his palm. "I'm really sorry about this."

"Apologies don't matter. Not to me. Not

to Gibbs. We're only two weeks away from your qualifying race. Do you know what that means?"

"I need more seat time."

Joe shakes his head.

"Okay. I'm listening."

Joe searches him. "Are you?"

"I am. Tell me what I need to do to win."

"What you need to work on is knowing when to go fast. And, more important, learning when to go slow."

"Precision."

"Yes. This track here is your first lesson in precision."

Joe takes another car out of the box. A junker. Cody follows him around to the start of the track.

"And how do we achieve precision? We set the perfect trajectory. Every. Single. Time."

Cody places his junker on the tracks. "I'm not sure I understand."

"I'll show you. Put your fingers on the sides of the car and pull back."

Cody extends the car back, putting strain on the launching device.

"Ease up."

Cody moves the car a smidgen.

"More."

He barely releases the tension.

"More. Come on. It's too tight. You'll spin out again."

"It's never gonna make it up the windshield."

"Trust me."

Okay, old man. Prove me wrong. I'm ready. This time Cody relaxes his grip.

"That's it. Now focus on the apex of that first curve. Keep you eyes on it. And when you're ready, release."

Cody's eyes drift up the track. He sets a mental trajectory.

One. Two. Three.

He opens his fingers and the junker flies up the windshield, across the hood, and into the first turn. It hits the apex dead-on, sailing through the loop. Cody rushes to the other side of the car as his Hot Wheels does the loop-de-loop and hits the straightaway, flying up the end ramp and into Cody's waiting grasp.

It worked! Holy cow! It was perfect.

"I did it. I did it!"

"Nicely done." Joe smiles.

"You're pleased?"

"Beginner's luck. Now practice. Again. And again. Until you hit it every time, no mistakes."

"Yes, sir." Cody darts back to the launching device. He places his junker on the track. Resets his trajectory. And releases. Another perfect run.

Again. Another precise execution.

"Three outta three."

"Good. 'Cause we're going to put this little lesson into practice later this afternoon. And your race car better not end up like that Firebird."

Joe tosses him a set of keys. "Here. Pull that LeSabre in here."

Cody steps outside, and a blast of warm spring air meets him.

Things are looking brighter here in Clarksville.

He rolls the Buick into the garage, thinking about the precision trajectories . . . and when he'll be able to break for lunch to give Amber a call.

CHAPTER THIRTY-SIX:
POUNDING THE PAVEMENT

From her van Amber watches Bree disappear behind the front doors of the school. She pulls away, heading toward the library first. She has six hours to implement phase one of her plan, and she needs every single minute to count. She starts with the librarian, who helps her polish up her thin résumé.

By noon Amber sets out into the business community of Clarksville to find a new job. The librarian suggests she focus on retail positions because her waitressing skills would easily transfer to customer service. The librarian coaches her to smile, look people in the eye, and not to seem too eager. Amber is unclear how to pull that off, because she is positive desperation is leaking from every single pore of her skin.

Regardless, she begins her trek at one end of Clarksville's main street and visits every shop with an OPEN sign. The florist requires floral-arranging experience. The fish market will keep her résumé on file. Three local gift stores are sympathetic but admit they hardly have enough business to keep their doors open, especially during the slower winter and spring seasons. There's a tanning salon looking for a part-time clerk for nights and weekends. Not a great fit for a single mom with a burns-never-tans skin type. Heading up the other side of the street, she finds that the shoe store just made a new hire and isn't looking. The movie theater is hiring but pays even less than Rosie's, and can only guarantee twenty hours a week. She stops in at Harry's and they like her résumé, but the owner is concerned that she's overqualified and would get bored with the usually slow weekday pace. And she wouldn't make nearly enough in tips. Dead end. Dead end. Dead end.

With an hour to go before Bree is out of school, Amber halts her downtown search. Tomorrow she'll look into the businesses on the outskirts of town — mostly big-box stores, a country club, three gas stations, and a few chain hotels.

Exhausted and feeling more dejected than ever, Amber ends her trek at the far end of the main street, where Joe's garage lies. A little company might be just what she needs right now.

As she nears the shop, she is excited to see Cody's Firebird in the parking lot.

She finds the two of them in the garage working underneath a race car. Pieces of the car in all shapes and sizes are scattered around the vehicle in every direction. Amber steps carefully around the parts as she approaches.

"Hey, guys?" Two heads creep out from under the chassis and look over in tandem.

"Amber. Hey, I was gonna call you later," says Cody. She likes the charge in his voice when he sees her.

"I should know better than to ask, but is she gonna make it?"

"She'll be under the knife a little longer, but the prognosis is good," says Joe.

"What brings you by?" asks Cody, rolling himself out from under the engine, greased up from wrist to neck.

"Just in the neighborhood."

"Glad you stopped by. I was wondering if everything was okay after I dropped you off."

"Well . . . let's just say . . . a meddling mother-in-law is not a great way to end an evening."

"Yikes. Hope no real harm was done."

"No, it's okay," says Amber. She doesn't

miss Cody shooting Joe a look to beat it.

"Well, we could use a break, couldn't we, Cody?" Joe gets up from off the garage floor. "I'll put some coffee on. We may even have a doughnut or two left from this morning."

"That sounds great."

Joe heads into the office.

"Patti Hill is your mother-in-law, right?"

"Yeah."

"She came in here once to pick up Bree. Seems like a nice lady."

"She has a lot of friends in town."

Cody pours degreaser over his hands and towels them clean. "You look a little tired," he says, tossing the towel into the trash bin. "You sure you're okay?"

"Yeah. We have a long history. You know. Family. I'm sure it'll sort itself out." She tries to keep it generic, but she's not sure she's convinced him, from the way his eyes lock on hers.

"Well, I'm here for you if you want to unload it."

"Thank you. And thanks again for Harry's."

"My pleasure. I had F-U-N, too. Get it?"

"Yeah, I get it. Ha-ha."

Amber giggles. Flutters.

■ ■ ■ ■

In a few minutes the three of them sit around Joe's desk in the main lobby as Joe passes out mismatched mugs of steaming black coffee.

"Smells amazing. I so need this," says Amber. "And it's nice to be the one served rather than serving."

"How are things at Rosie's?" asks Joe.

"Same as ever. Busy. Greasy."

Joe passes her a plate with a selection of packaged cookies and snacks from the vending machine.

"Doughnuts were gone. So this is the best I can do."

"I'm actually looking for work. Don't tell Rosie. I just want something with a future." Amber selects a package of vanilla crèmes. "Split it with you?" she asks Cody.

"Ah, I'm more of an Oreo man, myself," he says taking his selection. "How's the job market around here?"

"Dismal."

"I'll put the word out," says Joe, tearing into some peanut butter sandwich crackers. "Hey, you wouldn't consider part-time mechanic, would you?"

Amber laughs. "So I have to know. Is he

any good?"

"We'll see after the qualifying race," says Joe.

"What's that?"

"His come-back or go-home race," jokes Joe.

"So there's a lot riding on this, then?"

"Everything. Right, Cody?"

Amber can sense that underneath Joe's humor is a great degree of seriousness.

"Why don't you come see for yourself?" Cody tells her.

"Yeah, come on down to the racetrack. You can be the judge of his talent," says Joe.

"Oh, I wouldn't know what I'm looking at."

"There's not much to it."

"Maybe that's why you're crashing," jabs Joe. "If you can make it, I'd love to have you and Bree as our guests. You can sit by me. Best seats in the house."

"Thanks, Joe. I'll think about it and check my schedule." Amber sips on her coffee, the warm and familiar flavor bringing comfort after her difficult day.

"So . . . you don't know anything about racing stock cars? At all?" asks Cody.

"I've watched a few races on TV. Looks dangerous."

"Have you ever driven a race car before?"

"Nope." She licks the center cream out of her cookie.

"You ever want to?"

"Not really." Amber shakes her head and sees Cody's expression turn thoughtful. Her lips part in a small grin. "Why? What?"

Chapter Thirty-Seven: Ease Up on the Clutch

Cody secures Amber in the Firebird's driver's seat and secures her helmet. He then plunges into the passenger seat and straps in.

"There's a headset and mouthpiece attached to this. Joe'll be on the radio giving you the overall picture, and I'll be guiding you from the passenger's seat."

"Why are there three pedals down there?" Amber asks.

"Wait. You don't know how to drive a clutch?" He tries to form his next words. *This could be a very long afternoon.*

"Just joking," Amber cracks. "Yes. I know how to drive a stick shift."

"Whew. Okay." *See that, Joe. Her sense of humor is intact. She just needs someone to bring it out of her.*

"So just how fast does this thing go?"

Cody sees she's teasing again.

"Fast. But for now, we're going to ease on

out to the track. Ready?"

"Ready."

Cody keeps a keen eye on her as she pulls out in first gear and then grips the wheel with her hands at nine and three. She pulls the car onto the frontstretch at a snail's pace.

"That's it. You got it. We can go a little faster. If you want."

"You've probably never seen the track at this speed before, huh?"

Cody grins. "You're probably right."

"Did you even know your car could go this slow?" She laughs.

He loves the sound of her enjoying. Living.

"Good one, Amber. Don't let him give you any flack." Cody hears Joe's voice through the headset.

"You're both so hilarious. Okay, now try second," says Cody.

"At least someone respects that heap of metal," Joe calls out.

Amber shifts gears, grinding the gear just before she engages. She slacks off the clutch.

"Was that bad?"

Cody catches her wincing apologetically. "Like they say, 'Grind it till you find it,' " he teases. "Just give it a little more gas when you let up."

Amber tries again and they jerk forward, and the engine roars to life.

"Like that?"

"Just like that." She has a sense for the power.

"Smooth transition, Amber," says Joe. "Nice work. Maybe you can teach Cody a thing or two while you're out there."

Cody smirks at Joe as they pass him on the infield. He waves, smirking back.

"Okay, okay. I've got this," says Amber with a quick glance at Joe. The car bobbles toward the inside wall.

"Hey, eyes on the track."

"I tell him that all the time, Amber," says Joe.

"Doing good?" asks Cody.

"Yup." Amber nods, eyes never leaving the track.

"Okay, feel like you can shift up?"

"Yup. I can do it." She slips the clutch into third gear. "Wow, much smoother."

"Wait'll you hit fourth." Cody glances ahead as the pavement starts to move more quickly under them. "Okay, so just take it steady and get a feel for the track. We'll go around once, and then on the second lap we'll try to gain some speed."

Amber nods. "Bet this is how you impress all the ladies."

"You're actually the first one I've ever let drive my car."

"Uh-huh. And that's what you tell each of us."

Cody laughs. "Not true. Not true."

Cody sees they're exiting turn four.

"Okay, go ahead and give it a little more gas on the frontstretch here."

Amber accelerates.

"Second lap. Looking good," Joe's voice announces.

"You're doing great. Shift it into fourth, and we'll really open her up."

"You got it." Amber steps on the clutch. Cody winces as she grinds the gear. Amber backs off. "It's been a while."

"It's okay. Just hold the clutch down a little longer before you shift."

Amber depresses the clutch pedal again. Cody can feel the shifter sliding into gear. "That's it. Now ease up on the clutch and give it the pedal again."

Amber presses the gas, and they head down the straightaway, gaining speed. But as they come into turn three, Amber gives it some power, and the rear end of the car fishtails out to the side.

"Oh no. What'd I do?" Amber jerks the wheel and overcompensates. The car starts to spin out of control as they exit turn four.

She's white-knuckling the wheel. Rookie mistake.

"Ease off the wheel." The car makes a wide doughnut. Amber goes wide-eyed. "Let up on the gas!"

"Ease off the wheel, Amber!" Joe instructs from the headset.

"Foot off the gas! No gas! No gas!"

"Grab the wheel, Cody!" Joe shouts at Cody.

Amber's hands fly up. Cody reaches for the wheel. "Brake very, very gently."

But Amber instinctively slams on the brakes. They start to spin toward the inside.

Cody steers them just shy of the grassy infield, and they come to a halt.

Cody turns to look at Amber. Her face is ghost-white, and her wide-eyed look is locked over the hood.

Cody unlatches her chinstrap. "Breathe. Breathe."

They can hear Joe's anxious voice chirping through the microphone. "Are you kids okay? *Hello?* Amber? Cody?"

Cody ignores him for the moment. *I've scared her right out of my life. I know it.*

"Amber. Are you okay?"

Amber's eyes soften as they meet Cody's concerned look. She breaks into a huge smile.

"That. Was. Awesome!"

"Are you kidding?"

"No."

Cody bursts out laughing.

Joe's panicked voice calls out again. "Hey! You kids okay?"

"We're fine, Joe," Amber says.

"Well, okay. Looks like you've got the same problem Cody has on that third turn."

Cody laughs. "You ready to head back to the pits?"

"Can we go again?" she says.

"You sure?"

"I'm positive."

"Yeah, let's do it!"

Amber readjusts her chinstrap and starts the engine. She moves the gearshift into first when her phone rings from inside her jacket pocket.

"Sorry, I gotta take this."

"No problem."

Cody glances at her as she puts the car into neutral and fishes the phone from her pocket. *This is a good day for Amber. She needs this.*

"Hello?"

Cody watches as her carefree smile vanishes.

"She . . . what?"

Chapter Thirty-Eight: Bree and the Bully

"Fighting? Really, Bree?" Amber is livid as the minivan barrels down the tree-lined street from the school. Amber tries with difficulty to imagine the report she was given by the playground aide: Bree pinning Cole to the ground and giving him a fist-pounding to the chest.

After getting statements from both parties, the principal had thankfully shown Bree mercy because of Cole's previous rap sheet. This was Bree's first incident ever. There would be no suspension. However, there would be a formal apology and a restraining order on both kids. Bree and Cole were not allowed to be near each other in class or on the playground.

"Since when do you fight?"

"Cole started it!"

"Explain this to me. Every detail."

"David and I were on the swings, and Cole came over. He started making fun of

David's stutter."

"Okay. What exactly did he say?"

"He said, 'How's your little b-b-baby g-go-k-k-k-kart at S-s-s-Sunday Sch-ch-chool?"

"And what did David say?"

"He didn't say anything. He just took it. So I said, 'Stop it. You're not funny. You're just jealous.' And then David said, 'It's o-o-okay, B-B-Bree. Just ignore him.' "

"Has David been bothered by Cole before?"

"Yeah. Lots. So I told David that it's not okay. And then Cole started mocking me."

"And what did you do then?" Amber asks.

"He started getting in our faces. And I told him to leave us alone."

"And he didn't?"

"No. He said, 'Ma-ma-ma-make me.' He made me so mad, Mom!"

"And that's when you tackled him?"

Bree turns and looks out the car window. "What else was I supposed to do?"

"Turn the other cheek. Walk away." Amber feels confident in her answer. It's what they learned in church.

"It doesn't do any good to ignore him. He just keeps doing it. Cole bullies everyone," Bree says. "He needed to be taught a lesson. Dad used to say some things are worth fighting for."

"Aren't you supposed to go find a teacher who can help you? Isn't that what they teach you in school?" Amber is stumped. On some level, she knows Bree's right. Darren would have been proud that Bree was protecting a friend, but instigating the physical fight was not acceptable.

"You shouldn't use force or violence on someone unless they've attacked you first and you're defending yourself," Amber says, glancing in her rearview mirror and catching Bree making a face at the back of her mother's head. "Excuse me? What was that?"

"Nothing."

"Not nothing. You don't make faces at me, young lady."

"I wasn't."

"I saw you. So don't you lie, either. What's gotten into you, Breeanne Hill?" Amber glances back at Bree. She's staring out the window with an indignant look that tells Amber this isn't over yet.

"I miss Dad. He wouldn't yell at me."

"I'm not yelling!" Amber yells at her. She immediately regrets it.

They ride together in silence for a few blocks. Amber knows she needs to discipline Bree beyond the written apology, but what kind of punishment would be fitting? Sending her to her room? She'll just read a book and play with her toys. Grounding her from seeing David? That hardly seems fair, since David was the victim here. Making her do extra chores? Having her write an essay about fighting and bullying? Until now, Bree never warranted stiff discipline, and Amber is totally unprepared to dish it out. What would Darren do?

"Where are we going?" Bree interrupts Amber's thoughts.

"To Rosie's."

"For dumplings?"

"No, I have to work."

"Aren't you bringing me home first?"

"I don't have a sitter. You'll have to hang out for a while."

"Can I stay at Grandma's while you work?"

"No."

"Why not?"

"Because I said no." Amber was not about to explain that the line of trust between her and Grandma had been officially crossed. "And when we get to the diner, you are going to sit quietly in your booth and do your homework. Got it?"

Amber checks her daughter's response in the rearview mirror and detects the slight head tilt of attitude.

"I didn't hear you," Amber says.

"I got it."

An hour into the dinner shift, Amber ends up slammed with customers. She can barely keep up and her legs ache. Two more hours of this! She hears the front door *ding*. Another four customers enter. Another *ding!* A couple with a small child shuffle in. *Ding!* Amber can't take the time to inventory as she spies a couple leaving one of her two-tops and rushes over to clear it. After wiping it down, she quickly puts down fresh silverware settings. When she turns to grab two more placemats, Mike Nelson slides into the spot.

"Welcome. How are you tonight?" Amber doesn't wait for his answer as she dives behind the counter for a glass of water.

Out of the corner of her eye, Amber sees Bree's pencil hit the table again and again as she grows restless over a homework sheet. The *tap, tap, tap* intensifies from Bree's corner booth. Amber notices several customers glance over, clearly annoyed by the sound. Rosie notices, too, as she flies by with a tray of hot food and a disapproving look.

Amber sets a water glass and a menu in

front of Mike. "I'll be right back to take your order." She doesn't even give him a chance to respond before she's hovering over her increasingly agitated daughter, who sucks down the last of her chocolate milk.

"What are you doing? Stop making that noise."

"Mom. Can you help me with this? I can't get it."

"Honey, I can't help you right now. Do the ones you can do, and we'll work on the rest at home." It's late, near Bree's bedtime. But Amber still has an hour on the clock.

"Can I get another chocolate milk?"

Rosie swings past, hearing the request. "The chocolate milk's not free. And table eight is ready to order."

"You can drink water," Amber tells her daughter as she tries to ignore Rosie's chiding. She moves to the table next to Bree and sweeps up a three-dollar tip. Amber vents to herself. *Seriously? That was a thirty-five-dollar meal. This isn't even ten percent!* Amber angrily stacks dirty plates and cups in her arms.

"I'm hungry," Bree whines.

"When I get a break, I'll bring you some chicken fingers." Amber's voice tenses as she swings around to give Bree a warning look, and an empty coffee cup wobbles on the top of the stack of dishes. Her eyes go wide as she watches it sail off the stack, nose-diving for the floor.

In the nick of time, a hand reaches out and catches it just before it lands. Amber can't believe it.

"Oh my gosh. Thank you!"

"You're welcome." The hand presents Amber with the mug. Amber's gaze moves to Mike Nelson's calm face smiling back at her.

"Here," he says, extending his hand.

"Thank you. Get you something to drink? Soda? Iced tea? Lemonade?"

"Actually, I've been wanting to talk to you about something." Amber's expression tightens. He wants to talk about Darren.

"I just made a fresh pot of coffee. Bring you some?"

"Ah, sure. That sounds good. But, if you have a minute later, I . . ."

"Hey, you go to our church, right?" Bree appears at her mother's side and dives right into the conversation.

"Clarksville Community."

"Yup. That's my church, too."

She excitedly points to something on Nelson's jacket. "Hey! That's my dad's patch. Are you a Screaming Eagle?"

"Yes, I am. My name is Mike Nelson." He

offers her his hand, and she shakes it.

"I'm Bree Hill. Pleased to meet you." Amber watches the pleasant interaction unfold, trapped between them.

"I actually knew your dad," Nelson offers.

"You did? How?" Bree's eyes go wide.

"Well, we were in the same unit together." Amber continues to grow uncomfortable and afraid of what might come out of Nelson's mouth. Especially around Bree.

"Bree, I don't want you to bother this young man. Go finish your homework, please."

"Oh, I don't mind. I heard a lot of stories about this little one." Nelson smiles at Amber, letting her know there's no need to worry. But she does.

"Do you have any stories about my dad?" Bree asks eagerly.

"A few. A few." Nelson laughs.

"What's so funny?" Bree asks.

"I was just thinking about something your dad did in the field with a fire extinguisher."

"What did he do?"

Amber tenses. "Bree. Let Mr. Nelson eat his dinner in peace."

"I don't mind. In fact, she's welcome to sit with me. I could use the company."

Bree's eyes plead with Amber. "That's kind. But she needs to finish her math. Bree, take your seat. Now."

Rosie steams toward her with overflowing milk shakes in each hand. "There're tables waiting, Amber."

Nelson nods respectfully. "Well, it was nice to meet you, Bree. See you in church."

"Yeah. See you." Bree pouts back to her booth.

"I'm sorry if Bree . . . She can be a lot to handle," says Amber.

"I really don't mind. She seems sweet."

"Have you decided on what you'd like to eat?" Amber takes out her notepad.

"Cheeseburger. No mustard. And your waffle fries, please. Extra crispy."

Amber jots it down.

"Listen, I don't mean to stalk you or pry into your business or anything. It's just I've been looking for the right time to let you know a few things that . . . you know . . . might make a difference."

"I'm not . . . I can't right now. Okay?"

Nelson nods. "Maybe later. I'd be happy to come over sometime."

"I don't think it's a good idea right now."

"Sure. I understand."

"Your order should be right up." Amber beelines to the kitchen and hands in her slip to the cook. She downs a glass of water, taking a few minutes to collect herself until she hears Rosie's piercing voice from the service station nearby.

"Amber? Amber!" Amber ducks out. "Is she eating?" Rosie looks over at Bree.

"Rosie, come on. I'm completely out of options."

"We're starting to get a line up out the door. I need that table for paying customers."

"What am I supposed to do with her?"

"Not my problem. But when I look over there next, I'd better see a four-top of diners." Rosie saunters off with an armful of place settings.

Amber glances around the café, trying to formulate a plan. There are only two places she can put Bree in the tiny restaurant. The kitchen or bathroom? Nope. She's gonna have to sit in the minivan outside. And she's not gonna like it. At that moment she sees Cody sitting down on a stool at the counter. He motions for Bree to join. She gathers her things and hops onto the stool next to him. Amber bustles over.

"I heard you're looking for paying customers," Cody says with a broad smile that reassures her that everything is going to be all right. For the moment, anyhow.

"I am."

"Great. Then, we'll take two cheeseburgers, two fries, and two shakes." He looks at Bree. "What flavor?"

"Chocolate!"

"Two chocolate shakes. With extra whipped cream."

"And three cherries, please."

"One cherry," says Amber. "No whipped cream. You've had enough sugar for the day."

Cody shrugs at Bree. "Gotta listen to Mom."

Amber floods with relief, as Bree transforms into a well-mannered young lady with Cody at her side.

"Glad you showed up when you did," Amber says to Cody, feeling Rosie's inquisitive stare from across the room. "Thank you."

"Thought I'd better check on you after that quick exit from the track."

"Oh yeah. That." She looks at Bree. "It's a long story. She can tell you all about it."

"I've got all the time in the world," says Cody, settling in.

"I got in a fight at school." Bree is almost boastful about it. Clearly nothing Amber said to her in the car has sunk in.

"What? Oh, wow. This sounds like a good one."

"I'll get those orders going," says Amber,

heading back to the kitchen.

"So, did you start it?" She hears Cody ask as she leaves.

"No," Bree says simply.

"Okay. Well, did you win?"

Cody gives her a high five. He better not be encouraging this. Maybe he can talk some sense into her.

Amber heads to the kitchen as Bree starts her story. "See, this is what happened. David and I were on the swings, and this kid, Cole, comes outta nowhere and . . ."

Their voices get lost in the background of diner noise, and Amber finds herself both charmed and charred about Cody's carefree approach. She's not sure which side of the fence she should land on. Or which is going to be better for Bree in the long run. Parenting has definitely become more complicated without Darren to bounce things off of.

As she slips the ticket onto the order rack and spins it around to the kitchen side, she decides it's not worth overthinking. Bree's a good kid who's been through a rough ride. She'll keep an extra eye on her. Give her a little more attention. If she can.

CHAPTER THIRTY-NINE: NOT A CHARITY CASE

"What. Is. *That?*" Amber exclaims in disbelief. An emerald-cut diamond of at least one full karat gleams up at her from Bridgette's hand. Amber looks at her best friend. Shrieks! And throws her arms around Bridgette's neck. "Get in here!" She yanks Bridgette through the front door. "You need to tell me everything! When? Where? *How?*"

Amber draws Bridgette to the living room. "Last night. The old lighthouse restaurant on the pier. Dinner. Roses. Sunset. Romance. The perfect cliché."

"I love clichés. And I'm so happy for you."

They plop down on the couch. Amber hugs a pillow to her chest. "What about the wedding? Date set?"

"Next fall. November probably. At church, of course."

"Colors?"

"Burnt orange, gold, and mossy green. Very fallish."

"Beautiful. Your parents?"

"Love him. On board a hundred percent."

"His parents?"

"His mom could be my sister. We're really close."

"You lucked out, girl." Amber can't imagine Patti being anything close to a sister.

"And I want to ask you something. Will you stand up for me?"

"*What?* Yes! Of course!"

"Good. I was worried. I didn't know if you'd be —"

"Bridge, yes. I'll be there for you."

"I'm so glad. Now, enough about this . . . How was your date?"

"It feels like maybe it's all going too fast," says Amber.

"That must have been some strong coffee," Bridgette jokes.

"Coffee *and* a spin around the racetrack the next day," Amber reminds Bridgette with a smile.

"Do you like him?"

"He's nice. He has a good sense of humor. He's good with Bree."

"But?"

"He's a little intense at times. And I think he definitely has a few issues of his own he's working on while he's here."

"A wise friend once told me to get my

own life together before finding that special someone to share it with." Bridgette winks at her friend.

"Oh, Bridge. Please. I'm so far from wanting to get remarried."

"I know. I know. That's what I'm saying. No pressure. One day at a time."

Amber nuzzles up to her friend. "I'm happy for you."

"Now, listen, I don't mean to bring up bad stuff, but there's a rumor going around that you're close to losing your home. Is that true, Amber?"

Amber can't hide from it any longer. In fact, part of her is glad Bridgette said something.

"Probably. But I'm still working on it," she says with a touch of relief that her best friend knows.

"Why didn't you tell me?"

"It's embarrassing, Bridge."

"What do you need?"

"I've fallen really, really far behind."

"Okay. How much are we talking?"

"A lot. I actually . . . I don't know how I'm going to catch up," Amber confesses in a wave of release.

"Okay. Well, it's not impossible. Karena and Pastor Williams can get the whole church behind you. We'll take up a special offering next Sunday, and before you know it —"

"Whoa. What? Oh, no. I'm not some charity case."

"We do it all the time when people are a little down and out. Everyone chips in."

"No. Don't you dare." Amber glances at Bridgette with a look that says she's serious.

"I don't get you, Amber Hill. Everyone at church loves you. And even though you haven't been there in a long time, they're still your friends. And if they knew you were in this much trouble, they'd reach out in a second."

"They don't owe me anything." Amber's stubborn pride flares up as Bridgette struggles to get through. "I got into this mess by myself, and I have to figure a way out of it."

Bridgette backs down and softens her approach. "The church can help in other ways, you know — once you're connected to the only source that can give you what you really need."

"Jesus is going to give me a couple thousand dollars?" She doesn't mean to sound snide.

"Your debt is just a symptom. You wanna get your house in order? You gotta repair that relationship with God first."

Amber sighs. Not this again.

"All I'm saying is, don't stay too long on that island of yours. Pretty soon the life rafts will stop coming up to shore."

For all of Bridgette's patience and encouragement, she is a die-hard realist, and, no lie, her advice stings sometimes. Amber brushes it off. Warning heeded. She diverts the conversation back to wedding plans.

After Bridgette leaves, Amber looks down at her phone to check the time. Bree will be done with school soon. She also discovers Jim Wellington has left a voice mail. She presses play and taps the speaker button.

"Mrs. Hill, this is Jim. I'm afraid I have some bad news. Your loan was sold to a third party this morning. They are requiring full payment immediately. We're beyond working out a payment plan. I'm sorry, but it's really out of my court now. Amber, your house is going to be seized. It's urgent that we speak. Please give me a call."

"No, no, no. Come on."

Amber stabs at the speakerphone button and fumbles the phone into her pocket, her engagement ring and wedding band catching as she twists her hand back out. A round-cut diamond no bigger than a quarter karat turns up at her.

And she discovers her way out.

CHAPTER FORTY:
LOVED AND FLAWLESS

"Who dumped who?" says Wayne Kent, proprietor of Kent's Pawn & Collectibles as he sits on his stool behind a glass counter eating an enormous, mayonnaise-oozing sandwich. Chunks of lettuce and turkey fall from his beard to his belly and land on the glass countertop. Amber is disgusted but doesn't let it deter her from her mission.

She looks down at the diamond ring she has reluctantly slid off her finger and pushes it toward Mr. Kent. The neon sign in the window illuminates the counter and casts a soft, underlit red glow, making her seem like the villainess in some seedy noir flick. The irony of the moment hits her, and she uses every bit of strength in her soul to fight back the tears.

"Well, the way I see it," Mr. Kent continues, "the guy who gave this to you cared enough about you to pick the best diamond that he could afford. He didn't get you a lower-quality but larger stone just to impress you. You were truly loved when he gave this to you."

"Yes, I was. So what is it worth?"

Mr. Kent grabs his jeweler's loupe and lifts it to his eye to examine the stone.

"It's only about a quarter of a carat, but flawless."

"What does that mean in dollars?" Amber just wants the deal to be over.

"I'd say about four-fifty, five hundred."

"That's it? I need more," she blurts out. Five hundred would barely scratch what she owes on her mortgage . . . or that new lender . . . or Perfect Payday. But she's here. She's made her decision. And she doesn't know what else to do. Five hundred had to mean something to one of her creditors. If anything, maybe it could buy her time. Buy. Time. Her days since Darren left have been minimized to this vicious cycle of using time to buy time. It didn't make sense. What a terrible way to live. And it was failing her. Surely, this isn't what God — or Darren — had in mind for her life.

"That's the best I can do." He chomps down on his sandwich and a slice of tomato squirts out, dripping down his hand and into his shirtsleeve. "So what'll it be?"

"I have to." Amber's voice squeaks as a

lump in her throat forms.

Mr. Kent nods. "He ain't going to come in here looking for this ring, is he? I don't get involved in messy breakups."

Amber lifts her gaze to his bloodshot, saggy-lidded eyes. "He was killed in Afghanistan, and I need the money to keep a roof over his daughter's head. So I don't think there's much chance of him coming in looking for the ring."

"Okay, then." Wayne grabs a form from behind the counter and slides it across to Amber. "Sign this. If you don't come back for it in two weeks, it's ours to sell."

She looks down at her left hand, where her ring used to be. It's his to sell. She won't be back. That's for sure. She squints back the tears as she quickly scribbles her signature on the paper and heads for the door.

"Miss?"

Amber doesn't turn around. She can't face him. She just wants out of this hole.

"Miss? Hey, wait. Your want your money, don't ya?" Mr. Kent trails her to the door. How could she be so careless? He hands her a thin envelope. She quickly checks inside. Her marriage reduced to a few grubby hundreds.

As the lump fills her throat, she notices that he's slipped her an extra hundred.

Without a glance, Amber steals out the door, fleeing the barred windows and neon sign.

CHAPTER FORTY-ONE: THE REBOUND GUY

Patti is the first one present for Sunday brunch. She sucks down a cup of coffee before Bethany and Joanne arrive. Twenty minutes later, Gayle, Karen, and Kim make late entrances. There was a line at the valet. They all sense right away that something's eating at her. But Patti doesn't let on as she makes pleasantries over a second cup of coffee. How are the kids? The grandkids? Did this one perform well at his piano recital? Did that one recover from the flu? Are you going to Cabo this year?

Finally, Joanne turns to Patti. "You look like you're about ready to burst. What's going on?"

Patti releases. "Cody Jackson. That's what. He's going after Amber."

The women absorb the news with blank stares and polite sips of coffee. Patti waits for their responses. "Oh, come on. Tell me what you've heard about him," she insists.

"I've never met the guy. What I know I've heard from you," starts Kim diplomatically.

"Which is . . . ?" prods Karen, with a look to Kim.

"That . . . he's coming in a bit hot," says Kim. "And he's a bit of a showboater."

"Doesn't sound like Amber's type," adds Joanne.

"He's no Darren," Patti says defensively.

"Well, just how much time have they spent together?" asks Karen, trying to get all the facts.

"I know they've been out on at least a couple of dates." Patti isn't exactly sure about this fact, but she can only suspect the worst, since Amber is hiding the relationship from her.

"I met him once at Joe's when I dropped off my Mercedes," says Gayle, a trial lawyer. "He was very charming. A head turner."

"You little cougar," teases Joanne. Which doesn't please Patti.

"Hey, a single lady can enjoy the local scenery once in a while," returns Gayle, and the women all laugh. "Let the evidence show that Mr. Jackson was polite and friendly. I rest my case."

"Well, I won't argue with the attorney," starts Bethany. "But I will add that I've gotten to know him a bit at church — Joe has him going to Clarksville Community — and while his heart seems to be in the right place, he does seem a bit restless. I think he's basically a flash in the pan. And Amber would be wise not to get in too deep."

"If he's training with Joe, then we all know what that means," says Kim, who speaks from experience. "As soon as he gets back on that race circuit, he's outta here. And where does that leave Amber? Heartbreak City."

Patti nods. Exactly what she thinks.

"Patti, you can't expect Amber to become a nun," Karen adds gently.

"No, of course not. I don't expect that at all," says Patti. "I knew she would move on eventually. I just don't think now's the right time. The girl has some real problems to deal with, and adding a man into the mix, especially a hothead like Cody, will not benefit her situation one iota. Or Bree's."

"Have you talked to her about it?" asks Karen, always the peacemaker.

"It's like talking to a brick wall," answers Patti. "She isn't interested in a thing I try to do to help her."

"How serious do you think she is about Cody?" says Bethany.

Just then the waiter appears with their meals. Patti pauses until he's left the table.

"I know this about Cody. He's got Bree in his favor. They're building a go-kart together at Joe's. From what I see, she adores him." As she says it, Patti realizes how much the thought of this really riles her up.

"Sounds like maybe it's Bree you're most concerned about," suggests Kim, who has a way of cutting to the heart of matters.

Patti punctures her omelet with her fork, and the table goes silent for a moment while the ladies enjoy their first bites. Patti takes a sip of grapefruit juice to swallow down the wedge of irritation gripping her throat. "I don't want Bree getting attached to some guy who's only going to dump Amber the moment NASCAR calls him up. I don't think she deserves that kind of loss again. And I don't think Cody sees that at all."

"The rebound guy," says Gayle. "That's what this Cody is."

"We've all been there," says Joanne, with a knowing wink around the table.

"I haven't," says Bethany, who's been married to her high school sweetheart since she was nineteen.

"Be grateful!" adds Gayle.

"I think I need to do something before he gets his claws too deep in those girls," Patti says as she delicately pops a strawberry into her mouth.

"You've just got to let it run its course," says Karen. "Or Amber will resent you even more than she already does." A few of the ladies nod.

"Well . . . you could try cozying up to him," says Gayle.

"Are you crazy?" says Bethany.

"No. Listen. Get close to the enemy. Find out his game plan. Then, beat him at his own game." If anyone knew how to win a battle, it was Gayle.

"It's not a bad strategy, but I don't think it's me," says Patti. "I don't have the patience or the time for his kind."

"What about talking to Joe?" suggests Karen. "He loves those girls like they're his own daughters. Maybe he can offer some insight."

Patti admits it's not a bad idea.

"And there's one more thing. Amber's losing the house," Patti announces, and the ladies all stop eating and look up at her.

"Oh, Patti. That's awful. I'm so sorry," says Joanne.

"Is there anything we can do?" asks Bethany.

"I doubt it. She didn't exactly offer the information to me. I found out when I saw something in her mail," admits Patti.

"You were snooping?" says Karen.

"Not exactly." Patti can feel the tsk-tsks.

"And you don't understand why she's having a hard time trusting you?" says Bethany with a wink.

Patti has always expected and depended on this kind of honesty from the group. "What if I offer to help her catch up on her mortgage and other bills?"

"How much are we talking?" asks Kim.

"Thousands," says Patti.

"You could give her a bailout. But I'm not sure that helps her long-term," says Gayle.

"She'll just feel indebted to you," says Bethany. "I don't think that's the kind of relationship you're going for."

"She's gonna need a lot of support," says Karen. "And if you don't want Cody being the one to give it to her, you've got to find a way to make peace."

"You just have to keep trying," says Kim.

"That's what Paula told me. But honestly . . . how?" She poses the question to the group.

"Babysit?" says Bethany.

"Done."

"Invite her for dinner?" asks Kim.

"She claims she's always working. Or too tired."

"Coffee date?"

Patti shrugs. They run out of suggestions.

"That's what I thought," says Patti. "It's impossible."

"Well, it is with that attitude," says Gayle, and she changes the subject to an upcoming fund-raising gala she is coordinating.

Chapter Forty-Two:
The Last Fight

On Monday morning, Kendra Drake is about to sit down with her morning coffee and a spreadsheet when Amber bolts past her on her way to barge through Jim Wellington's closed door.

"Mrs. Hill . . . Mrs. Hill . . . May I help you?" Kendra leaps up, spilling her coffee all over the paperwork on her desk.

Amber flashes Kendra a look of hurt and fury as her hand reaches for Jim's doorknob. "I need to speak to Mr. Wellington."

"Mrs. Hill. Please. You can't go in there. He's with someone."

Amber steps aside, and Kendra rises from her desk. "I can try to help you."

Amber pulls the dingy envelope from Kent's Pawn Shop & Collectibles out of her purse and sets it on Kendra's desk.

"He told me I'm losing my house, and I can't. Not now." Amber chokes back tears.

"What would you like me to do?" Kendra's voice is unaffected, and Amber knows that it's not her fault. But it grates on her.

"I know it's not the full amount, but it's everything I've got."

Kendra opens the envelope and quickly does the math. "I think you'll need to speak to Mr. Wellington about this." She hands it back to Amber.

"What has he told you?"

How publicly mortifying will this become? Kendra must know how to read minds, because she says, "It's my job to keep all of our clients' business in strict confidentiality."

At that, the door to Jim's office opens, and he escorts a client to the door. Amber catches his eye, and he motions for her to wait. She backs down. After Jim sends his client off, he immediately turns his attention to her.

"Amber. You got my call?"

"I did." She sees Jim's face flood with compassion but has a hard time meeting his gaze. She hands the envelope to him. "Pay the new lender. Stop the foreclosure. Please."

"Why don't you come into my office? Let's talk." Mr. Wellington extends his arm to usher her into the frosted-glass-walled room. Amber can't go. She can't withstand another dead-end conversation. He's just going to tell her that there's no hope. She looks down at her naked ring finger. She can't face that raw rejection right now. Amber backs toward the door. She knows she's losing this battle. Better get out of the fight before it turns too bloody.

"Please. Just take it and do what you can," she pleads in a quiet voice.

"Mrs. Hill. There are a few legalities I need to discuss with you in light of your situation."

Amber shakes her head. "I've fought so hard."

"It's not the end of the world. Please. Let me help you transition through this . . ."

"I have to go . . ." Amber's words trail off as she reels for the door. Outside, the world is nothing but a blur of sounds and colors. She stumbles along, following the sidewalk blindly right past her van . . . downtown . . . and then cutting into the neighborhood until she finds that she has walked all eleven blocks home.

CHAPTER FORTY-THREE: TELLING BREE

Amber's gaze is drawn to Matt, bathed in lamplight in front of Bree's window. The shades are drawn on the evening, and quiet has settled over the house. Amber marvels at the inch of Matt's stem poking through the dry topsoil. A tiny leaf is on the verge of unfurling. Look at that. She got it to sprout. Getting it to mature will be a whole different story. If Matt is to survive, he will need year-round warmth that he's never going to see in Clarksville. And he will need a yard . . . a yard that she'll soon be losing.

From the bathroom, Amber can hear Bree finishing up with her teeth. She pulls herself away from the plant and selects three books for bedtime. She turns back the covers on Bree's bed as she hears the bathroom door creak open. Bree coasts into her bedroom, balancing a plastic cup filled with water for Matt.

"Did you see Matt?" Bree asks her mom,

pride on her face as she gives him a drink.

"I did. Nice job, honey."

"When he gets bigger, can we plant him in the front yard?" Bree sets the empty cup on her desk and slides into bed under the covers. Amber tucks them up under her chin.

"Which story tonight?" Amber shows her the three books she's selected. Bree points to one. Amber cuddles up to Bree, setting the books aside for a moment.

"Aren't you going to read it?"

"Yeah. But first, Bree, there's something I have to tell you."

Bree nods. "Is it serious?"

"It is."

"Did someone die?"

"Oh. No, honey. No one died." Amber sees the fear wash out of Bree's eyes. "It's different than that. We're going to have to move soon."

"Move where?"

"I'm not sure yet. Out of this house."

"Far away?"

"No. No. We're not moving away. We're staying here in Clarksville."

Bree looks relieved. She sits up, leaning on the headboard with a thoughtful expression.

"Do you understand what I'm saying?"

"I think so."

"You won't have this room anymore. Or this yard to plant Matt in."

"I'll have a new room?"

"Yes."

"Will it be a big house?"

"We don't need a lot of space for just the two of us."

"I like that," says Bree, with a little glow on her face.

"You do? Why?"

"Because it means we don't have to do so many chores."

Amber is a little surprised at how well Bree is taking this. "How do you figure that?"

"Less space to clean. More time to have fun."

It hits Amber. Fun. When was the last time the two of them had fun together? Goofing off? Laughing? Just enjoying each other? She can't remember.

"Can I take Matt?"

"Of course you can. So, you're okay with moving?"

Bree doesn't miss a beat. "Yeah. It's a new adventure. And adventures are fun!"

There's that word again. *Fun.* Amber turns to Bree. "We could use a little more fun here, couldn't we?"

"Yeah." Bree nods.

"You know what?" says Amber with a wry grin. "I have a surprise for you."

"What?"

Amber shakes her head. "Tomorrow. You'll find out tomorrow."

"Noooo. Tell me now!" Bree pleads.

"But then it wouldn't be a surprise." Amber tickles Bree's belly. Bree lets out a giggle.

"Tell me now! Tell me now! Tell me now!"

"Never!" Amber tickles her again. Bree shrieks with laughter, tumbling off the bed onto a pile of pillows. Amber dives after her with tickle hands . . . and they forget all about the storybook.

CHAPTER FORTY-FOUR: THE QUALIFYING RACE

Race night. Cody is suited up at the pit and ready to hop into his car for a couple of warm-up laps when Joe enters with a serious look. He motions to him.

"What's up, Joe? I was about to take her for a spin."

"Someone wants to see you."

"Who?"

"Just come on."

Cody follows Joe to the grandstand, up the elevator, and into an upper-level suite with a desk that overlooks the raceway.

Wow. This is the way to watch a race.

Below them, fans are filing into the stands with their colored flags, hot dogs, and bags of peanuts. On the track, engines roar as half a dozen race cars zoom by on their warm-up laps.

As they step out onto the deck, Cody immediately notices a familiar face. Gibbs. He goes weak in the knees as Joe gets Gibbs's attention. *Why didn't he warn me!*

Gibbs, a man in his sixties with sleek silver hair, a golden Florida tan, and not an ounce of body fat, turns to Cody with a bleached-white smile. He slides his sunglasses off to get a better look at Cody, who is doing his best to wipe the surprised look off his face. "Good to see you again, son."

"You, too. Sir." Cody shakes Gibbs's hand and tries to calm his nerves.

"I've been getting a few updates from Joe here. But thought I'd come out to see your progress for myself."

Cody's stomach flip-flops. "That's very generous of you. Joe's been a great help. I've been working real hard."

"That's what Joe says."

I sure hope so. I've been busting my butt for him.

"I've also got a little news for ya. I think I've found you a new sponsor."

"Great. That's great." Cody looks to Joe. "You been holding out on me?"

"No. And don't get too excited until you hear everything," adds Joe.

"Sure. Well, who is it?"

"I can't disclose all the details just yet, but let's just say it's a household name," Gibbs tells him.

"Big money, then?"

Gibbs nods.

Yahoo! My ticket outta Clarksville.

"Don't worry about the money. Worry about winning," says Joe.

"I've had quite a time convincing them that you're a caterpillar ready to become a butterfly," says Gibbs. "You understand?"

"I do, sir. And I'm ready." That flip-flop in Cody's stomach makes another appearance.

"It's all riding on this race, son. If you place tonight, they'll grant you the sponsorship."

"I see." The nerves start to tingle up Cody's legs.

"Do you?" asks Joe. "He means that if you don't place, they're going to go with another driver."

"They like you, Cody. They want you to succeed. As do we. They're willing to make a big investment. They just need to feel secure about it paying off."

"I got this." Cody looks Gibbs in the eyes.

"That's what I need to hear. Now go get 'em." Gibbs slips his sunglasses back on and turns to the track. "Good luck out there."

"Thank you, sir. Don't you worry."

Cody feels a tug on his sleeve. Joe rushes him out of the suite to the elevators. As soon as the elevator doors touch closed, Cody

300

explodes.

"Why would you tell me this right before the race?"

"I didn't want you brewing in it. Gettin' all heady about it."

"And so *this* is your strategy? I'm freaking out, Joe!"

"Why? You should be thrilled."

"Because it's my first race back."

"Isn't this exactly the kind of opportunity you've been hoping for? Shed this Podunk town. Move into the big leagues."

The elevator doors open and they step out, beelining for the gate that will let them back onto the field.

"Did you call him down here, Joe? Did you think this would get me to perform better?"

"You need strong motivators." Joe flags one of the members of the safety team in an orange vest to let them through the gate. "Can we get back in, please?"

"Yes, sir. But there are still a few cars on the track. I need an all-clear from traffic control. Gimme a minute to work on that."

"All right. All right. Just let them know I've got a driver out here who needs immediate access."

"You got it, boss." The safety in the orange vest scampers off with his walkie pressed to his mouth.

"I don't know why you're so nervous. All you gotta do to win is listen. To me." Joe taps Cody's ears for emphasis. "I'll guide you right into first place."

Cody is about to protest when he hears a voice at his back.

"Cody! Cody!" Cody turns and recognizes those pink tennis shoes running up.

"Hey, Bree! Great to see you!" Cody gives her a fist bump. "You come here all by yourself?"

Bree giggles and points behind her, where Amber jogs around the corner of the stands to catch up. It was amazing what a simple pair of jeans and boots did for a girl.

"Bree! I told you to . . . wait!" Cody flashes her a smile. "Oh. Thank goodness."

"I'm so glad you guys made it," says Joe. "I've saved you a special seat. Out there."

Joe points to an RV set up in the pits.

"Wow! There's a deck on the roof. We get to sit up way up there?" says Bree. Joe nods.

"Hey, I'm glad you're here," says Cody.

"Are you nervous?"

"Not an ounce." *Now that* you're *here.*

"Okay, Cody, I've been doing some research, and I have some advice for you," says Bree.

"She's been waiting all day to tell you

302

this," Amber adds.

"I'm sure it's very important." Cody kneels down to hear her over the crowds and engines. "Okay, shoot."

Bree's look turns serious as she places her hands on her hips. "Drive fast and turn left."

"Got it, kiddo. Thanks." Cody laughs and turns to Amber. "She knows what she's talking about."

"Thanks for inviting us. And good luck out there." Cody can't help but notice how soft and beautiful Amber's blond hair looks flowing from beneath the brim of her hat.

"Thank you." *You have no idea how much I'm gonna need it.*

"We've been given the go-ahead!" says the guy in the orange safety vest as he reappears.

"All set, Speed Racer?" says Joe.

Cody motions for Amber and Bree to follow Joe as the gate swings open.

This could be the best or worst day of my life. And everyone's gonna have a front-row seat to see how it unfolds.

Cody sighs as he steps out onto the track and heads for his race pit. He glances back to see Amber smiling confidently at him. Above her, on the suite deck, Gibbs kicks back, sunglasses lasered in his direction.

No pressure. No pressure at all.

The green flag drops. Cody floors it as the ravenous pack of race cars roars down the frontstretch and into the first turn. In car number 55, he blasts past several cars, taking fourth position, and steers the car into the backstretch.

"Looks good, Jackson. Steady into the third," Joe's voice pipes through the headset. "Let's try to keep all the paint on the car this time."

"Copy that."

Cody blasts smoothly into and out of the third and fourth turns. Perfect precision and timing. He downshifts and jams the accelerator to the floor. His car tears down the frontstretch, dead center and heading for the lead in a three-wide of racers.

"Hold that line."

"That's the plan." Cody maneuvers his car to the low line into the second turn and makes an attempt for the lead. The other two drivers quickly edge him out.

Come on. I had that!

"You had that!" Joe yells.

"I know. Going again."

"If forty-six and twenty-three don't change position, you can slide in between them from the outside after turn two."

Cody careens down the frontstretch as he dives into the first turn and jams the accelerator.

"Watch twenty-three! He's squeezing past on the inside!"

Cody narrowly misses his opportunity to pass. He steadies just enough to block 23 from taking the lead.

"Where's forty-six?" Cody demands, his eyes darting to the rearview mirror. "I can't locate."

"On your tail. On your tail. Just outside. Stay ahead of him!" Cody glances back at his mirror, where he sees car 46 kissing his outside bumper.

"Yeah, I got eyes on him."

"Edge slightly to the outside. Block him."

Cody executes the move perfectly. Driver 46 is forced to back off.

"Nicely done. He's behind you half a car length. Outside."

They come out of turn two, zipping down the backstretch. Cody struggles to stay with the pack and keep 46 at bay. They are now a three-wide as they lap the track once. Twice. A third time. Cody executes the turns gracefully — but impatience starts to creep into his craw.

"I'm deadlocked, Joe. I gotta break free."

Cody sails around turn four, heading into the frontstretch again. No change in position.

I gotta win this. Even if it's my way.

"This is getting boring, Joe."

"You're doing great. Stay focused. Wait for your opportunity."

"I wait too much longer and they're gonna push me back."

"Twenty-three's getting antsy. Lean to the outside again," says Joe.

Cody's eyes are locked on the windshield as he takes a fifth lap with these two neck and neck. The fire in him burns off any remaining nerves. Adrenaline surges. Everything he's ever wanted and worked for is riding on this. Only a few more laps in the race.

"I'm gonna go for it."

"Hold steady. You don't need to win this. You just need to place."

"I can do this, Joe."

"You're packed in there like sardines. It's too risky."

"Third place doesn't cut it."

"Listen to me. It's too tight. Wait for my call. I'll let you know when the pack loosens. At that moment, pull back ever so slightly. Then use the Hot Wheels move to slingshot into the third turn. You can pass them on the high line and then dive into the apron and first position."

It's a nice plan, old man. But there's no time like the present.

Cody's foot hammers down the gas pedal.

"Cody, slow down! You're closing in too tight on the lead."

That's the whole point, Joe!

As they take turn two, 46 slows, edging just inside Cody's car. Cody takes advantage and cuts sharp to outside to shake him off. This sends him bumper to bumper for position with 23. Cody surges forward in a reckless move. He slams the gas to the floor, nosing ahead of the lead car as they whine down the backstretch into the third turn on the middle line.

"You're doing it again! You're coming into the curve too hot! There's not enough room to hit the high line!"

Cody ignores him and accelerates, using the momentum to surge past the lead. He slingshots around the turn.

I did it! I did it! Yes!

"That shouldn't have worked, kid. Your guardian angels must be working overtime."

"I got this, Joe!"

Cody hits the gas to finish the pass. But at the very last moment, his bumper clips 23's fender and sends his car into a tailspin. He barrels out of control down the middle line, heading toward the wall. The racers behind him jerk their cars to the high line, barely evading a collision as tires squeal, leaving smoke trails.

Cody white-knuckles the wheel and gives it all he's got to steer himself to safety.

"Aim for the walls!"

Cody does his best, gripping the wheel to the inside.

The car sweeps the wall. Cody steers to avoid a crash, but he can't seem to regain control. He fights with the wheel.

"Hold 'er steady. You blew the back right tire."

I lost. It's over. I was so close.

"Bring her home, Cody. Get outta there. You're done."

An angry beat pounds in his chest, flowing all the way up to his temples.

I blew it. I can't believe it.

"Cody! Cody! Watch your —"

Before he can check his rearview mirror, Cody is surrounded by the sickening sound of metal impact. *POW!* Tires screech. Plexiglas spiderwebs, obstructing his view.

And in the next second, Cody finds himself airborne.

CHAPTER FORTY-FIVE: TERROR ON THE TRACK

Smoke enshrouds Cody's car and billows across the racetrack, blocking Amber's view. She's terrified to her core. Her world jolts to a halt as the remaining cars whiz by, barely dodging the wreckage.

Something catches Amber's attention out of the corner of her eye. Parts from Cody's car are spinning off the roadway and pinging the sidewalls. The red flag drops. The other racers downshift and idle to a stop along the backstretch.

Joe and his pit crew bolt past her toward the crash.

Bree is already down the ladder and running as Amber descends from the rooftop of Joe's RV to chase after her.

"CODY!" Bree sprints across the infield. Amber tries to catch her, fearing what might be a horrible scene, and runs after her.

"Bree. No. Wait!" She can't keep up with her.

Amber is relieved when Joe glances back and sees Bree following in his tracks. He whips around and stops her cold. "Bree. No. Go back to your mother."

His stern command sends Bree into tears. Amber rushes in and pulls her close.

"What are you thinking? It's dangerous. You can't go up there." Amber draws her in tighter.

Bree starts to sob. "Is Cody alive? Is he gonna be okay?"

Amber lifts her gaze to the smoky crash site. All she can hear is the crew shouting at each other. At Cody. Nothing is making sense to her in this moment. "I don't know, Bree. Come on, we need to get out of the way."

"God, please let Cody live," Bree says in a barely audible voice as Amber leads her back to the staging area. "Please God, protect Cody."

Amber's legs grow weak, and her stomach flip-flops. It's that same feeling she got when the news about Darren came. Her peripheral vision goes dark. She's going to pass out. A fog sweeps over her. Black spots straight ahead. She can't pass out. Not with Bree here. Stay with it. Deep breaths. In: two, three, four. Out: two, three, four.

Amber finds a row of chairs in the staging

area and locks in her focus. She just needs to make it to the chairs. She grips Bree's hand a little more tightly and pulls her toward the tented area.

"Mom, are you okay?" Bree asks.

"The chairs. Need. To. Sit," Amber mumbles as she treks forward. What if he was . . . what if he didn't make it? She can't take another loss like this. And Bree . . . how would she ever forgive herself for letting Bree see this? Sirens scream down the track and arrive on the scene. This is serious. Really serious. Flip. Flip. Flip. Her stomach contracts. Tighter. Tighter. It's going to eat itself.

"You look like you're going to throw up," says Bree.

Her vision widens. Light enters. Focus sharp.

"I'm good," Amber says as she tries to relax her face into a reassuring smile. She quickly gains access to a chair. Bree kneels next to her, and the two of them hold each other until the sound of sirens stops.

Bree turns a worried glance to the crash zone, the smoke now starting to clear.

"Don't look, honey. Don't look over there." Amber is grateful to see that a fire truck and ambulance are now blocking the view of the collision area. "Just close your eyes."

"And pray?"

"Yes. Pray."

Bree squeezes her eyes closed even as tears slip through and roll down her cheeks to her chin. Her lips move silently in prayer. Amber hugs her tighter. How could she be so foolish as to get involved with this wild card? The fear turns to anger, and blame rises quickly. Why didn't she see how dangerous this is? How dangerous *he* is? If he were a safe driver, he wouldn't be training with Joe in the first place. And why, for Pete's sake, hadn't Joe warned her before this? Now look what he's putting Bree through. Look what he's putting *her* through!

Amber squints at the track. Out from behind the fire truck and haze a silhouetted form emerges, striding hastily in their direction.

"Cody?"

Bree opens her eyes. "Cody!" She leaps up and runs from the staging area.

He's a little shaken but, amazingly, unscathed except for a small cut above his brow. A small smile parts his lips when he sees Bree running toward him. A wave of relief washes over Amber, calming the fringes of her nerves. But disquiet lingers in her spirit. She made a mistake about Cody. She put herself and Bree in the path of peril. And she won't do it again. She can't.

Amber makes her decision and surges toward her daughter, yanking Bree right out of Cody's arms.

"Let's go," she barks.

"Mom, what are you doing? Mom!" Bree stumbles backward, trying to get her balance. Amber prods her toward the direction of the exit.

"We're going home. Right now." Amber won't look at Cody.

"What? Mom! No!"

"Amber, hey. It's okay. I'm fine. Everything's fine," Cody calls after her.

Amber looks askance at Cody as she drags Bree across the infield. "No. It's not fine."

Cody trots after, but Amber won't have it. "Don't." She shakes her head at Cody.

Picking up the pace with Bree at her side, Amber glances back for one last look at the crash.

"Amber. Please. I want to talk to you." Cody starts to trail her across the infield.

"Cody Jackson!" Amber hears Joe's commanding voice above the simmering crowd and idling engine noise. "Let. Them. Go."

She stands at the gate, waiting for the man

in the orange safety vest to unlock it. Across the track, Cody holds off, his eyes pleading with her. She turns away.

She tightens her grip on Bree's hand as the gate swings open, freeing her from the disastrous moment.

Chapter Forty-Six:
Still Don't Get It

Cody wanders from the track to his pit, glancing up to the box suite where he's expecting to see Gibbs glaring down at him. Instead, the box is empty.

Not a good sign.

"Get over here. Now!" Joe screams from the pit, where the tow truck delivers the debris that used to be car 55.

I'm sunk. Utterly finished. It's back to driving a freight truck and making frozen-food deliveries.

Cody traverses the infield like a dejected puppy, locked in Joe's disgusted stare. The pit crew bustles around the car, trying not to meet Cody's gaze.

They're out of a job. And it's my fault.

Cody approaches, keeping the car between them, maintaining a safe distance from Joe's wrath.

"Guys, can you give us a second?" The pit crew scatters out of sight. "Gibbs already texted me. You've been dropped."

Cody doesn't dare utter a word as he absorbs the anger pulsating from Joe's body. "You have ten seconds to say your piece."

"I had a clear line. I decided to take it. I would've made it, too, if the lead hadn't decided to cut in at the last minute. I had it, Joe. You saw that, too. I know you did."

"Are you done?"

"You gotta take opportunities when they come."

"You endangered lives. Racing is dangerous enough without you adding recklessness to the mix."

"I took a calculated risk."

"Is that how you see it, Cody?" Joe's voice rises to a fever pitch. "Look at this car. This is what your calculated risk has gotten you. And this scrap heap is going to become one sad metaphor for your entire life if you don't learn to listen."

"Patience . . . precision . . . apexes . . . slow turns . . . blah, blah . . ."

"I didn't ask you to slow down. I asked you to listen. The winning opportunity was just seconds from reach. I could see that from my vantage point. You couldn't."

"This isn't a Hot Wheels track. You can't just slingshot me to success."

"That's the thing, Cody. I know I can. But

316

you won't let me. We're not a team. You only think about what matters to Cody."

It jabs. Sharp and deep. *What if I had listened to Joe? Would I be on that winner's stand right now?*

"And Amber can see that, too. Why do you think she bolted?"

He hadn't thought about the effect his attitude and decisions might have on Amber. Or Bree.

"You think she sees this heap as just a calculated risk? No, sir. If you care for them, show it. They've lost enough already."

Cody nods. It's sinking in. Fast.

"And by the way, you owe me two cars now."

"How on earth am I gonna pay for this?" Cody stares at the heap, his despair mounting.

"I reckon that's worth about four weeks' work at the garage."

"Are you kidding me?"

"No, I'm giving you grace. And I'd say you'd better take it. Especially since your schedule's been freed up considerably."

Cody's tough-guy facade instantly fades.

CHAPTER FORTY-SEVEN: A BLIP ON THE RADAR

Amber figures the stress of the day is what causes Bree to fall asleep on the couch a full two hours before bedtime. And she is grateful for the few extra moments alone. To recoup. To think. She brews herself a cup of tea and curls up in the bay window that overlooks the front yard as the light fades and the sky turns purplish-red in the afterglow of the sunset. She realizes this will probably be the last time she sits in this spot. Her favorite spot to cuddle when Bree was just a baby. Where they would easily take up residence for the afternoon. Nursing. Sleeping. Reading. Sometimes snow fell outside. Other times a rainstorm beat on the windowpanes. Together, they enjoyed a safe, cozy window on the world. Waiting for Daddy to come home from work.

A low rumbling noise rattles the dirt-spotted panes and Amber glances outside to see Cody's Firebird approaching the curb.

Patiently. She's not surprised he showed up after the way she abandoned the racetrack.

She watches Cody in the driver's seat as he takes a moment to smooth his hair. He stares out the windshield pensively, then glances toward the house. Amber ducks behind the curtain. It's silly. But still. She keeps an eye on him as he exits the vehicle and walks up the sidewalk with gravity in his step. In a beat, Amber hears his knock.

She moves quickly to answer the front door before he rings the bell. Bree is asleep on the couch, and she doesn't want her seeing Cody.

Opening the door, she knows what she needs to do.

"Hi," she whispers.

"Hey," he replies nervously.

Amber puts her finger up to her lips. "Shhh. Bree's asleep on the couch. Mind if we talk on the porch?"

"Sure." Cody steps aside, and Amber closes the door behind them.

"Hey. I've been trying to call you," he starts. "Are you both okay?"

"Yeah. We're fine."

"Why did you split like that? Was it something I did?"

Amber doesn't even know how to start. Direct is probably best. "I can't do this . . .

319

this, whatever it is . . . You're a great guy, but . . ."

"What? Come on. Don't give me that lame line. What's the real problem here?"

Amber struggles to answer. "If you can't see it . . ."

"I guess I can't." Cody is really blindsided. Which only makes it harder.

"I can't handle what you do. I don't think you see how dangerous it is."

"Of course it's dangerous. But I've got it under control."

"Didn't appear that way." Amber gets defensive.

"No one was hurt."

"I was. I was hurt, Cody." Her tone turns. "You could have died!" It feels cathartic to let it out. "Joe's advice will save your life. Why don't you listen?"

"You're right. I'm not going up to Indy. Gibbs dropped me."

"Does that mean your career's over?"

"I don't know. But I want to keep trying."

She was hoping he'd say he was done with racing.

"I'm not going to die."

"You don't know that. You *can't* know that." Amber reaches a frustration point. She has to stand her ground. Promises mean nothing to a heart with renewed fear.

"I wish I could feel differently about this, I really do, but Bree and I can't handle another . . ."

"I get it. And I'm not going anywhere. I like you, Amber. I want us to be something more."

"I'm so sorry, Cody. I can't."

Amber turns and heads inside, gently closing the door. After a few moments, she hears his cowboy boots clap down the front steps.

Amber returns to her spot in the bay window. A low fog has rolled in, creating a hazy atmosphere. She peers over at Bree's sleepy figure and assures herself that she has made the right decision. Cody may be done with Gibbs for the moment, but it won't be long before Joe whips him into shape and he's snatched up by some other owner. And then, gone. And Clarksville will just be a blip on the radar of his ever-expanding career.

It's not a good idea to get any closer. Tomorrow she'll let Bree know.

No more go-karts.

CHAPTER FORTY-EIGHT:
HEIRLOOM RING

Amber sizes up Bree as she spoons cereal into her mouth at the kitchen table. She hates that she's going to have to spoil Bree's day right off the bat. As she wrestles in her mind how to break the news, her phone vibrates on the table next to her.

"Who is it?" Bree asks.

"Cody."

"Aren't you going to get that?"

"Nope."

"Why?"

"Because we're eating breakfast." Amber flips through Bree's homework sheets. "You missed a math problem here."

She pushes the paper to Bree and hands her a pencil. The phone stops ringing.

"Are you mad at Cody 'cause he crashed his car?" Bree asks.

"I'm not happy about it."

"So you're just not going to talk to him?"

"Finish that problem." Amber taps her

finger on the sheet.

"He wasn't hurt."

"This time." Amber flashes Bree a look. Bree picks up the pencil and quickly scratches down the answer to the problem.

"There." She pushes the paper back to her mother. Amber shuffles the stack together.

"Everybody makes mistakes," Bree says before slurping up the rest of the milk from the bottom of her bowl.

Amber feels it best just to be direct and honest. It worked with the house news. Perhaps Bree will take this just as well. "Bree, I've decided that I'm not going to see Cody anymore. And I don't want you hanging out with him anymore, either."

"What? Why?"

"It's just not a good idea."

"What about kart club?"

"No more karts." Amber grabs Bree's cereal bowl and slides from the table. "Now. Grab your things. We have to get going."

"Wait. Why can't we see him?" Bree's face fills with confusion.

"Cody is a nice person, but he has a dangerous job."

"So what? Dad had a dangerous job."

It punches Amber in the gut. *Yeah, and he didn't come back to us.* "Cody'll be leaving

Clarksville pretty soon. It's best we focus on other things."

"I don't understand why we can't just be friends till he leaves."

"Get your things." Bree stares at her. "Go. Come on. Chop-chop."

Bree rushes out. Amber places the breakfast dishes in the dishwasher and throws a few things together for Bree's lunch. She heads to the foyer for her purse and Bree's backpack.

"Bree! Let's go. We're gonna be late!" Amber calls up the stairs just as Bree's pigtailed mop appears at the top with her pink helmet tucked under one arm. It's gonna be a fight.

"You can leave that here, young lady. You're not going to kart club today."

"Just because you don't want to see Cody doesn't mean I don't," Bree huffs back at her.

"I'm picking you up after school, and that's that."

Bree stands defiantly on the top step.

"But we're doing test-drives today," Bree begins to whine.

"Put the helmet down and get down here." Amber jabs her arms into her jean jacket and slings her purse over her shoulder. "We have to go."

"I want to drive my kart!"

"I said no."

"I'm going!" Bree clutches her helmet to her chest. Amber marches up the steps. Bree doesn't budge.

"Put it down." Amber points to the wooden bench in the hallway.

"No." Bree moves off the steps into the hallway, away from her mother.

"Let. It. Go." Amber reaches over and tries to pry the helmet from her grip.

"Mom! Noooo!" She eludes her mother's grasp and in retaliation throws the helmet across the floor. It rolls into the wall with a thud and makes a small dent in the plaster.

"Now look what you did!"

Bree flails herself down the stairs. Worried that she'll misstep, Amber hastens after her daughter. Bree flies out the door without her backpack. Through the stained-glass window in the old oak front door, Amber can see Bree making a beeline for their van.

That went well. She sighs and grabs Bree's backpack, locking the door as she exits.

As Amber sails down the front sidewalk, something planted in the yard catches her eye. She marches across the lawn and finds it's a large sign announcing: PUBLIC AUCTION — FORECLOSED PROPERTY. Amber explodes, ripping it out of the ground and sending it across the yard.

"Amber?"

She spins around to see Patti strolling up the sidewalk. *Where has she come from all of a sudden? And why does she always look so amazingly put together?*

"Hi, Patti."

"I was on this side of town making a My-Way delivery when I drove by and saw this sign."

"I . . . we . . . we're on our way, actually," Amber replies impatiently as she steps toward the van. Patti looks into the van and sees Bree pouting in the rear seat. She gives a little wave, and Bree waves back; her frown stays put, and so does she.

"You're losing your house, Amber," states Patti.

"I did everything I could, Patti."

"Everything? Really? You're spending your time running around town with Cody Jackson, some fly-by-night. How is that doing everything?"

Something inside Amber gives way.

"Enough. Okay? What is it you want?" Amber is a three-count away from unleashing a tirade on Patti.

"No grandchild of mine is going to be out on the streets."

"Don't be extreme."

"What's your plan, then? I've asked you before, and I get nothing. So what am I to assume?"

"I'm working it out. Don't worry." But Amber is sure that her worried face and Patti's worried face are the causes for Bree's brow wrinkling with worry in the van window.

"Why don't I take Bree for a while? Just until you can get things straightened out."

"What? No . . . Patti . . ." Amber stops herself from marching Patti off her lawn and runs her fingers through her hair in exasperation. That's when Patti gasps. Amber jerks her eyes to see what's wrong. Patti looks aghast as she reaches for Amber's left hand.

"Where's Darren's ring?"

Oh, that eagle eye! Amber does not owe her an answer and snaps her hand back from Patti's grasp. Without missing a beat, Patti jumps in with her know-it-all reply.

"You took it off for Cody, *didn't you*?"

"Patti, no. Please. It has nothing to do with Cody."

"Then where is it?"

"None of your business." It slips right out, sounding so schoolgirl-like.

"You better believe it's my business. That was my mother's ring!" Patti's indignant look meets Amber's reddening face. She had indeed completely forgotten. And she pawned Darren's grandma's ring. His favorite grandparent. The one he went to visit every Sunday. The one who came to every one of his football games until she got sick. The one he had escorted down the aisle at their wedding to be seated in the position of honor alongside Patti. It was her last outing before she passed. How could Amber have let that important detail escape her? *Darren, forgive me. Please.*

"You sold it," Patti says in disbelief. "You actually sold it. That's what you meant when you said you did everything. Oh, Amber. I don't even know what to say."

Amber feels the weight of Patti's disappointment, but she holds her tongue, defaulting instead to a defensive stance. "I'm sorry. I had to. I've lost everything, Patti."

Patti glances at Bree, who's watching bug-eyed from the backseat of the van. "Not everything." Her heels click down the sidewalk back to her car.

Amber gets into the van and tosses Bree's backpack onto the backseat. "You forgot this."

Bree's accusing look insults her from the rearview mirror. Her voice pleads, "What did you say to Grandma?"

"Nothing." Amber turns on the ignition and throws it into drive.

CHAPTER FORTY-NINE: NEVER MEASURE UP

It takes Patti two cups of decaf and a half-hour call to Kim to settle her down from the morning's interaction with Amber. When she finally does, she chooses to work on her MyWay inventory as a way to calm her mind and get herself back into the day's work flow. MyWay has always been the steadfast thing she can throw herself into when chaos invades her peace. Once she's in a better frame of mind, Patti plans to follow up with new clients and prep her house for the evening's beauty seminar that she's hosting with some of the town's more influential women. She is halfway through restocking the antiaging moisturizers when the doorbell rings. It's not uncommon for clients to pop by in the middle of the day for a product pickup or tea. Patti flips on the front burner and places the kettle over it. Wanting to look her MyWay best, she

dabs on some lip gloss and heads for the
door.

She squints through the peephole to see
who's on the other side of the door. A man
in a leather jacket sways nervously on her
front porch.

She opens the door, and his gaze snaps to
her face as she waits behind the screen door.

"Hello, ma'am. Do you remember me?
Cody Jackson?"

"I know who you are."

"Well, I was wondering if I could have a
moment of your time."

"Maybe. What's this all about?" Patti
keeps her distance behind the screen.

"Amber."

"I'm not sure there's much I can offer on
that subject."

"Maybe you can just hear me out first?"

Patti reads his demeanor as sincere. Plans
whirl inside her brain. This may be the
perfect opportunity to steer him away from
Amber.

"All right." Patti unlocks the screen door.
"Why don't you come in?"

"Thank you, ma'am."

"And, please, it's Patti." She leads him
through the house, stopping short in the
foyer.

"You have a beautiful home here."

"Thank you."

"I guess business is going well." Cody tries to break the ice.

"Never better."

"Have you ever thought about advertising on a race car?"

"Actually, I hadn't thought of that before."

"I'm looking for sponsors."

"I guess I'd have to talk to Joe, then, right?" This is not where she thought the conversation would lead.

"Right. Sorry. That was kinda forward. And anyhow, it's not why I'm here. I just thought that . . . You know, Patti, you're a real inspiration. I hope Amber can see that someday."

She's not holding her breath about that. She puts on her pleasant MyWay persona. "So, what *can* I help you with, Cody?"

"Yes, well, actually, I came here hoping to get a little advice. Amber's been through so much with Darren's death, and . . ."

"We both have, Cody."

"Yes. Of course. I recognize that. Which is why I want to be honest with and respectful of both of you . . . but I don't know how to reach her."

"That makes two of us." Here's her chance! "Best thing to do right now . . . just let her go."

"I can't. I really like her. I've tried to go slow. To understand what she's been through. But she pushes me away. Can you help me get through to her?"

"Cody, I wasn't exactly thrilled to hear you two were dating."

"We're not. But she doesn't want to see me anymore. And I don't understand."

News to Patti. *Hmm. This changes things. Score one for Amber.* "I'll be honest, I'm glad to hear it."

"I would never do anything to hurt her. Or Bree."

"You're a nice-enough guy. But you'll never measure up to what Amber had with Darren."

"I wouldn't even try to compare myself with or replace Darren, but I know I can give both Amber and Bree the kind of love they deserve."

"What? And then go off and get yourself killed in some car crash? It's irresponsible. At least my son died serving his country, not showboating around some track."

The comment lies there between them, flat and cold. Patti's hurt look unearths her true feelings. She's meant every word. Cody slowly turns toward the front door.

"Thank you for your time, Patti."

Patti makes no effort to get the door for

him. She waits until Cody sees himself out, and then returns to her desk as the kettle begins to scream from the kitchen.

CHAPTER FIFTY:
A BETTER HOME FOR MATT

On her break, Amber texts the one person who has served as her surrogate mom since freshman year, when her own parents died in a car crash and she was forced to move to Clarksville to live with her grandparents. She waits to hear back, checking her phone every few minutes. Two anxious hours go by before Amber gets a response: *Come by the house after work.*

The diner slows after the lunch rush, and Amber scurries to get her side work done. When she tells Rosie about the auction and that she needs to find a new place to live, Rosie starts to chide her, but then excuses her to leave an hour early. Paid. Rosie has a soft spot. When she wants to.

When Amber shows up at Karena's doorstep, Karena already has a plan in place.

"My great-uncle has a hunting cabin over by the lake. He's living in Florida now, and he's willing to rent it to you for a steal.

Hundred bucks a month. If you want it."

"Wow. Thank you, Karena." Amber is humbled by Karena's quick actions and the affordable offer.

"It's small. Only a one-bedroom."

"Okay. Can I take a look?"

"Well, I don't have a way to get in yet. But you can drive by and peek in the windows. He's FedExing me the keys if you say yes."

"Yeah. I'll do that."

"You'll drive by?"

"Yes. And I'll take it."

"Sight unseen?"

"How bad can it be?" Amber tries to smile.

"Just giving you full disclosure. It's a hunting cabin. AKA: bachelor pad. And he hasn't used it in several years. So I make no guarantees on the clean factor."

"I don't have a lot of choice or time right now, Karena."

"When do you need to be moved out?"

Amber glances down at her white diner tennis shoes, stained with ketchup and grease. "It's going to auction in a week."

Karena nods. Amber feels no judgment. "Okay, sweetie, then let's do this." She puts an arm around Amber's hunched shoulders and wraps her in a hug. Amber melts into Karena and realizes how good it is to have someone else bearing the burden with her.

By the weekend, Amber has her most important and essential belongings packed up. The boxes are loaded into Joe's pickup truck and make their way to the hunting cabin across town. The rest of her things have been donated or thrown away. Her meager belongings add up to what they did when she and Darren moved into their first apartment right after they were married. Just a few boxes of the essentials.

Amber and Bree spend their last night in the house in sleeping bags on the floor of the living room because Joe and his buddies had graciously relocated their furniture earlier that afternoon.

In the morning, they wake to the sun warming the room. They slip on their work clothes and give the house a final cleaning. When it's finished, Amber stands alone in the middle of the foyer and looks to the dining room, living room, and upstairs. Empty walls. Empty floors. Empty shelves. Empty. Empty. Empty.

She spies the case displaying Darren's medals still sitting on the fireplace mantel. The last item left in the home. She tucks it safely into her tote bag, tears stubbornly filling her eyes. She wipes her cheeks when

Bree comes down the stairs carrying her little clay pot.

"You ready, sweetie?"

Bree nods as she shows her mother what's left of Matt. He's withered to a faded green nub.

"Oh dear. Matt doesn't look so good. You wanna put him in the Dumpster on our way out?"

"No. I think the new house'll be better for him." Bree tucks the pot under her arm.

"I don't think he's coming back."

"He might. We just gotta have a little faith."

Amber keeps her mouth shut and reaches for her purse. Matt did not survive in the conditions in here, and no amount of faith is going to bring that seed back to life.

Bree stretches out her hand, and Amber takes it.

"Are you sad?" Amber asks.

"A little."

"Me, too." Amber looks at her daughter. "I'm sorry this is happening. I tried really, really hard to —" The lump in Amber's throat chokes off her sentence.

"I know you did," Bree says, squeezing her mother's hand. "And I think Dad knows, too. It's gonna be okay."

"I hope so." And they walk out hand in hand . . . with Matt.

CHAPTER FIFTY-ONE:
A MOTHER'S LOVING TOUCH

Patti hears from Karena that Amber is moving today, and she takes the day off to help. Or to at least be available in case Amber calls for help. She never does. Not one to wait, Patti texts Amber around nine to prompt an invitation. No response. Now it is noon, and Patti knows Amber is not going to get back to her.

So she is here instead.

DARREN HILL, BELOVED SON, HUSBAND, AND FATHER, 1984–2014 stares back at Patti from the hard marble gravestone. She kneels beside it, cleaning the face with a cloth and plucking stray weeds from the plot. She straightens the American flag, planting it securely in the soil at the top of the gravesite. Last, she swaps a wilting pot of daffodils for a fresh planter of yellow daisies, giving the whole site a mother's loving touch.

Looking at the stone just makes her

wound of loneliness throb and ache until the pain is so intense that everything inside her feels punctured.

"I don't know what to do anymore, son. Amber's losing it. Literally. She lost the house today. I don't suppose she's been around to tell you much of what's going on. I don't understand why she doesn't visit your gravesite. It's beyond me. She should be embarrassed. And then running around with that hotshot race car driver. I know. I know. She has a right to move on. But this guy is a subpar choice. Thankfully, it's fizzled to nothing. But that and losing her home makes me doubt the choices she's making. And in some way I feel like it belittles you. Don't ask me how. It just does.

"I don't know why I'm still so angry. I don't even know what I'm angry about. Or who I'm angry at. I'm just so angry. A lot more than I'd like to admit. And it seems to always get directed at Amber.

"Maybe it's because I wanted to see what you could have been. What you could have done with your life. I wanted to be at that college graduation. I wanted so much more for you.

"And I'm just angry at anything and anyone that prevented that for you. Airborne. Amber."

As she says it out loud, the answer blares. The two things Darren loved the most, she has resented all these years. Conviction pierces her, dissolving the anger into regret.

"Oh, Darren. I'm so sorry." Cleansing tears flow.

"What can I do? I'm worried I've lost them. Please. I just don't know what to do anymore."

Patti hangs her head. No more words come.

The sun's rays fall over her body, melting the chill and spreading warmth to her core. It's the nicest, most peaceful feeling she's been granted in a while.

She stays kneeling bedside her son's grave for a long, long time.

CHAPTER FIFTY-TWO: THE HUNTING CABIN

The mud-brown hunting cabin, with its peeling paint and sloping roof, is a great big disappointment and a great big relief all wrapped up together. Amber pulls her van into the dirt drive. The grass is withered in patches and struggling to survive everywhere else. Straggly remains of bushes line the front of the shack. Scraps of garbage have blown into the crevices of the cheerless landscape, and the windows are blocked out with some sort of black material draped on the inside. Amber struggles to take in the enormity of her downfall.

"Are we gonna get out?" Bree asks from the passenger seat, the wilted Matt cupped safely on her lap.

"Yeah, honey. And . . . um, welcome to our new home."

Bree doesn't say anything as she unclicks her seat belt, scrutinizing the new dwelling with her little brown eyes.

"Do you think there are any kids to play with around here?" Bree scans the sparse lakeside neighborhood, where most of the homes look unoccupied. Probably seasonal rentals.

"Yeah. Probably." Amber hadn't even thought about the neighborhood friends Bree is leaving behind.

She makes herself exit the van and unloads the last few boxes onto the drive. Bree steps out, balancing her mustard plant in one hand. Amber is not blind to the healthy skepticism growing on Bree's face as she scans the cabin.

"Joe says he put our boxes in the living room. Shall we take a look inside?"

"I think it's haunted!" Amber follows Bree's eyes, glued to a wispy curtain flapping in the breeze through a screenless back window.

Amber smiles. "No. It's not. I bet Joe left a window open to air the place out for us."

Bree shakes her head. She isn't buying it.

An SUV pulls in, and Karena and Bridgette emerge with cleaning supplies and fresh energy.

"Hey, you two," says Karena. "Thought you might need a hand."

Bree rushes over and gives them both a hug. Amber strings along behind her, glad for their perfect timing. "Hey, ladies. This is a surprise."

"Many hands, light work. More girl time," Bridgette adds.

"You guys, really? You've done enough already," says Amber.

"You're gonna need all the help you can get. I stopped by yesterday, and I don't think Great-Uncle Charlie ever put a mop to this place."

"Ugh. That bad, huh?" Amber says.

"Hey, a little elbow grease, and this will feel like home before dinner," says Bridgette.

"I really think it's haunted in there," Bree insists as a tiny gray patch of fur scuttles along the side of the house.

"There're mice!" Amber shrieks.

Bridgette jumps back into Karena's arms.

"Okay, okay — now I'm really glad you're here!" says Amber.

Karena produces a package of three mousetraps. "Uncle Charlie already warned me. You ready to go in?" she asks. "I promise it's not haunted. But I can show you a few places I used to use as hiding spots when I was a kid!"

Bree grips Karena's hand. Amber grips Bree's hand. And Bridgette takes Amber's hand. The three of them nod, and Karena leads them into the compact hunting shack decorated in "early attic" and a thick layer of dust. After walking through three cob-webs and finding a dead mouse in the sink, Amber retreats to the living room. "Let's get those traps set up. Now," begs Amber with a wilting look.

"I know it's a bit of an adjustment, Amber, but this can be a good home. You just need to have a little faith to see it," says Karena.

"I know. I'm trying." *There is a bright side to this. There is. There is. I know there is.*

"Maybe a coat of paint will help," Bridgette says. "And the price is great. Think how much you can save."

Amber desperately wants to believe this is better. But she can't help comparing the downgrade to what she just came from.

"Mom, there's a bucket of dirty water in the tub with some green stuff floating in it," says Bree, wrinkling her nose as she comes from the back of the cabin, where the bathroom is located.

"Oh, disgusting," Karena and Bridgette chime in tandem.

"We'll take care of it, honey," says Amber. "Why don't you unpack your clothes into the dresser for me?"

"Okay. And where can I put Matt?" Bree says, Matt still cradled in her hands.

"I'm not sure Matt is gonna need —"

"The bedroom window gets the most light," Karena offers.

"Can I put him on the windowsill, Mom?"

Amber shrugs. "I guess so."

After she leaves, Amber turns to Bridgette and Karena. "That plant isn't going to grow. It's nearly dead."

"Maybe. But I love that Bree has the faith to believe it will," says Bridgette.

"Childlike faith. The most precious gift of God," adds Karena wistfully.

"I could use a little of that right now."

"Oh, I know it's still there, Amber," says Bridgette. "Buried but fighting, just like that little sprout in Bree's pot."

"Give it time. Whether you believe it or not, God's got you in the palm of His hand at this very moment — dust, mice, dirty buckets, and all."

"With a beautiful plan for the rest of your life," adds Bridgette, not dropping her usual air of hopefulness. She knows Bridgette means well. But at the moment, it's just totally annoying.

"All I feel is defeated . . . and grimy. Let's degrunge this place," Amber says, heading to the bathroom. "Starting with the shower." She looks inside the tub and her stomach turns. "Ladies. This is the last straw!"

Karena and Bridgette rush to her side. The bucket of floating algae stares back at them.

"What was Uncle Charlie thinking?" Karena asks.

Amber tips her gaze toward the ceiling. "That's what." She points at a sagging spot in the ceiling where water has leaked through for who knows how long.

"I'll let Uncle Charlie know he's gonna be getting a repair bill soon," says Karena, clicking her tongue.

"Let's hoist this outta here and then give this bathroom a scrub down," says Bridgette. "Girls, hands on the handle. We got this!"

Three hands latch on to the bucket's metal handle. "One, two, three!" says Karena. And they lift the five-gallon bucket of filth over the edge of the tub and waddle out of the bathroom, through the house, and into the yard, where the bucket's contents get dumped near a tree.

Amber sees a hose connected to a faucet on the side of the cabin. "I think I'll rinse it out and use it for something. It's still a good bucket."

"Amber, that bucket is a nice metaphor for your life," says Karena.

"You've completely lost me."

"That dirty bucket of water is like all the stuff you've been holding on to. Anger. Fear. Sorrow."

"It's called grieving, Karena."

"There's nothing wrong with grief. But when it starts to clog up your life like that bucket of algae, that's when you need to clean it out. How much of your grief have you shared with God?"

Amber doesn't answer.

Karena points to a clean bucket overflowing with water. "Give Him every nasty, despairing feeling that you have, and He will refresh your life with new springs of water," says Karena in that singsongy church voice she uses when she gets preachy.

Amber does an inward eye roll. *Here she goes again.*

"Doesn't that sound good?" Karena brings them all in for a hug. "We can do it right now with a prayer."

Bridgette and Karena bow their heads. Amber loosens herself from the huddle.

"I'm gonna rinse that bucket now," she says, heading to the spigot on the side of the house. One look at the rusty knob gives her pause. She attempts to turn it on, but it won't give an inch. She keeps wrestling with it, wrenching her wrist with the torque.

Does everything in her life have to be

jammed up?

She kicks at the spigot, cracking the knob at the base. Water fire-hoses her. An instant soaking.

Friendly laughter breaks out from across the yard as Bridgette and Karena dash to her side.

"You feeling refreshed yet?" Karena says.

Amber shakes off like a dog, spraying them both.

Amber tucks Bree's sleeping body under the covers and slips into her half of the queen bed they now share. She lies back, window cracked open to let in the spring breeze. She listens to the sounds outside of the cabin. More nature. More darkness. More stillness. A thousand times quieter than their house in town.

The black drapes covering the windows have been torn down and her sheer curtains make shallow breaths in and out of the window frame. The mingled smells of disinfectant, lemon, vinegar, and wood soap have overpowered the musty, mildewy odors that were trapped in the cabin. She and Bridgette put a temporary patch on the shower ceiling. And now Amber's skin feels refreshed and silky after a long shower in the spick-and-span white ceramic tub.

Today they made a good start on the cleaning. But it's only the tip of the iceberg. There's so much more to do. The graying walls of the bedroom beg for a fresh coat of paint. And she'll want to install some shelves in the closet. The old shag carpet on the bedroom floor still carries a faint odor of kitty urine and mildew. When Amber peeled back a corner of the carpet, she found gorgeous oak floors hiding underneath. Perhaps she can convince Great-Uncle Charlie to rip out the carpet and let her refinish the wood, the way she and Darren did in the upstairs bedrooms of their house. Her old house. Former home. Former life.

She reaches for the night-light, her gaze landing on her Bible that she knows Karena placed there — *Hint! Hint!* — when she was unpacking the bedroom. It doesn't bring feelings of anger or disgust. In fact, Amber finds some comfort seeing it there.

She leans over and takes the Bible, cracking it open to reveal the still-sealed letter from Darren tucked in the middle. Her eyes land on his familiar handwriting, yet it feels oddly distant having this piece of Darren in a space he's never occupied. These were Darren's last words to her. She considers opening it but, like so many times before, can't bring herself to do it; questions paralyze her. What if there is nothing special in here at all? What if it's just a record of events on the field? But what if it is of lasting importance? What if it could change her world? What if she's withholding something Bree needs to know? Or what if the words are so powerful they slice open her wounds all over again? Would she ever recover?

No. Not today. She can't hear Darren's last words today.

Amber tucks the letter back into the Bible and lays her head on the pillow.

Her body is exhausted from the hard day's toil, but her restless mind spins with one disturbing thought. How are she and Bree ever going to be able to crawl out of this hole she put them in? She doesn't mean to be ungrateful. There's a roof over their heads. Food in the fridge. But if God has a beautiful plan for them, why do things look so dingy and helpless? And why can't she get out of this funk?

Amber thinks of that filthy bucket and its soupy, moldy contents. She feels the weight of her own inner sludge. She fears that if she pours it all out, she'll just be empty. Clear to the endless bottom. The transparency is frightening.

The wind picks up and blows the wispy

curtain across Matt's pot. Amber realizes that Bree has balanced him crookedly across the window ledge, an accident waiting to happen. And she can't bear the thought of cleaning up one more thing in this place tonight. Amber slips out of bed and stabilizes the pot inside the ledge. She sees that some of the dirt has been knocked to one side. Amber pats it evenly around the green nub.

There. That's better. Wait. How crazy is this? Here she is, up at midnight, fussing over this silly wilted sprout that she doesn't believe has a chance.

But why else would she be doing this unless she thought it might actually . . .

Childlike faith.

Maybe it *is* still there. Sunk somewhere at the bottom of that gloppy bucket.

Maybe Karena was right. It can't surface because of all the sludge.

CHAPTER FIFTY-THREE:
I SAID NO!

Bree isn't in her classroom after school. And she isn't in the gym or the playground. The teacher hasn't seen her leave, but her coat and bag are not in her storage cube. Amber is on the verge of panic as she dials Patti. Is this one of the days Patti picks her up? With all the moving and her fight with Patti, Amber isn't sure if their old arrangement is even still in effect. She hasn't communicated with her since auction day.

"Patti. It's Amber. Is Bree with you?"

Patti says no and asks why.

"Because she isn't at school. And she should be."

Patti reminds Amber that it's Wednesday. Kart club day.

"Of course," says Amber nonchalantly. "I've been so busy I forgot what day it is. Thanks for your help." She quickly hangs up in a panic, cutting Patti short.

Kart club! That kid better be there. And if

she is, boy, is she in trouble!

During the two-minute drive from school to Joe's Auto, Amber gives herself a small moment to play out what is about to happen at Joe's. She is furious that Bree has disobeyed her. She doesn't want to overreact. But here she is again, faced with the discipline dilemma. If she grounds Bree, what privileges could she possibly take away from her? She doesn't have a TV or Internet at the cabin. And the only other things that are important to Bree are David, Matt, and church. Positive things don't deserve negative consequences. *Why can't she just listen?*

Pulling into Joe's, Amber decides to think about it later. Now, she has to extract Bree without making a huge scene, and — if possible — avoid Cody. She swings her van into an open parking space and looks over to see Cody's Firebird, inflaming her annoyance. She gets out and slams the door.

Amber pounds into Joe's, stone-faced and exhausted, and is met by a bustle of kids and karts. The smell of the sawdust and paint overwhelm her as she searches the area for her daughter. Out of the corner of her eye, Amber sees Cody's lean, muscular figure zigzagging through the maze of materials toward her.

Before she can dodge him, Cody meets her at the door with a smile. "Hey, Amber. It's good to see you. How have you been?"

"Where's Bree?" Amber says curtly.

"By her kart. Over there. Outside. She's giving it a test-drive."

Amber's gaze stretches out over the parking lot to where Bree's pink go-kart weaves around an oval track made from old tires. She's wearing her pink helmet and is intensely focused on her driving as she glances back, trying to get David off her bumper.

It will be punishment enough to drag Bree from this.

"The kart looks great, doesn't it? She did such a good job," says Cody proudly.

Amber ignores Cody, her eyes on Bree as she heads outside toward the track.

"Amber. Wait!" says Cody, going after her.

Bree's kart pops around the corner, and she sees her mother standing in the middle of the track. Her eyes go wide, and she immediately knows she's in trouble. Her foot comes off the gas as she swerves to the left and coasts to a stop a few feet beyond Amber.

"Bree. Come on. We're going."

"I don't wanna go," she calls from her kart, not looking back.

At that moment, David's kart rounds the

corner and he nearly runs Amber over. Amber leaps out of the way as David slams on the brakes, skidding to a stop next to Bree.

"Amber. Please. Get off the track!" Cody insists as he blows his whistle and the other riders pull to the side.

Bree doesn't budge.

From the sidelines Amber hollers, "You're done with this. Let's go, young lady!"

This hits Cody like a ton of bricks. "You're pulling her from the club?"

"I *pulled* her from the club a couple of weeks ago. But she came here anyway. Without my knowing it. She's probably been coming all along."

Cody nods slightly. It's true.

"That's not fair," David whines from his kart. Amber shoots him a look, and he bows his head into his chest, afraid to say another peep.

"Amber, wait a minute . . ." starts Cody, moving toward her across the track. "I'm sorry. I didn't know, or I would've told you."

"This is not your concern. Bree, get your things."

"No!" Bree grips the wheel tighter with both hands.

Amber marches back out onto the track to Bree's kart. She grabs her by both arms

357

and yanks her hands off the wheel. "Get in the car! Now!"

"Mom! *No!*"

Amber lifts Bree out of the kart and stands her on the track. "I went to school looking for you. You outright disobeyed me."

"I don't see why . . ." Bree quickly shuts up under Amber's seething expression.

"Hey, Amber. Everything okay here?" Joe's voice from the garage suddenly makes Amber realize that she is creating the exact chaos she'd hoped to avoid. She glances around. Joe's gentle eyes scrutinize her as he methodically wipes his hands on a grease cloth. "Something I can do to help?"

"No, Joe. We're just leaving," Amber says as she takes Bree by the arm and marches her to the van. Bree's face turns red as she holds back her tears.

Amber opens the door, and Bree jumps into the van. Cody dashes around to Amber's side.

"Amber, please. She's just a kid. She loves it here. And we love having her here."

"You don't get to decide, okay? Stay out of this." Amber gets in the van and angrily backs out.

The drive to the cabin is tense and silent. Neither speaks for several miles. Bree stares angrily outside, her helmet still on.

"You okay?"

"You never let me do anything."

"That's not true. This is the only thing I don't want you doing."

"Why? Because it's fun? I never have any fun, except when you're not around."

"That's not fair." Amber pulls up to a red light. "I'm doing my best here, Bree. I really am."

"Dad would let me have a kart!"

"Well, Dad's not here, is he?" Amber thumps her thumbs against the steering wheel, completely unprepared for Bree's next remark

"I hate you! I wish you had died instead of Dad!"

The words slice into Amber, taking her breath away.

She turns to Bree, who is unbuckling her seat belt. "What are you doing?"

Bree grabs the door handle and launches out of the car, leaving the door wide-open.

"BREE!" The light turns green. The car behind her honks its horn. Bree runs a few feet ahead, then jerks in front of Amber's van without looking. The car behind her lays on the horn again, and then veers out from behind her. Bree dashes across the street at the same time the driver accelerates on Amber's left, heading straight for Bree crossing its path. Amber can see the inescapable collision coming.

"BREE! BREE!"

In the split second before Bree steps in his path, the driver sees Bree and slams on the brakes. Bree whooshes by, narrowly missing the car's front bumper. Unfazed, she doesn't even look back as she pounds across the street. Amber watches her disappear into the neighborhood as she fumbles to release her seat belt.

The driver yells a profanity at Amber and speeds away. Amber's heart races, and she leaps from the van. She blinks back frightened tears. Where did Bree go?

CHAPTER FIFTY-FOUR:
MATT'S DEAD

For the next twenty minutes, Amber wildly traverses the streets in her van, searching for Bree. They are only blocks from the cabin, so after she has combed the neighborhood, Amber heads home, hoping Bree went there.

Storming through the front door, Amber immediately spots Bree's helmet tossed aside on the floor. *She's here. Thank God!*

"Bree? Bree! Where are you?" Amber dashes to the back and sees the door to their bedroom closed. She tries the knob. Locked.

"Bree. Open this door. Are you okay?" She bangs on the door. "Get out here right now."

She listens. Silence. "Bree. Come on. You almost got hit back there. I need to know if you're okay!"

More silence. Amber grows impatient, pacing in small steps in front of the door. She raps on it again, harder.

"Open this door right now, young lady!"

Nothing.

"I'm breaking the door, Bree. If you're in there, get away from the door. Okay? On three."

Amber steps back. "One. Two. Three!" She slams her body into the flimsy door. It splinters off its hinges and crashes to the floor. Amber bolts in.

A breeze whips the flimsy curtains in and out of a wide-open window. Matt isn't on the sill. She looks to the floor. Dirt spilled everywhere. The once green little sprout is now a dried, brown corkscrew. Amber knows in this moment that Bree is gone.

"BREE!" She leans out the window, yelling into the world. Peering down, she can see little tennis-shoe prints leading away from the house and across the yard.

Amber rushes back out into the street, frantically searching for her daughter.

"BREE! BREE!" Her voice reaches hysterical levels as she circles her yard in random directions. Finally, collapsing in a heap on the front lawn, Amber reaches for her phone. It only rings twice on the other end before —

"Karena. I need you."

CHAPTER FIFTY-FIVE: THE SEARCH

Amber sits under a tent set up in the church parking lot to shelter her and the volunteer searchers from the steady rain pelting down. It's been five hours now, and no Bree. Amber's stomach, emptied by several rounds of vomiting, spasms in the void. Her tears have long since dried up, replaced by fright and a pounding headache. Flanking her with wool blankets are Karena and Bridgette, who nestle in close.

"You should go warm up inside," says Karena. "I'm worried you're getting sick."

But Amber refuses with a deadened look. "If Bree is outside somewhere, then I'm going to suffer with her."

"At least drink some tea." Bridgette hands her a thermos. Amber tries to choke down a few sips.

After a minute, Rosie, Amber's friends from the diner, and a good handful of church members circle around Amber.

Nelson wheels from group to group, passing out flashlights. Cody and Joe diligently hand out water bottles. Pastor Williams steps into the tent holding a picture of Bree.

"Okay, everyone, as most of you know, we're looking for this little girl." He holds up the photograph. "Breeanne Hill. Or Bree, as we call her."

At this, fresh tears start to flow down Amber's cheeks. Bridgette squeezes her close.

"We're going to start by canvassing the area in a five-mile radius from the Hills' cabin. I want you to divide into groups of three to five. There are maps that outline which group is searching which quadrant. Talk to neighbors. Talk to anyone you see on the street. Ask to look in yards, sheds, barns, vehicles. Be nosy! Police have posted an Amber Alert. So make everyone you know aware of this. Okay? You've got your supplies. Flashlights. Hand warmers. Water bottles. Stay with your party. Keep in touch, and call in if you find anything. Anything! You can call the police number directly. Karena and I will also be here working the phones. Any questions?"

The group mumbles a collective no.

"Okay, pray as you search, people. We're gonna bring our Bree home tonight!" Pastor

Williams nods reassuringly to Amber. The groups move hastily to their vehicles, and a stream of headlights convoys out of the parking lot into the night.

Pastor Williams joins Amber, Karena, and Bridgette. He leads them in a prayer over Amber. But Amber doesn't close her eyes. She just stares helplessly into the darkness as the rain picks up, cascading in sheets from the inky sky.

CHAPTER FIFTY-SIX: AFRAID TO KNOW

From the corner of the tent, Cody watches Amber, her pain so palpable that it actually makes his heart ache. He starts toward her. "Amber, I'm so sorry. We're gonna find her. I promise."

Amber slants her gaze to Cody, but no words form. Cody lingers, struggling to offer more, when Joe intervenes. "Don't worry, hon. We're going to find that little stinker. Got it?" He gives Amber a wink, and he's sure for a second that her eyes believe him.

Joe grabs Cody, pulling him out of the tent. "You'll do her more good looking for Bree. Let's head out, okay?"

"Yeah. You're right." Cody steals a glance back at Amber, who has buried her head in the blanket. Just then, Nelson wheels up to him.

"Hey. I was wondering if I can hitch a ride with you guys. The legs aren't much help right now, but my eyes are good," he says with an eager smile.

"Yeah, man. Of course."

"Why don't you guys take Cody's Firebird, and I'll ramble behind in my truck. We can cover more ground that way," Joe suggests, and he heads off to his old Ford pickup.

Cody leads Nelson to his Firebird and helps him into the passenger seat. They take off out of the parking lot and cruise slowly down the street, windows open. On high alert. Cody keeps his gaze bent for any signs of Bree as the rain splats through the open window. He doesn't care how wet he gets. All that matters is getting Bree back.

After a few blocks, Cody tries to take the edge off. "I hear you were in Darren's unit."

Nelson scans the lawns, sidewalks, and trees in the same way he once scanned the buildings in Afghanistan for insurgents. "Yeah. I was transferred there about a month before he was killed."

"Did you know him well?"

"Better than most." Cody detects painful memories lodged in his voice. "He saved my life."

"Really. Wow!" Cody is hesitant to ask, but does anyway. "What happened?"

Nelson is silent. "Hey. Over there. I saw

something move."

"Where?" Cody slows.

"In the bushes by that house."

Cody stops the car in the middle of the street. He and Nelson shine their flashlights in the direction of a mulberry bush along-side a house. He catches a glimpse of black fur as it slips between the slates of a white picket fence and disappears.

"Cat," says Cody, flipping his light off. He continues on. "Does Amber know what happened with you and Darren?"

"I really doubt it. Every time I try to talk to her, she avoids me like the plague."

"Maybe she's afraid to know."

"Seems like it," says Nelson.

"Would it help her to know the truth?"

"I think it would. But she's got to be ready to hear it."

"But I mean, if you have the key to relieving some of this pain she's going through, then . . ."

"Look, man. I've tried. Let's focus on finding Bree. Okay?"

Cody nods. He gets it. He's pushed too far, too fast. Nelson's right. The best and only thing Amber needs right now is Bree.

CHAPTER FIFTY-SEVEN:
FINDING OUT ON FACEBOOK

Patti is tucked serenely into her king-size bed between the folds of her thick comforter. She's engrossed in a compelling novel propped up on a pillow on her lap. The first time her phone dings from the nightstand, Patti ignores it. But when the *ding* goes off four times in a row, she reaches over and checks. She is astounded to find that her in-box has exploded with messages. She clicks on the one from Kim first.

Kim: Any word yet?

Word about what? Patti follows the Facebook link Kim has attached. It's from the Clarksville Community Church page.

Community Alert: Bree Hill, nine-year-old daughter of Amber Hill, disappeared this afternoon and has not returned home. Search parties being dispatched from Clarksville Community Church. Please pray for her safe and quick return. To

volunteer to search, contact Karena Williams.

*What? What's happened to Bree? And why
didn't Amber call me?*

Patti throws the covers off and jumps out
of bed. She yanks on a pair of yoga pants
and a hoodie while dialing Amber's cell. Of
course, it goes right to voice mail. Patti flies
down the steps, not stopping to turn off any
lights. She leaves the house unlocked and
jumps into her car.

On the twenty-minute drive to the church,
Patti makes calls to her key MyWay consul-
tants. And one to Angela Brice.

She rolls into the empty church parking
lot, immediately spying the tent and its four
inhabitants bunched up together. Why on
earth are they all not out searching for Bree?

Patti scuttles from her car as the wind and
rain pick up. She bolts for the tent. "It's
kind of hard to find her if you're not out
looking." Her eyes dart to Amber. She has
that same traumatized look that she saw at
the hospital after receiving the news about
Darren.

Patti stays fixed on Amber as she looks to
Karena.

"Miss Patti, glad you're here," says Karena, standing to welcome her. Pastor Wil-

370

liams joins Karena at her side.

"We're doing everything we can to find your granddaughter," says the pastor.

"Why is it that I had to find out from Facebook that my own granddaughter is missing?"

Bridgette looks at Amber, who stutters out an answer. "I'm sorry. I just . . . I didn't think . . ."

"No, you didn't." Patti is unsuccessful in keeping calm.

"I'm sure it won't be long before they bring her right back to us," Pastor Williams says.

Patti breezes right over his comment, her focus still lasered on Amber. "Why did she run? What happened?"

"She was upset."

"About what?"

"She was unhappy with me," Amber says.

"What did you do to make her run?"

"What did I do? Why do you assume it was my fault?"

"She's a good child. She wouldn't run off for no reason," Patti digs.

"She was mad! She was mad at me because I didn't want her hanging around with Cody. There. Isn't that what you wanted?"

Patti can't respond.

"Miss Patti. Won't you sit with us and

pray? We know this is upsetting, and prayer is the most effective thing we can do at the moment," suggests the pastor.

"No. No, I won't sit around. In fact, why are you all sitting around?" Patti glares at Amber.

"We were out earlier for about five hours," explains Karena calmly. "Now we're staffing the phones and assisting volunteers."

"And praying," adds Pastor Williams.

"Amber" — Patti holds her gaze on Amber — "stop feeling sorry for yourself and get out there. Do you hear me? Your daughter needs you."

"Patti, I can't do this right now," Amber says.

"You can, but you won't. Shameful! I have every MyWay associate and customer in three counties on the lookout."

The flashing strobes of a police car capture everyone's attention.

"That's my ride. Officer Brice offered to take me out on a search. So that's where I'll be. I am asking you to please call me if anything comes up. Got it?" She locks eyes with Amber for a second. "I don't want to find out any more news via Facebook."

CHAPTER FIFTY-EIGHT: THE ONE PLACE

Amber stands up on shaky legs as she watches Patti take off.

"She's right. I've gotta head out to look. I can't sit here any longer."

"Amber, don't let her get to you. You need to rest awhile," says Karena.

"It's okay." Bridgette jumps to Amber's side. "I'll go with you."

"There's one place we haven't looked. It's just a short walk from here." Bridgette nods and opens her umbrella for Amber as they dive out from under the tent and into the rain.

Bridgette and Amber briskly walk arm in arm several blocks down from the church toward a closed wrought iron gate.

"I don't think we're gonna fit through those bars," says Bridgette. Amber grins.

"But Bree sure could have. She's such a little wisp."

"Look, we're here. Lemme just try this."

Bridgette holds the flashlight on Amber as she wriggles the latch. After squeezing it with all her might, the latch snaps free. The gate releases, and the ten-foot iron entrance creaks open. Amber and Bridgette enter the Clarksville Cemetery.

Amber marches toward the section of military gravesites. "Bree? Breeanne Hill? Are you here?"

"Bree, honey! If you're here, please come on out! It's okay!" Bridgette calls.

"I'm not mad, baby! Please. Where are you?" The rain tapers to a fine mist. Amber slows to a hurried walk. Bridgette keeps up, closing the umbrella and panning the cemetery with her flashlight.

"Make sure we look inside those private mausoleums, too. Maybe she went in one to get out of the rain," Bridgette says.

"Look at us. Traipsing through graves for my daughter. What have I done, Bridge? How did I get to this point?"

"Amber. Life happens and we all make choices we're not proud of. What's more important is what you choose to do now."

They wind through the uniform white stones, scanning the area, passing within several feet of Darren's grave. She's been here only one other time. When Darren was laid to rest. Amber had planned to take Bree out of school that day. The memorial service had been held weeks before Darren's body had been transported back to Clarksville, and Bree had been in attendance. The laying to rest was a formality when his body arrived. A ceremony. It would mean little to Bree. Only make her feel sad. Make her cry. Amber had been looking for any excuse not to put Bree through it. When she arrived at school to pick Bree up, she found her laughing and playing with her friends on the playground at recess. Carefree. Happy. Maybe it wasn't right, but Amber couldn't bring herself to tear Bree from her little solace. She left school and met Patti at the gravesite. Patti had vehemently disagreed with Amber's decision. The incident marked the beginning of the great rift between them.

"Bree? Are you here?" Amber calls out as Bridgette searches the area with her flashlight in a 360 of the area. Listening. Watching. Waiting.

"I don't see her. She's not here," Bridgette finally concludes.

"I just thought maybe . . . but . . . this is stupid." Amber turns from Darren's grave. "How would she know? I've never taken her here." Amber's despair and regret deepens. "What if we don't . . . if we can't find her? She'll be out here all alone. Unprotected.

Oh, Bridge, I can't lose her!"

"No, no, no. Amber, don't you talk like that." Bridgette scoops up Amber by the arm. "Let's keep looking."

Amber trudges forward with Bridgette, clinging to her optimism with all her strength.

CHAPTER FIFTY-NINE: COUNTY ROAD 40

Patti rides shotgun with Officer Woody Brice, a calm but tough spirit with ten years on the Clarksville police force and a young family at home. His wife, Angela, is a faithful MyWay customer, and their daughter, Lily, is in Bree's class. Patti knows how close to home this situation must hit him, and in this moment, she is grateful for that unspoken compassion.

"I figure since the search party is combing the neighborhoods, we should patrol the highway coming into town. If I were a kid running away, I wouldn't try weaving through side streets. I'd just hightail it down the main road."

"Sounds like you've had some experience in this area."

"Just a little. Unfortunately. Seems like we get a couple of runaways a year. Thankfully, they always turn up. A friend's house. A hunting shack. The park."

"I can't thank you enough." Patti's quiet words are few as fears feed on her imagination. Officer Brice makes the turn from downtown onto County Road 40, heading south out of Clarksville. He puts on his emergency strobes but keeps the siren silent. The *whoop-whoosh* of the wiper blades clearing the misty windshield fills the space between them. Within half a minute they are coasting at twenty-five miles per hour along the forested landscape just outside of the city. The pulsing blue-and-red glow of the strobes cast a spooky glow on the wooded area. Patti can't imagine her little girl out here. Alone. Unprotected. She rolls down the window for a little fresh air. The cool night air somehow makes her feel like Bree is within reach.

They travel for another mile. A truck speeds up behind them and then comes to a crawl behind the trawling squad car. Officer Brice waves it by, and soon the road is void of traffic again. Patti tilts her head slightly toward the open window, eyes on the pavement ahead, seeking out any sign of her granddaughter.

The oncoming headlights of an SUV crest a small hill and dim as they pass. Patti's eyes adjust to the darkness again and catch a flicker of movement.

"What's that?" She points up ahead as the squad car's headlamps start to envelop something bumping along the shoulder.

Straining his gaze, Brice sees it, too. He lets his foot off the gas and creeps the car along the shoulder until it comes to a stop.

Patti can now make out the pink camo go-kart chugging over the pitted ground. "It's her! It's Bree!"

"Will you look at that?" Patti detects relief in Brice's voice. He presses a button once, and the siren makes a double warning chirp. Up ahead, the kart slows.

"Bree! Bree!" Patti hangs her head out the window. "Stop!"

"Ms. Patti. Please. Can you keep your head inside, please?"

Patti unlatches her seat belt and reaches for the door handle.

Officer Brice places a gentle grip on her arm. "Ms. Patti, I know you want to go to her. But I need you to stay in the car. Police protocol. Okay?"

Patti nods, but she looks unsure as she takes her hand off the door handle. It's the hardest thing she's had to do all night.

"You'll have her in your arms soon enough."

Patti watches Officer Brice exit the car with his hefty Maglite. He illuminates a wide path along the shoulder to the kart. Patti can clearly see their interactions. She leans her head out the window so she can get every word.

"Hello, miss. I'm Officer Brice from Clarksville. How are you tonight?"

Bree's inquisitive face peers out from the kart, squinting back at the officer. Patti exhales in relief. "Are you Breeanne Hill?" Officer Brice asks with a solemn look.

"Yes," Bree answers.

"License and registration, please."

"I don't have those things," says Bree, making Patti want to giggle. "How fast was I going?"

"Well, miss, I'm afraid this vehicle isn't licensed for the road. I'm gonna have to ask you to come with me."

"Are you gonna take me home?" Bree's face crinkles at him.

"Your mom would sure like that." Officer Brice plays diplomat.

Patti is eager for her response, hoping it won't cause trouble.

Bree thinks about it for a second. "In that police car?"

"Yes. Have you ever ridden in one before?"

Bree shakes her head.

"Well, it's a lot of fun. You don't wanna miss this opportunity."

Good angle, Brice. That'll reel her in.

"What about my kart?"

"Not to worry. I'll put it in the trunk."

Bree relents, and Officer Brice helps her out of the kart. He directs her to the squad car, and as Bree approaches, she sees Patti in the passenger's seat.

"Grandma?"

Patti leaps from the car and grabs Bree in her arms. "Bree! My peanut! We were worried sick about you. Are you okay?"

"I'm fine."

"Good." Patti can't let go as she smothers Bree in affection. "Don't ever do that again, okay?"

"Am I in trouble?"

"No. No, honey. Not at all. You just gave us quite a scare."

Brice rolls up, pushing the kart. "Ladies, shall we?" He opens the back door for them.

As Brice secures the kart in the trunk, Patti and Bree slide into the backseat together. Patti sends out a quick text and a tweet. *We have Bree! Safe and sound.*

They pull into the church parking lot to find Amber, Karena, and Bridgette helming the waiting search party, which has returned to greet them.

"All these people were looking for me?"

Bree asks Patti with a stunned look.

"Yes, peanut. Everyone loves you a whole lot."

Patti opens the door for Bree and Amber scoops Bree into a big hug as she floods with emotions. "Bree! Oh, baby!"

Patti climbs out of the car and gives Amber her moment. Joe and Cody help Officer Brice unload the kart. Patti gives Officer Brice a warm squeeze on the arm.

"Thank you so much. Tell Angela I have a special MyWay gift coming for her and the girls. And you can expect a healthy donation to the police fund from me this week."

"I'll do that. And thank you in advance, Ms. Hill." Officer Brice starts for the door when Amber rushes to his side.

"Thank you, Officer. Thank you so much." She gives him a hug. "Bree, what do you say?"

"Thank you, Officer Brice."

"You're welcome. You're a good little driver, Bree. But let's keep that thing off the highway for now, okay?" Bree nods emphatically. "Get home safely, everyone. And have a good night."

The crowd murmurs their thanks and farewells as Officer Brice takes off. Amber pulls Bree aside from the crowd.

"Bree, please don't ever, ever, ever do that

again. I was worried to death. Promise me. Okay? Promise me?"

"Are you mad at me?"

"No. I was just very, very, very scared that I had lost you. And I can't lose you, do you understand?"

Bree nods slightly as Patti jostles in from behind and takes another turn at a hug. "We're just glad you're safe." Patti catches Amber's resentful stare.

"Okay, Bree, it's been a long night. Let's head home."

Bree unfurls from Patti's hug. She stands there, expressionless. Thinking.

"Everything okay?" Patti asks.

Bree shakes her head.

"Do you feel sick?"

"No," she whispers.

"Are you hungry?" Amber asks. "You must be starved." Bree looks up at her mother with hollow eyes. "I'll make you whatever you want once we get home. Come on."

"No."

"No, what?" says Amber. "No, you aren't hungry?"

"No, I want to go with Grandma." Bree's voice grows louder. Patti steps closer to Bree. What did she just say? She glances over and sees Karena and Bridgette and a few searchers turn their heads.

"Honey, you're not staying with Grandma," Amber insists.

"I want to live with her." Bree nudges closer to Patti.

Patti lights up at the thought. This is what she's been trying for. Hoping for. For Amber's own good. She seizes the moment.

"Amber, we're all on our last emotional nerve. Maybe it would be best for her to stay with me. A least for a little while."

"No, Patti. My daughter is coming home with me. End of story."

Patti braces. She knows enough to expect a fight. It would be hard to accept a daughter's rejection. But now that Bree has opened Pandora's box, she won't back down. "Amber. Consider this the gift of some well-deserved time alone to get your house in order."

"A gift? How dare you?" Patti glances at the crowd, their attention drawn to Amber's insistent tone. "Breeanne Hill, you're coming home with me!"

"No, I'm not going with you!"

Amber reaches over and grabs Bree's coat, but Bree slips away and darts behind Patti. Patti instinctively protects her.

"Amber, hey, what are you doing?" says Bridgette, stepping up and then quickly withering under Amber's daggered look.

Patti knows she's stepped into dangerous territory, but she's not going to back down when it comes to Bree's well-being. She nods to Karena for help.

"I think it's best if everyone takes a deep breath," says Karena, slipping from the tent to Amber's side. She takes Amber by the arm and gently draws her away from Patti. Amber squirms.

"Bree. What are you doing? Why are you running from me?"

Patti blocks Bree from Amber's view. "Go get in the car, Bree."

Patti sees the stung look in Amber's face as she watches Bree run toward Patti's car. She feels a twitch of pain for her daughter-in-law. But enough is enough. She is saving Amber from herself. And although it's an ugly moment, it's the right thing to do.

Amber tries to pursue her daughter, but Patti intervenes, blocking her path to Bree.

"I'm not gonna force you, Bree. Please. Come home with me. Bree? Did you hear me?"

No answer. Bree opens the car door and hops inside, slamming the door behind her.

"She's in good hands, Amber. You know that. Please, take all the time you need," Patti says, trying to convince Amber. "She'll come around."

"Amber, let her go," says Bridgette, coming up from behind.

"So, you're both on *her* side?" Amber says bitterly.

"Go home and get some rest," says Karena. "You'll see things differently in the morning."

Patti takes this as her cue and gets in her car. She can hear Amber's weeping even over the sound of the engine.

In the beam of her headlights Patti notices the rain picking up again. She pulls out of the parking lot, glimpsing Amber leaning into her van, wet hair matted to her head, jacket soaked, devastated as her daughter drives out of view.

She glances over at Bree. Her head is resting against the leather seat and turned away from her mother's view. As hard as this is, this is exactly what Darren would want. She knows it.

"I'm sorry I made you worry." Bree's thin voice breaks into Patti's thoughts.

"I know you are. It's okay now."

They head through the dark streets of Clarksville.

"Do you have ice cream?"

"I do, peanut. I do."

"Cookie dough?"

"Yes. And chocolate chip."

Of course, if Darren were here, none of this would be happening.

CHAPTER SIXTY:
ON HER KNEES

As Patti's taillights vanish down the street, Amber's misery morphs into anger. She rips herself from Karena and Bridgette and throws herself into her van.

"Are you sure you're okay to drive?" pleads Bridgette. "I can take you home."

"I'm fine." She slams the door and peels out on the wet parking lot pavement. She knows everyone is still staring at her. And they're probably talking about her, too. She has lost her daughter publicly and made an utter fool of herself in front of at least two dozen church members and friends. The labels fly around in her brain. Unfit parent. Widowed wreck. Pathetic waitress. Lost soul.

After a few minutes, she finds herself in the middle of town. Thankfully, no cars are around as she blows through the flashing yellow stoplight. She keeps driving. Eyes traveling with the faded white line that keeps her inside the lane. She hits the edge of town, which leads away from everything familiar.

Where am I going?

Amber makes a wide U-turn right in the middle of the highway and circles back toward Clarksville, winding through several side streets until she stops dead in front of her old house. In that brief second, she forgets she doesn't live here anymore.

What am I doing here?

She lets off the brake and coasts forward.

Where do I live now?

Her frazzled brain struggles for a second to recall the way to the cabin. Once it does, she tries to think of a reason to return. To do what? Sit there? Without Bree? The thought levels her.

Where else could she go? Karena's? Bridgette's? Rosie's? Of course. And they would gladly welcome her into their homes. But then what? It won't shed the hollowness.

Where do I belong?

What if I am truly lost? A lost soul.

Amber pilots the van back toward the highway heading out of town. She picks up speed, still unsure where she's headed, steering past the church. The white steeple, lit up with several spotlights, looms large and expectant against the dark stormy sky.

When you're lost, come home. The words whisper to her spirit, stilling her wild mind.

Amber slams on the brakes, skidding to a stop in front of the main entrance.

This used to be your real home. Remember?

Is her mind doing strange things? Or did God speak to her just now?

Either way, it's time to reckon with Him. She spills out of the car and charges up the front steps of the building.

"First of all, God, I used to have faith. I used to believe You were good."

Neither the church nor the voice offers a response. She scans the dark and empty night. This is crazy. But she can't stop. It feels good to yell at God.

"Then, You did this to me. You took away my husband, my home, and now my daughter. I tried everything I knew how to do." She pleads with the cross atop the steeple. "So why? What did I ever do to deserve this? I gave You everything! Hours and hours in that building. This is a pretty crappy reward for being faithful."

Hands on her hips, Amber glares at the front doors of the church. Was the joke on her? One big, cruel, empty hoax? If He didn't produce an answer, she could never step foot here again.

"So? What are You gonna do? How are You gonna fix this mess? 'Cause I'm done. It's on You now."

Amber pauses. The night remains still. Nothing stirs around her. She listens. Tiny tremors quake her knees. She bolsters her hope a second longer.

"Yup. That's what I thought." She pivots, storming down the steps.

And then . . . a flicker. The stained-glass window on the front of the church, right below the steeple, suddenly illuminates. Amber rises, gazing at the luminescent art. Jesus the Good Shepherd, holding the little lost lamb, a circle of children gathered at his feet. In all her years at the church, Amber had never really seen this. She studies the beautiful image.

She is that lamb that Jesus has been holding in his arms. This whole time.

The front door creaks open. Amber's eyes travel from the window to a wheelchair rolling out. Nelson. "Thought I heard some yelling out here." Behind him are Karena, Pastor Williams, Bridgette . . . and Cody.

Nelson wheels up to Amber with a smile and reaches his hand out to her.

"What are you all still doing here?"

Bridgette takes her other hand.

"Praying. For you," says Cody.

Amber glances at Pastor Williams and Karena, who are sharing a peaceful look. "Won't you come in?" the pastor says.

Cody holds the door for her.

And Amber steps inside.

CHAPTER SIXTY-ONE: WHAT HAPPENED THAT DAY

"There's something that I've been wanting to tell you," says Nelson as he positions his chair next to Amber. She sits in the front pew of church, exhausted.

"I think I'm ready now." Amber lifts her gaze to him.

Nelson breaches the awkward silence as he locks his chair and fumbles with his footrest. "I just hope you can forgive me."

"For what?" Amber gives him her full attention. She recognizes that familiar lump forming in her throat. "It's okay. Whatever it is. It's forgiven."

"Sergeant Hill was the closest I ever came to having a big brother."

Amber nods, bracing herself for the final puzzle piece to Darren's death.

"We were on patrol, and it was getting to be around dusk. We were in our Humvees on this desolate stretch of desert on this low road between several dunelike ridges. This one wise-cracking guy from Texas, Corporal Schaefer, was making us all hungry talking about the perfect barbecued ribs. And we were thinking about hunting one of those skinny little mountain goats they have up there in those hills."

Amber laughs a little.

"I was begging them to stop talking about food, because my stomach was growling something fierce. Darren gave me his last protein bar. And then we started talking about how we'd all be home soon, and Darren said we should all have a barbecue cook-off to see who could make the best ribs."

"That sounds like him for sure." Darren had a great love for his five-burner, cast-iron grill — a piece that was especially hard for her to get rid of when she had to sell it early on.

"So anyhow, we kept going until we reached this one place. There was a burned-out car and all this debris. Clearly there had been a battle there before. It was that kinda eerie feeling you get, you know? Right before something's about to go down?"

Nelson looks away for a moment. An uneasy silence replaces their levity from just moments before.

"Darren got real quiet and wouldn't take his eyes off the road. When we saw that, we all turned real nervous. Then all of a sudden he yelled, 'STOP! STOP!' And we looked a few feet ahead of the truck, and there was this small metal object sticking out of the dirt right in our path."

"A bomb," mouths Amber.

Nelson nods. "Darren got out and went to the front of the Humvee. Schaefer and I jumped out after him, to cover. He went to the bomb and saw that there was a wire, and the Humvee was right on top of it."

"Darren yelled at the guys to get out of the truck. And that's when we saw the insurgents. Above us on the ridge. But it was too late."

Nelson's eyes rove to the front of the church and stare blankly at the altar. Amber waits, not daring to move.

"The first hit knocked most of us to the ground. We scattered everywhere, and then everyone was firing at once. Darren wanted us to get to cover behind the second Humvee, about twenty feet away. He went first, bullets flying around him.

"I got hit in the leg. And then right here." Nelson touches his left side. "Went close to the spine. Knocked out my nervous system from the waist down. Everything went numb. I was pretty sure I was gonna die. I started breathing real heavy and things sounded really far away.

"I could hear Darren's voice right up next to me, telling me to hang on. To breathe. He asked me to nod if I heard him. And I did. Just barely. Then, he told me God had bigger plans for my life than dying in that desert."

Amber can't take her eyes off Nelson. "You were there when . . ."

"He dragged me to safety just as this RPG went screaming by. Darren ducked out to fire a round, and that's when he was . . ."

"Shot."

"As he was dying, he yanked this off and held it out to me." Nelson removes a thin leather strap from around his neck and holds it out for Amber to see. On the strap is a worn metal piece formed into the shape of a cross.

"He told me God loved me more than I could imagine."

Chapter Sixty-Two:
The Necklace

Nelson places the metal cross in the palm of her hand, still warm from his skin. "It should belong to you."

Amber is in awe of the gift, and completely at a loss as to how to respond. "Where did he get this?"

"He made it from bits of shrapnel he found after our first firefight."

Amber runs her fingers over the pitted metal. The long spine and its crossbar cocked at a slightly imperfect angle.

"His sacrifice saved me, Amber. And I'll never be able to repay him for that. But I plan to spend my whole life passing on that grace to others however and whenever I can."

"Thank you." She kisses the cross and winds her fingers tightly around it. "And thank you for having the courage to tell me. I've been so afraid of the facts. They seemed like they might be too raw for me. But now

I can only see how sacred that last moment was. For both of you."

"Amber. I'm sorry he chose to save me rather than come home to you and Bree."

"I'm not. I mean, there's not a moment I don't wish he was here again. But how can I be angry or resentful knowing that Darren's last act was one of unconditional love? Anything else would be selfish . . . which is exactly how I've been living."

The world flip-flops around Amber, aligning itself in a whole new way. She slips the necklace over her head, awash in fresh reality. She will live her life differently from this moment. She will live in faith and joy and sacrifice — as one who is deeply, deeply loved. Because she is. And always will be. Nothing can take God's love from her.

Nelson grabs the arms of his wheelchair, and with every ounce of strength that he can find, pushes himself up to a shaky standing position. Amber reaches over, anticipating a sudden collapse. Instead, Nelson straightens, tall and proud, growing steady. He pulls his right arm up into a salute.

Amber's eyes gleam through the tears as she embraces the solemn moment. Nelson releases the salute, and Amber bolts from her pew to hug him.

CHAPTER SIXTY-THREE: CAN WE TALK?

"Grandma? Hey, Grandma?" Patti opens her eyes to see her granddaughter standing over her. "I have an idea for something to do today."

"Oh, do you? What time is it?" She glances at her digital radio clock — 6:13 a.m. She rolls over and props herself in a semi-sitting position on her decorative pillows. What does it matter how early it is? She barely slept all night. Might as well get up and make use of the day. "What's your idea, sweetie?"

"Hannah gave me some more of these." Bree holds out a snack-size plastic zip bag for Patti. She can't see a darn thing.

"Hand me those glasses on the night-stand." Bree obeys, and Patti slips on her reading lenses. She takes the bag from Bree. "I still don't see anything in here, Bree. Is this some kind of joke I'm not getting?"

"No. Look. In the corner. See?" Bree's

voice is eager. Patti pulls the bag closer to her face. *Well, look at that.* Three itsy-bitsy dust-colored seeds are wedged into the bottom corner of the bag.

"Do you see them?"

"I do," says Patti.

"What are they?"

"Matt number two."

Armed with a light breakfast and a cup of coffee, Patti sets up a gardening station at the kitchen table. She helps Bree pack soil into some clay pots.

"What happened to the old Matt?"

"Oh, you know. Circumstances beyond his control."

Patti almost giggles out loud. When did her granddaughter become so adult?

"I see."

Bree pats down the soil. Patti nods and takes a sip of coffee. "What's the story behind the mustard seed? Why not a bean seed or a marigold?"

"Because the mustard seed is the most powerful seed in the whole world!" Bree says in an action-hero voice that makes Patti laugh out loud this time.

"Super seed!"

"Yeah! Super seed!" Bree tucks one of the seeds beneath the dirt and pours water on it. "So powerful it can move mountains!"

"That is definitely a superhero seed." Patti stirs more cream into her mug. "How does a seed move a mountain?"

"No, it's faith that moves the mountain."

"You're not speaking my language, little one." She ruffles the top of Bree's head.

"God can do anything if we have just this much faith." Bree pinches the seed, and it disappears between her fingers.

God can do anything, huh? Can He bring your mother back around to her senses? Can He restore this family? Those are some pretty big mountains to tackle. It may take a whole packet of mustard seeds.

"Do you have mountains in your life, Bree?" Patti fishes for an explanation for why she ran away.

Bree brushes off her hands and wipes them on a towel. "Well, I miss Daddy a lot. That feels like a mountain."

And there it is. She should have pieced it together sooner. Bree is acting out because she misses Darren. The same thing happened with Darren when his dad left. "Well, peanut, I'm not sure about moving that mountain, but I do know something that can help."

"What?"

"A memory."

"I don't understand." Bree presses the last seed into the pot.

"It's okay to miss people we love. And when we do, we can think of a good memory to make it a little less difficult." Patti sees that Bree has softened into the back of her chair. "Why don't you try? Tell me about a good memory you have of your father."

Bree nods. Patti pours more milk into Bree's glass.

"I can't . . . I can't think of one."

"I'm sure you will. Why don't I go first?" says Patti. "I have a story that I'm not even sure if your mom knows about."

"Really?"

"Did you know that your dad built a go-kart when he was your age?"

"He did?" Bree's eyes register curiosity as she brings the milk glass to her lips.

"He built it with his dad, your grandpa John. This was about a year before we got divorced. It was all black, with gold racing stripes."

"Cool!"

"Very cool," says Patti reaching for an album from the cupboard over her countertop-desk space. "I think I even kept a photo of it. He and his dad built it in the garage, and they were planning to race it at the annual Boy Scout Derby races."

Patti pages through the album until she finds the photo for Bree.

"It kinda looks like a bee," says Bree. In the picture, a young Darren in plaid shorts and a T-shirt stands next to his gold-striped kart, with his dad at his side.

"And that's your grandpa John."

"Where's he now?"

"Well, that's a long story for another time, peanut. So anyhow, your dad and Grandpa John put this superpowered lawn mower motor in it. Like one of those industrial-size mowers that cuts the grass on football fields."

"Those things are huge!" Bree can't take her eyes off her daddy's picture.

"I warned John — Grandpa — that it was probably too powerful for that little kart. I was afraid they were going to blow a tire or that the whole thing would fall apart if it got going too fast."

"Did it?"

"Well . . . not exactly."

"What happened?"

"They took it out for a test-drive one evening after supper. Around the block. They had that thing purring down the road. It worked too well. That kart started to gain speed. Faster and faster. Your dad tried to slow down. But, as we found out later, the

403

gear had stuck. Grandpa John was flailing down the street trying to catch up, but that kart just zipped outta sight."

"Where did he go?"

"Grandpa and I jumped in the car and chased him down just in time to see your dad miss a turn in the road and go sailing into Mrs. Dobkin's yard. He crashed through the rotted wooden fence and drove the car headlong into her koi pond."

"Wow!" Bree glanced up at Patti with wide eyes. "Was he okay?"

"More than okay. Practically giddy. Barely fazed, he floated out of the driver's seat and waded to the edge of the pond. Not a scratch."

"Was the car ruined?"

"Completely. The engine was three feet underwater."

"Did he and Grandpa get it fixed in time for the race?"

"I'm afraid not. He never got to compete. Grandpa John wasn't around for the race the next year. And Darren didn't have anyone to help him rebuild the kart."

"That must have been hard for him," Bree says.

"It was. But I'll never forget the huge smile on his face as he crawled out of Mrs. Dobkin's pond. He had just had the thrill ride of his young life. And lived to tell about it."

Bree laughs.

"That was your daddy. He lived a full and adventurous life. He wasn't afraid to try new things. You're a lot like him, Bree." Patti wraps Bree in a hug, and Bree melts into her. "Feel better?"

"Yeah."

Patti slips her fingers under the plastic overlay of the album page and extracts the photo of young Darren and his yellow-jacket kart.

"I think you should have this."

Bree takes it. "Thank you, Grandma."

"You're most welcome. Now, why don't you get on upstairs and put on your clothes. They're freshly washed."

"Thanks, Glam-ma." Bree gives Patti another hug and scurries off. Patti sweeps up the loose dirt from the pot. She places Matt 2 on the windowsill.

"Grandma?"

Patti turns to see Bree has returned and is standing in the doorway. "Yes, honey?"

"Can you pray with me?"

Patti's insides freeze up. Pray. She hasn't got a clue how to do that. "Sure. Of course." Bree takes both Patti's hands in hers. "Why don't you start?"

Bree closes her eyes. Patti does the same.

"Dear God, thank you for Grandma and Matt Two. Please help him grow. Be with Mom and help her to be happy again. And I'd really like to race my go-kart, so if . . ."

The front chimes clamor. Saved by the doorbell! Patti's eyes pop open.

". . . Amen." Patti gives Bree's hands a squeeze. "Okay, scoot upstairs. I'm going to answer the door."

Patti peers through the peephole and quickly unlocks the door. Amber has a latte in one hand and extends a second one to Patti.

"I come in peace," she says with a friendly smile. "Can we talk?"

Patti shows Amber into the kitchen, and she takes a seat at the kitchen island, on a stool. Patti remains planted on her feet, unsure about where this is going.

"How's Bree?"

"She's fine. She's upstairs getting dressed."

"I didn't come here to try to get her back. I know that's probably what you're thinking."

Patti follows Amber's gaze to the windowsill. "I wouldn't blame you if you did," she answers.

"I mean, of course I want her home. But that'll come. Hopefully soon. I know I've been a terrible parent since . . ."

"Not terrible, Amber. Just traumatized."

"It's not an excuse. I pushed away everything and everyone in my life who was offering me support. I was selfish."

Patti allows time for the confession to unwind.

"I overlooked that Darren is your loss, too. He was my husband, but he was your son. And I . . . I'm so sorry."

"Thank you, Amber." Patti barely manages to get it out.

"I'm not going to pretend that we don't have some issues to work through. And I know that I have a lot of issues to work through. But I'm willing to make an honest effort if you are."

Faith the size of a mustard seed. An answer to a prayer that had just been uttered. All of it was happening right here in the hearth of her home. She had done nothing to deserve the mountains that were being moved. Was this the amazing grace of that hymn? It was opening her heart, melting away that old grudge.

"I resented you a lot in those first few years. And, I guess, if I'm being honest, until just recently. But I was being selfish, too. I wanted what I wanted for Darren. And neither you nor the Airborne fit into that plan. I was devastated when both took him away from me."

"Thank you for explaining that, Patti. That means a lot to me." Amber stares into her latte.

"Darren loved you so much." She now understood why Darren was unrelenting about his relationship with the Lord. It set free every fear, frustration, anxiety . . . and regret. And left nothing but peace in their place. A peace Patti had never experienced before. A longing to reconcile.

"I regret we weren't closer when Darren was alive. I regret he's not here to be a part of this. And I am more than willing to try to be a family with you now."

Amber's huge grin welcomes Patti in for a hug.

"I feel so much better. Thank you, Patti."

"Me, too. But I have to ask. What brought about this sudden change? The Amber I saw last night is not the one who's standing in my kitchen right now."

Amber holds up the metal cross draped around her neck. "This. It was Darren's. Nelson gave it to me."

"That's beautiful. I sense a story," Patti says.

"Yes. One that Bree needs to hear, too."

Amber hands Patti the necklace.

"Oh, Amber. I can't. It was given to you."

"And now I'm giving it to you." Patti is on the verge of tears, and her trembling hands refuse to allow her to undo the clasp. Amber takes over, securing the necklace around Patti's neck.

"Thank you," she manages in a whisper as she straightens the cross. "Before Bree comes down, I want to show you something." Patti goes to the cupboard, reaches into a drawer at her counter workstation, and removes a small box.

"I have a standing order with the local pawnshops. They call me if anything interesting comes in."

She hands it to Amber and watches her open it.

"My ring." Amber's tone is genuinely grateful.

"*Our* ring. Our family heirloom. Let's make sure to protect it so it's there for Bree when she needs it."

"Absolutely." Amber tucks the ring back into the box.

"Mom?"

Patti looks up to see Bree sliding sock-footed into the kitchen.

"Are you here to take me home?"

"No. Unless you want me to." That old rehearsed resentment starts to clench at Patti's heart. She wills it away. Where to stay is Bree's choice. Patti knows she loves them both. And she can see that it's not a competition anymore. They're a family.

"Bree, I owe you an apology," says Amber.

"You do?"

"I haven't been there for you like I should have. I love you, and I'm going to do better. I'm so very sorry. Will you please forgive me?

"I forgive you, Mom."

"Thank you."

"I'm sorry I said I hate you."

"I know you didn't mean it."

Bree circles her arms around her mother's neck, and Patti's heart unclenches.

CHAPTER SIXTY-FOUR: THE LAST LETTER

Amber leads Bree and Patti to Darren's gravesite. When they get about fifty feet from the stone, Patti stops.

"Go ahead. You two need to do this on your own."

"Are you sure? I want you to be there."

"No. I'm sure. They were his words to you. And Bree." Amber sees a small pain seeping into Patti's face.

"You can read it later. Okay?"

Patti nods, and Amber feels free to move Bree to her father's grave.

They draw closer. "Can you see it yet?"

Bree scans the stones until she finds Darren's. "That one." Excitement and awe fill her voice.

"I'm sorry I didn't take you here sooner."

"It's okay. We're here now."

"You ready?" Amber stops them in front of Darren's gravestone. She pulls the unopened but well-worn and familiar envelope

411

from her coat.

"It came in the mail a few days after the soldiers came to tell me he had died. I couldn't . . . I guess I didn't want there to be last words."

Bree takes Amber's trembling hand in hers.

"Here. You want to open it?" Amber hands Bree the letter. She slices it open at the crease with her thumb and hands it back to Amber.

Amber draws in a deep breath and kneels to Bree's level. Bree squeezes her hand.

Dear Amber and Bree,

I miss you both so much. This will be the last letter you get before I come home, so I guess I'd better make it a good one. I'm so ready to be with you both. If I have learned anything these past fourteen months apart, it is this: The only way to keep moving when the road seems dark and broken is to live in His love. When you choose Him, He puts peace in place of fear. It can be hard to do that every day. Especially here, but I try, because this road leads to Him, and back to you. Stay focused on Him. See you soon. I love you with my whole heart.

Darren/Dad

Amber folds the letter, unable to catch her breath. Bree's arms fold around her.

"I've been hurting so much that I lost sight of the most important blessing that your dad ever gave me."

"The house?"

"No. You."

Peace flows in waves over Amber. Looking up, she sees that Patti is coming up behind them. Amber extends a smile and an embrace.

"Mom, can we try not to be sad anymore?" says Bree.

"I . . . Yes. But . . . I'll be honest. I'm not even sure I know how anymore . . ."

"All you have to do is just think of a good memory about Daddy." Bree smiles at Patti, and Amber senses some secret bond between them.

"Okay. I can try."

"Show her how, Grandma!"

Patti turns to Amber with a playful smile. "Have I ever told you about Darren's go-kart adventure?"

"What? No. This oughta be good."

As Patti starts the story, Bree's hands slip into Patti's and Amber's. Gratefulness swells in the midst of fallen heroes . . . Darren's legacy . . . and a family restored.

As the earthy spring air enters her, Amber feels her life starting a new season.

And soon, she is laughing.

Chapter Sixty-Five: Cody's Camaro

Cody puts the finishing touches on a door panel paint job on a Jeep SUV when he hears the familiar clinking of a car engine parking near the office door.

Amber.

Cody brushes his hair off his brow as Amber springs out of the van with a huge smile. Bree bounces from the passenger side.

Wow. Something big has happened.

Cody wipes the grease off his hands as Joe steps in from the office to join them all.

"Hey, Cody! Hey, Uncle Joe!" Bree wraps her arms around Joe. Cody greets her with a fist bump.

"Gimme those keys and I'll pull that van of yours in here. Take a look at that rattle," says Joe.

"Ah . . . Oh, well, that's not why I stopped, but sure . . . I probably should."

"Only take a second. On the house."

"Thanks, Joe." She tosses him the keys.

He heads out, and Cody clears away a few boxes so they can fit Amber's van in the stall.

"Actually, I came by to say hello. Heard you're gonna be sticking around Clarksville for a bit."

"I am."

"I wanted to thank you for everything you've done for me. And especially for Bree."

"Can I drive my kart?"

Cody looks for Amber's approval.

"Yes. You can."

"It's around back with the others."

Bree takes off.

"You seem . . . different." Cody quickly corrects. "Good different."

"I am different. A lot's happened in the past few days. Good things."

"With me, too."

"You wanna talk about it?"

"Maybe sometime." *I really don't want to muck up this moment.* "You?"

"Maybe sometime."

"Sounds like we both did some growing." Cody likes the comfortable feeling settling in between them. "I may have pushed things too . . . too fast. I mean, I know I did," says Cody. "But if you're willing to give me a second chance, I promise you I'm going to listen and take things slow . . . as a team."

"I pushed you away out of my fear. And I know what to do with that fear now. It's not going to run my life anymore."

"I think we both deserve second chances."

"Isn't that what grace is all about?" She smiles at him and brushes her hand against his arm.

Yes! Thank you, God! Now, please don't let me mess this up!

Whoa. Did I just say a prayer?

Bree zips past them with a huge grin on her face as she circles the parking lot in her kart.

"Slow down, Speed Racer!" Cody calls to her. "She's a good little driver. Really has a natural feel for the road."

"That kart has been her lifeline. I'm just sorry I didn't see it sooner."

"She may wanna consider a career in racing."

"Whoa. Don't push it, buddy."

"I'll teach her everything she needs to know."

"That's exactly what I'm afraid of," teases Amber.

Cody flags Bree to the garage. "Nice job there!"

"What? Do I have stop?" Bree says.

"Just for a second. There's something I want to show you two," says Cody.

Cody leads Amber and Bree out of the garage to a vehicle blanketed by a large brown tarp.

"Is that . . . don't tell me they were able to fix that thing."

"Not a chance. But Joe and I worked out a plan. He had this little beauty tucked away in his junk heap. I restored it for him as a way to pay off my wrecked one. I'm going to be taking it around the local circuit for a while. Until I improve a little more."

"That sounds like a good plan."

"Come on! Let's see it!" Bree dances around the car.

"Drumroll, please!" says Cody, pulling the tarp off.

The tarp slips to the floor, unveiling a restored Camaro decked out in pink camouflage. Exactly like Bree's go-kart. Cody pins his gaze on the girls, eager for their raw reaction.

For a moment, they are speechless as both sets of eyes pop in amazement.

"Cody . . . you . . . I can't believe this," Amber barely whispers.

"It has the Screaming Eagle logo on it!" Bree says, running up to the car to glide her fingers over the hood.

"Oh my goodness. Cody, does this mean . . . ?"

"You're racing for my dad!"

Bree's eyes start to tear. *What? Bree crying! Oh no, that I really can't take.* Cody kneels beside Bree.

"That's right. I'm dedicating my next race to him. Saturday. Will you be there?"

Amber nods. "We can't wait. Right, Bree?"

"Thank you!" Bree wraps her arms around Cody's neck and leans into his ear. "I'm glad you and my mom are friends again."

Cody sighs and hugs Bree back. *Me, too.*

He finally took the right risk.

CHAPTER SIXTY-SIX:
WINNER

Once again, Joe invites Amber and Bree to a bird's-eye view of Saturday's race from his RV rooftop. This time Patti joins them, as do Rosie, Karena, Bridgette, and Hannah. They are even able to hoist Nelson and his wheelchair up there via a crane.

All through the race, Amber notes that the announcers can't seem to say enough about Cody's pink Chevy Camaro decked out with the Screaming Eagle logo and Darren's unit number.

Amber observes that, for the most part, Cody is driving obediently under Joe's command. Even though there are several times he tries to talk Joe into a risky maneuver.

Amber is all nerves through much of the race, especially as Cody approaches the final two laps. He's been holding third position for most of the race. Her stomach ties up in knots. She braces herself next to Joe, bending her ear to hear his every instruction to Cody.

"Bear down on the lead from the outside," Joe shouts through the headset. "Good. Now let off the gas. Head for the high line out of the third turn."

Amber watches as the pink camo falls slightly behind, allowing him to take second position.

"After you hit the apex, make a sharp turn to the low line right onto the edge of the apron. Now! Now!"

It sounds dangerous to Amber, and she can't believe what she's seeing as Cody's car hits the apex of the turn and then rips diagonally down the track out of turn four, slicing between the first-and-second position cars.

"Yes!" Joe yells, jumping up and down. "Yes! Hit it hard. You got this!"

Cody blasts down the frontstretch in first position. He's several car lengths ahead as he approaches the first turn of the final lap.

The knots in her stomach unravel. "Goooooooo!" Amber screams, her own voice drowning in the shouts of everyone around her.

He manages to hold position out of the second . . . down the backstretch . . . no one can touch him as he enters turn three . . . and he turbo boosts out of the fourth.

Cody's car zips down the frontstretch and across the finish line. The checkered flag shoots up over the track.

Amber and Bree throw themselves into each other's arms, screaming their fool heads off and dancing around the roof.

Cody is finally . . . a winner.

CHAPTER SIXTY-SEVEN:
GOD BLESS THE BROKEN ROAD

Amber ambles outside at the hush of daybreak. The gentle, warm light of the rising sun creeps across the lawn in front of the cabin. She collects an armful of wildflowers that have sprung up around the outside edge of her yard. To brighten the dining table for breakfast. Along with the blueberries she picked from a wild bush near the lake.

The grass needs mowing. And the weeds around the outside of the cabin are thigh-high. She'll have to dig them out. Deep roots. Maybe she could plant some flowers in their place. Hostas up the sidewalk would be an inexpensive fix for a lush effect. And what about an herb garden on the side where there's shade in the afternoon? Fresh basil and mint. Yum.

Amber drinks it all in. A restorative gift. A blessing. All of it so beautiful to her now. Every last little paint-peeled board and cracked shingle. The screenless windows and the sagging front stoop. The dirt drive. Her rust-bucket minivan with the cracked windshield and leaking oil.

And, of course, the blessing . . . still dozing inside.

"This is the day. This is the day. That the Lord has made." Amber tiptoes over to Bree's side of the bed, waking her with the familiar song. *"That the Lord has made."* She pauses a moment.

"We will rejoice," Bree sings softly, coming out of her sleep.

"We will rejoice," Amber echoes.

"And be glad in it."

"And be glad in it." Amber takes a seat on the edge of the bed next to Bree.

Bree scoots herself up from under the covers.

Amber hands her a yellow-striped sailor shirt and a navy skirt. "I thought you might like to wear this for church."

"Do you think it'll fit?" Bree looks at the garments.

"Only one way to know." Amber helps Bree change, finding that the clothes fit to a tee since Bree has grown in the last two years.

"How does it look?"

"Perfect." Amber adjusts the neckline. "Now finish getting yourself ready and meet me in the kitchen. I'm making pancakes." Amber plants a kiss on Bree's forehead. Bree hops out of bed and pulls the skirt on.

"I like your dress. You look pretty."

"Why, thank you." *I feel pretty. And very much alive. Thank you, God. I never thought I'd be here again.*

Amber lights into the kitchen, gathering the ingredients she needs for breakfast.

"One cup water to two cups pancake mix. One teaspoon butter or oil. One egg." She reads from the back of the box. "And blueberries. Definitely blueberries."

Amber grabs a measuring cup from the cupboard and heads to the sink. She lifts the glass up to the window to make sure the water line is level on the one-cup line.

That's when she sees it. Through the glass cup. On the windowsill.

"Bree! Bree! Come here!"

"What?" Bree calls from the bedroom.

"You've got to see this!" Bree dashes to her mother's side. "That wasn't there yesterday, was it?"

They peer down at Matt 2, soaking up the sun. He's now a sturdy sprout about the height of a quarter, with one tiny leaf unfurling at the base. Vibrant. Reaching for the light.

Bree shakes her head. "Wow! Hey, Matt Two! Welcome to the world."

"His soil looks dry." Amber pours the water from the glass measurer into Matt's pot. "Drink up, little Mustard Tree Matt. You're gonna need it."

Bree can't stop staring at the plant. "I didn't doubt for a second you'd be back."

"Maybe you should bring him to Sunday school and show Hannah and the kids."

"No. Let's wait until he's bigger and stronger. I don't want to disturb him."

"But didn't you say that plants like voices? Think of all the people who will talk to him at church." Amber winks at her daughter.

"Good point. He'd like that."

"Why don't you grab a shoebox and that sweater he likes so we can transport him safely?"

Bree rushes back into the bedroom.

Amber's thoughts remain on the thriving green sprout in the pot. If God can use faith the size of a mustard seed and as fragile as this plant and turn it into a strong, rigid tree, able to withstand any element . . . then . . .

God, I'm just coming out into the world again, but I'm still as weak as Matt right now. Please make me an unwavering tree of faith someday.

For the first time in over two years, Amber enters the sanctuary of Clarksville Community Church. She and Bree travel down the center aisle, making their way to one of the front pews, where Hannah and Nelson are sitting. Amber nods to Joe and Cody as she passes by and slips into the row in front of them.

"It's good to see you here." Joe pats her shoulder as Amber takes her seat. Amber turns slightly to give him a smile.

"It's good to be here."

"You look radiant," Cody adds.

"Thank you. I feel radiant."

In the front, seated behind the pulpit, Amber sees the choir, with Bridgette and Karena in their usual places, both beaming as they make eye contact with Amber.

Pastor Williams appears at the pulpit, and Amber rises with the congregants.

"This is the day that the Lord has made!" proclaims Pastor Williams.

"We will rejoice and be glad in it," Amber responds with the enthusiastic crowd.

"Amen! This is truly a joyous day for many reasons. And one of those reasons is that a dear sheep of this fold has returned to us. Amber Hill, we're so blessed to have you back."

The crowd breaks into applause. *If even one sheep should lose its way. It's so nice to be home.* Warmth flows through Amber, rising to her cheeks. She really didn't expect such fanfare. Nor does she think she deserves it.

Pastor Williams settles the crowd. "We are also so grateful because this talented young lady has decided to pick up her guitar again and bless us today with a song to start our time of worship. Amber? You ready?"

The pastor's head turns to Amber, and she slips out of the pew as the rest of the congregation take their seats. She moves to the front of the church, gazing at the familiar family staring back at her. Bridgette hands her a guitar, and Amber finds her place at the mic stand, placed off to the side of the choir. Her fingers find the strings and form a familiar position. She strums a light chord and steps closer to the mic.

"Sometimes God's plan for our lives is not what we hoped it would be. We get stuck and we find we're on a very broken road that we would have never chosen for ourselves. And when that happens, it's easy to become fearful and angry. I spent a lot of time being those things. I was turned inward, thinking I could help myself, instead of outward toward God to be my strength.

"I'm grateful now. Because that road brought me back to Him. And I can see now, looking back, that He was sending me blessings all along the way, including all of you. I was just too self-absorbed to see them."

Amber, deep in contemplation, barely lifts her eyes beyond the end of the mic. Everything about her is steady and strong. And real.

"I'm proof that anyone, no matter what the broken road they're traveling, can learn to let go of fear. Anxiety. Pain and grief. Surrender it all to God. He's always there for you. Even when you feel like you can't see Him. He's ready to show you the way. Ready to bless you."

When Amber finally raises her glance across the packed sanctuary, it's completely silent. Not a single movement. All eyes turned to her.

She scans the crowd. Cody sends her a reassuring nod from his seat. Hannah has her arm around Bree, who is leaning against her. Beside them, Nelson occupies an aisle space, sitting somehow straighter, somehow stronger than she's ever seen before.

And then, a flicker of movement catches Amber's glance as the side door to the sanctuary opens and a straggling worshipper enters.

Patti. In her Sunday brunch best.

She starts down the side aisle, her eyes locking with Amber's for a moment and unleashing a small, knowing smile. Amber returns it with a grateful one.

She strums the opening bars of the song as Patti quickly makes her way to the front and finds Bree, who loops her yellow-striped sailor arm through Grandma's.

Darren, can you see this?
This is the day the Lord has made.
I am rejoicing!
And so glad to be in it.

Amber draws in a breath, and her lips part. The melody drifts through the church.

Praise . . . after a long, dark journey.

ACKNOWLEDGMENTS

Thank you to the Source of all Creation. None of this exists without You. Thank You for seeding this idea, guiding the story, and protecting this project and everyone involved — both the motion picture and the novel. A little mustard seed of faith started this story and carried it through. You have truly blessed the road that brought this story to life.

Thanks to Harold Cronk, the film's director, for that call one summer day that started off: "Hey, I have this idea . . ." We built a beautiful story on screen and on page! May its blessings and impact reach further than we could have ever imagined and go deeper than we would have dared dream.

To my parents, Ron and Gail, and my in-laws, Gordon and Mina, who have always been there for me and showed me what faith looks and acts like. Thank you for also being on set to cheer us on and be background talent. It's fun to see your faces on that fifty-foot screen! And it's no coincidence that you are all in that church scene together. You have always been an active part of the church — a legacy that has been passed on and on.

To my sisters, Melanie and Amy, for the quiet, gentle ways they have been blessings in my life and in this project. The encouraging e-mails, texts, and Facebook comments have sustained me. Our roads have all been broken in different ways, but they always lead back to one another. I am so grateful.

To Amy S., who drove eight hours to be background talent and spend the day with me at church scenes during filming, and who offered her loving support through every step of this process. Our adventures continue . . .

To seasoned author and former classmate Travis Thrasher, who answered my slew of novel-writing questions. Who knew back in our college days in Chicago that we'd end up connected in this way? Thank you.

To Kyle L., a former NASCAR mechanic (and now friend), who helped me tweak the racing scenes to sound exciting and authentic. Thank you for indulging my racetrack ignorance and making this novel better!

To my agent, Julie, thank you for believing in me and opening amazing new doors! I'm sure signing on with me has been an unconventional ride. I promise you more adventure to come!

To my editor, Beth, for seeing the potential in this project, and for her patience and encouragement. You can't imagine how relieved I was after sending you the first draft to hear you say, "You did a fantastic job!"

To Steve and Bess. What a gift your friendship has been! All because of this story.

To the amazing cast and crew of *God Bless the Broken Road.* During the shoot, you all rose to the task, day after bitter, cold Michigan day. You were never mediocre. You were always excellent! Thank you!

And to Ryan, my husband. You were there when *GBTBR* was just that little mustard seed of a story. You understood (and graciously endured) my crazy hours, late-night meetings, and bouts of writer's angst. You flew to the set three times during filming to be a part of the Clarksville world. And then on the way back to LA, you took the wheel thirty-four of the thirty-six hours across the United States as I furiously pecked out this novel on my dinosaur MacBook, barely looking up to see the country go by. The journey has been so much bigger than just this project. You never doubted. You never let me quit. Thank you for blessing me with your love on all the roads we've traveled together. I love you.

ABOUT THE AUTHOR

Jennifer Dornbush is an accomplished screenwriter and penned the script for the film version of *God Bless the Broken Road.* This is her first novel. She lives in Los Angeles.